GABRIEL IS CURSED

NYMPH'S REVENGE BOOK 2

JULIA GOLDHIRSH

To my mother who instilled in me a love of nature and who proofread all of my books without a single complaint.

CHAPTER 1

The only things remaining from their battle with Nightshade were the broken mirror and a gnawing sense of dread.

Nightshade's plans ran through Gabriel's mind like a mantra. *We'll kill those damned humans for what they've done.* But the information only came in fragments, and the location and details of the poisoning eluded him, making him restless.

After hours of lying on the floor beside Rose's bed and staring up at the holes in the wooden ceiling, Gabriel drifted off.

Remnants of Nightshade's memories cycled through Gabriel's mind as he slept. The nymph stood before a muddy brown river as it turned soot black. Red and orange flames licked at the trees of the forest and children screamed.

Belladonna tried to douse the flame, but it only leapt higher. Beside her, a nymph boy cried out. "Please save him. Nightshade, you told me you'd save my friend."

The fire blackened the tree from root to the treetop, but it still raged, leaping from tree to tree, killing even more nymphs in its wake. The water in the river only stoked the flames. There was no saving the forest.

Nightshade threw a glass bottle filled with muddied water to the ground. It shattered into tiny pieces. "They'll pay. Water for water and blood for blood."

Nightshade stormed out of the forest towards a factory. It was the source of the tainted water. *Strange. I don't remember seeing that building,* Gabriel thought.

Nightshade's eyes darkened as he approached the building. People rushed in and out of it as they headed to and from work. In his hand were two dangerous items: a discarded bottle of alcohol and a match. "The very things they discarded in my forest will kill them. If they weren't so selfish, they wouldn't need to suffer." Belladonna raced towards him. "Don't do it. Whatever they did, it doesn't justify mass murder."

Nightshade sneered. "If getting revenge for my people makes me evil, then it's a small price to pay."

"If you do this, then you will be my enemy. I'll make your life a waking nightmare."

Nightshade smirked. He stared at Belladonna as he threw the alcohol to the ground and lit the match. "I'd love to see you try."

He threw the match into the alcohol, and the factory went up in flames.

* * *

ROSE WOKE to the all too familiar thump of a fist slamming against the wood of her parent's front door, accompanied by the shatter of glass and a spine-chilling yell. No light streamed through the window of her bedroom. Next to her, Gabriel still slept soundly on the floor beside her bed.

As the banging continued, her father shouted, "I'm gonna get you for this. I'll beat you black and blue, you ungrateful wench."

A shiver snaked its way up her spine at the slurred words. She crept out of bed and left her garden-shed-turned-home, being careful not to wake up Gabriel.

There was still a large hole where her front door used to be, a remnant of Nightshade and Belladonna's battle. As she tiptoed through the greenhouse, she passed some scorch marks on the foot-path and overturned earth where Gabriel had dug his heels in when attacking Nightshade.

After sneaking through the greenhouse, she fumbled with the latch until the door popped open. She poked her head out to see what damage he was causing this time. The shards of glass from the broken beer bottle shimmered in the moonlight. Rose wrinkled her nose in disgust as her father swayed on his feet.

Her father continued to bang on and tug at the door, but it wouldn't budge.

If mother locked him out, maybe she's ready to seek help after all, Rose thought as she watched her father struggle with the door. After several more minutes, he realized he wasn't getting in and ground his teeth together in frustration. He yelled, "When I get back inside, I'll make you pay for this in blood." Then he stormed off.

Rose tucked her head back inside the claustrophobic greenhouse and guided the door shut. When the door closed, she cringed at the slight clinking sound it made and whipped her gaze to her retreating father's back.

Her knees buckled when her father didn't turn around. She crept back to her room through the hole in the garden shed, and when she reached Gabriel, she bent down over his prone form.

He'd risked his life for hers, but why? Despite her pleas, he'd slept on the floor after the battle, refusing her offer of the bed. Why did he value his life, his comfort, so little? What was wrong with him? Rose's forehead scrunched up as she watched his sleeping face.

When she pushed back hair from his forehead, he cried out in his sleep. "No. Please, don't." His hand flailed forward, reaching out to her, and she grabbed onto it.

"It's okay," she said, but he tossed and turned, muttering nonsense. He didn't wake.

She gave his shoulder a light shake. "Gabriel, wake up," she said.

He rolled over. "Why are you doing this?" he mumbled.

She shoved him harder.

At that, his eyes flew open, and his gaze fell to where her hands touched his. She pulled away, and his eyes narrowed at Rose. "What do you want this early?"

She huffed and lifted her chin. "You were talking in your sleep. Loudly. You seemed upset."

A grin spread across his face. "Is that why you were holding my hand?"

Her face flushed. "You... tried to grab me in your sleep, so I stopped you." Rose's gaze flickered to her parents' house and back to Gabriel.

Gabriel reached out for her, but she pulled away. "Something tells me my talking isn't the only reason you woke me up."

Guilt turned her stomach. He'd already done too much, but leaving her mother would be a death sentence with her father still in the picture. She couldn't leave her to be tortured by the monster who was supposedly her father.

Lailah didn't have many choices. Financial independence wasn't exactly easy as a single woman in the early 1900s with no living relatives, aside from her previously invalid daughter. The silence stretched out, and she bit her lower lip, knowing she would not like what she had to do next.

Her words came out just above a whisper. "Will you help me get my mother out of here too?"

He cupped his ear. "I'm sorry. Could you repeat that?"

Rose rolled her eyes. "Forget it."

His easy smile cracked the silence. "I'm sorry. I was only joking. Of course, I'll help you, but we'll do it later after I've had some sleep. I'm still exhausted."

The tension in Rose's shoulders relaxed a little. She could always count on him to come through when it mattered. Rose wrapped him in a hug. "Thank you."

"It's no problem," he said with a yawn. "Since you're up, I'm taking your bed." He crawled under her covers and drifted off to sleep. She watched over him until he was snoring away. Then she went out to the garden to come up with a plan.

The sun filtered through the glass panes of the greenhouse, staining the sky a salmon pink. She grabbed a stick and started drawing a map of her parents' house in the dirt near the walking paths. Their room was on the top floor, so she'd need someone to watch the ground floor in case her father came back.

She only had vague memories of the top floor, but the layout of the first floor had been burned into her mind, untouched by time. *Maybe my trauma will pay off after all.* She sighed.

Even though she hadn't seen it in eight years, she still remembered the placement of the kitchen cabinets and the gas range. She winced as memories of her father flickered through her mind and she felt the phantom burn of the stove. Her hands shook as she stared down at the faded red marks on her hands, a constant reminder of that night.

Rose gulped, pushing the thoughts aside as she continued drawing the house's layout. When the sounds of Gabriel yawning reached Rose's ears, she strode to her room to get him, tugging him over to the map.

"You need to know where everything is before we do this. If my father catches us, it could be dangerous for both of us."

He listened intently, his eyes skimming over the map. "Is he the one that caused the injury to your hands?"

Rose's face flushed, and she crossed her arms, hiding them behind her back. "Yes. He's violent and fast, so if he shows up, hide."

Rose's heart hammered in her chest, her breath catching when his fingers lazily traced her arm until he reached her hand, drawing it from behind her back. "You need not be self-conscious of the scars. Every part of you is beautiful."

Her mouth went dry, and she gulped. "Do you think me easily swayed by false sweet talk?"

"Who said it was false?" His eyes warmed her from head to toe. His face was so close to hers, but she couldn't bring herself to kiss him.

She'd drunk poison and because of that he'd had to walk right into Nightshade's territory to find a cure. Those thoughts sobered her. She didn't deserve his kindness. The color left her cheeks, and she cleared her throat.

"Anyway. Getting back on topic. You should find some pans near the stove that would be heavy enough to cause him some serious harm."

Rose looked him up and down. "Do you think you can take him in a fight?"

Gabriel flashed her a cocky grin. "If I can keep my horse in line, I don't think your father will be a problem."

Rose's heart squeezed in her chest, and she pulled him into an embrace. He rested his hand on her head, and she buried her face into his chest. "Thank you. I don't deserve your kindness."

"You deserve a much better hand than the one you've been dealt, but you should learn to be more careful about drinking strange liquids after I warned you they might be dangerous."

Rose rolled her eyes. "Perhaps I was a bit too desperate to escape the greenhouse before."

Gabriel gave a short laugh. "You don't say?"

Rose's gaze turned serious, and she squeezed Gabriel's hand. "When we go in there, I'll do my best to avoid getting caught, but if it gets too dangerous, run. I don't want you getting hurt because of me."

Gabriel stroked her hair. "I can't promise that. I don't want to leave you behind, not again. Your safety is more important."

Rose looked up at him. Wanting to say more, but unable to find the words, she lingered in his embrace for another moment before pulling away.

Gabriel helped Rose pack a few of her skirts and blouses, some bread from one of her mother's most recent deliveries, and the remaining pieces of Belladonna's shattered mirror. She tensed up when she saw the charred grass beside the mirror, a reminder of the battle that had happened only two days ago.

After sunset, they waited for her father to leave the house for his usual night on the town, or rather his night at the town bar, before they snuck into the house.

Rose carefully picked the lock and painstakingly turned the handle so it wouldn't creak. She cocked her head, but only heard the ghostly bellows of the frogs. She placed a finger to her lips, urging Gabriel to be quiet. However, as they entered the house, his feet thudded on the wooden floors.

She leaned close to his ear. "Stay here and keep watch while I get my mother."

Gabriel took her hand in his. "Be careful."

Rose gave his hand a squeeze. "The same goes to you." She slipped her hand away from his. After one last glance back at him, she continued down the hallway until she reached the stairs.

She crept up the staircase, being careful not to lean on the creaky, wooden banister or step on the squeaky board in the middle of the first flight of steps.

When she arrived at the top of the stairs, she snuck down the hall until she reached her parents' room. Rose opened the bedroom door and found her mother in bed asleep.

Rose's gaze darted around the dim room, searching for demons she knew weren't there. "He's not here," she whispered to herself, but the heart racing in her chest said otherwise.

They needed to work fast so they could leave before her father came back. Rose gave her mother's arm a gentle nudge. "Mother. Wake up. I'm getting you out of here."

Her mother didn't stir, but she didn't want to risk being too loud. Rose shook her again, but she still snored away. Bile rose in her throat as panic gripped her. She yanked the bed sheets off, and the snoring stopped.

Her mother sprung upright in bed, her hands protecting her face, her eyes wild.

As Lailah saw red eyes and dark hair, recognition flashed through her eyes, and her shoulders relaxed, but her mouth gaped open in surprise. "Rose? What are you doing here? It's dangerous. He could be back any minute." Her gaze searched the room in a panic.

Rose placed a hand over to her mother's mouth. "Shh. I'm here to help you. Pack some clothes and personal items. We're leaving. Now."

Lailah shook her head. "If I leave, he'll hurt me… and you. I can't."

Rose put both hands on Lailah's shoulder and looked into her eyes. "We don't have time to argue about this. I have a friend here. He's going to help us escape. You'll be safe, I promise." Lailah mumbled the words back to herself like a prayer. Rose shook her shoulders, which brought her out of her daze.

Her mother rushed to pack some things into a small, worn cotton bag which already had some Victorian style corsets, a wrinkled striped blouse with long sleeves, and a long, checkered skirt in it. It looked like the remnants of an old escape plan that never happened.

Rose's eyes darted to the clock on the wall and then back to her mother. Her heart thumped in time with each tick. The walls closed in. It had already been thirty minutes. This was taking too long. They needed to leave, *now*.

She tapped Lailah on the shoulder. "Let's hurry. We don't know when he'll be back."

Her mother flinched away from her touch. Rose rolled up the sleeve of Lailah's night shirt and saw a violet bruise the size of a fist blooming on her shoulder. Her eyes narrowed. "Did he do this to you?"

Her mother gave a slight nod as she shrunk away from Rose, her gaze focused on the floor. Rose sighed. "Sorry. Here, let me help you." Rose shoved the remaining clothes into her mother's pack before grabbing her by the hand and leading her to the staircase.

They tiptoed down the stairs and Rose kept the pack precariously perched on her shoulder, gritting her teeth together as she attempted not to jostle it. Her mother trailed behind her, and she kept looking back, pointing at where she wanted her to walk.

The crash of a glass bottle shattered the silence as they reached the first step, sending a shiver down Rose's spine. Rose pushed Lailah back, so they were both hidden by the wall in front of the stairs.

A slurred voice shouted, "Where are you, you whore of a wife? I've got a surprise for you." He clenched a jagged bottle in his fist.

Lailah's hand gripped onto Rose's wrist so hard that it ached, and she looked back to see her mother's entire body tensed and her eyes wide. Lailah's mouth gaped open, and Rose clamped a palm over it, barely stifling the whimper that clawed out of her mother's throat.

Rose leaned in so her lips brushed Lailah's ear. "Be quiet. We don't want him to find you. Gabriel's going to take care of him."

Rose frantically searched for Gabriel but didn't see him. Fear settled into her stomach. *What if he left? No. He wouldn't, right? He must've hidden when he heard the door open.*

The tension in her stomach eased when she glimpsed a pan peeking out of the kitchen's entrance.

Gabriel crept along the walls of the kitchen, towards her father. She held her breath when he raised the pan above her father's head and then brought it down with full force, hitting him with a swift *thwap*.

Her father yelled out in pain, and his hand flew to his head. Then he swiveled around to face Gabriel. His eyes gleamed with hate, and her body screamed at her, telling her to run, but she remained still in their hiding place, taking shallow breaths that she hoped weren't loud enough to draw his attention.

"Who the hell are you?" He stumbled closer to Gabriel, who tried to swing the pan at him again. But this time her father caught it. He lashed out at Gabriel with the broken bottle, and it grazed his arm, leaving red tracks on his skin and staining the glass.

Gabriel clenched his hands together in a fist, and his nose wrinkled. He crouched down and rushed her father, hitting him square in the chest. They both tumbled to the floor.

Gabriel turned to the stairwell and yelled out, "Run. Now."

Rose grabbed her mother's hand and sprinted through the living room, past Gabriel and her father. She gave them a wide berth as her father squirmed and bucked under Gabriel's weight. He pinned her father's arms and legs, holding on for dear life.

As they ran through the front door, Gabriel slammed his fist into her father's head, causing the man's head to snap to the side in a jarring motion. Gabriel yelped when his knuckles connected with her father's jaw. His skin split open and blood trickled from his knuckles, but the punch had the desired effect.

His eyes rolled back in his head, and he went limp like a puppet with its strings cut. When Gabriel wiped his forehead, it came away with blood. He gave a nervous laugh. "I think I got him. Now let's get out of here."

They raced out of town in the dead of night. The only sounds accompanying their departure were the chirp of crickets and the whisper of leather as he untied the horse's ropes from the post.

Rose clung to her mother. "I'm sorry I blamed you for his actions. It's him I really hated."

Tears streamed down her mother's face, and she opened her arms. Rose curled up in them as she sobbed. The clop of hooves against the soft ground reminded her they were both finally leaving their former prisons behind.

Rose's head smacked into the wall of the cart when it came to a stop. She rubbed her sore temple and narrowed her eyes at Gabriel's back. "Sure, drive like you're in a horse race. It's not like I needed my head or anything."

When he turned around, he gave her a sly smile. "My sincerest apologies. If you'd like, I can nurse you back to health to make up for it." He winked.

Her cheeks heated, and she turned her gaze to the floor of the mail cart, scooting herself over to the ledge. "That won't be necessary. Just be more careful next time."

As Rose slid to the ground, she surveyed her surroundings. A familiar grey-blue house stood before her. The forest green trim snaked around the house like vines.

Rose turned back to Gabriel, her brow raised in question. "Why are we at your house?" She thought they'd want to get as far away as possible with her father still on the loose.

He clenched the reins of the horse so tightly that his knuckles went white. "I'm just going to grab a few things before we depart... some keepsakes. You might want to pack some food for the journey," he said with a tight-lipped smile. The tension in his grip kept her from asking any further questions.

They all headed into the house together, and Gabriel wandered off toward his room. Rose made no move to follow him. Her mother gazed around the house in awe. As if to herself she said, "He seems kind...but sad."

"He's been that way since we met," she said and pursed her lips together. Her eyes skimmed the house, and she thought about his mention of food.

"Mother, why don't you help me grab some food. We'll need it for our journey. I'll go check on him."

Her mother shook her head, and her lips curled up in a wistful smile. She slid a strand of Rose's hair between her fingers. "I'm afraid I can't do that."

Confusion and worry twisted her stomach. "What do you mean? Aren't you coming with us?"

She shook her head, and her gaze flickered to the hallway Gabriel had gone down. "You've grown up to be so beautiful... just like a rose. However, you need room to grow. I'd be like a flower pot that's too small, holding you back. You go on with Gabriel. I'm going to stay in town and solve my own problems. But thank you, my darling, for giving me the strength to take the first step." She gave Rose a kiss on the forehead and turned, walking towards the mail cart before Rose could protest.

Her mouth dropped open and a thousand questions flooded her mind as she stared at her mother's retreating back. Lailah was speaking in riddles. *What did she mean hold her back? What would her mother do if he came after her? Why would she risk staying so close to the man that harmed her? Where would she stay?*

Rose couldn't accept her mother's decision. Her legs moved before she could think. Her face flushed with anger as her hand caught her mother's wrist and squeezed it so hard that she winced. Her mother halted halfway out the door.

Rose's voice rose to a yell that burned her throat, sounding too much like her father's. "You'd throw away everything after what we tried to do for you? If you go back there, he'll kill you. Gabriel could have gotten injured or killed. We both put ourselves in danger for you. Where are you going to go? We risked everything for you!"

Rose's voice cracked when she met her mother's tear-filled gaze.

She let go of Lailah's wrist and saw a pink mark where her hand had been. "I'm sorry, mother. I didn't mean to."

Lailah shook her head and placed her hand over Rose's. "I understand you're worried, dear. It might not seem like it, but I'll be okay. I won't go back to our old home, even if it means working at one of those factories that wheeze smoke from dawn till dusk. I'll find a new place to live somehow."

Rose's heart squeezed at the thought of her working from dawn to dusk, coughing from the smoke. She didn't like the thought of her slaving away in a factory, but if she was safe from him, that was what mattered. She let out a breath. "Just promise me if he comes after you, you'll leave town and never come back."

Lailah pursed her lips. "I promise."

Maybe I take after my mother, she thought as she reflected on her own actions. Taking poison in an attempt to flee her glass prison had been dangerous, but there was always a reason behind her risks. Rose hoped that her mother wouldn't come to regret this decision.

Her mother cupped her cheek, and Rose's gaze flickered to the hallway. Gabriel still hadn't returned. "I'll be right back, Mother."

Her mother gave her a knowing look. "Check on him. I won't leave just yet."

Rose smiled and strode down the hallway to check on Gabriel.

She snuck down the corridor that led to Gabriel's room and poked her head in the door, but he wasn't there. *Where is he?*

She heard muffled sobs through the walls. *The woman's room.* An image of the room she'd stayed in before flashed through her mind.

As she crept closer to the room, the crying got louder, echoing through the hallway. She pressed her back flat against the wall, then poked her head into the slightly ajar door.

Tears streamed down Gabriel's face. His chest heaved as he cried. He held a thin, silver ring in his palm.

"I'm sorry I couldn't save you. Somehow helping Rose feels like a redemption I'll never get with you. I loved you," he whispered. He pulled a small photo out of a crevice in the dresser drawer, kissed it, and slid it back into its hiding place. Then he tucked the silver ring safely away in his pants pocket.

Rose wanted to reach out and embrace him, but instead she turned away. She'd just intruded on a private moment, and the thought made her skin itch and her fingers fidget.

After the sobs had subsided and he'd wiped his eyes, Rose made her presence known with a light rapping on the door despite it being ajar.

"Gabriel. Are you there?" Rose peeked her head through the crack in the door.

Gabriel's back straightened in alarm and he tucked his soiled handkerchief into his pocket, but the red-rimmed and blotchy skin gave him away. She wanted to pull him into a hug, but refrained herself. She hadn't realized how much the woman's death still pained him and wondered how long ago she'd died.

He smoothed his pants with his hands and straightened the collar of his cream-colored shirt before saying, "Oh, Rose, how long have you been there?"

"Not long. I just wanted to know what our plan was since you saw some of what Nightshade was plotting."

His sullen gaze took in the room one last time. "Let's go talk about this somewhere else." He shuffled out of the room and over to the study, where he collapsed into an armchair. His body sank into the cushions, and he rubbed a hand over his face.

When Gabriel gestured to the chair across from him, she plopped down, eager to hear where they'd be going next.

His mouth opened and closed, but no words came out like a marionette doll without a puppet master. Rose tilted forward, her hand reaching for his, but she stopped herself. Her hands folded into her lap instead.

After several painfully long moments, he shook his head. His gaze moved to hers, but it was unfocused. "Nightshade's allies plan to make humanity pay for destroying the forests. But when I saw his memories, it wasn't clear where he would carry out this plan."

He paused, his gaze catching on something behind them. She turned back to see a painting of a flower. "That's a beautiful painting."

"She'd always been an amazing artist." The ghost of a smile played across his lips. "Sorry. There are a lot of memories in this house."

Rose shook her head. "There's no need to apologize, Gabriel. You can tell me anything."

The start of tears shone in his eyes, and he stared down at his hands. Her heart squeezed as she remembered the silver ring. "Where was I? Right, Nightshade had memories of a nymph who lived in Lullin, an ally of his named Hawthorne."

Gabriel's gaze unfocused once more, his eyes looking at her but also past her. He mumbled something under his breath, but she couldn't make out the words.

This time Rose didn't hesitate. She reached over to place her hand over his. His fingers felt like ice. "You rarely lose focus like this. Are you okay?"

Gabriel looked down at her hand on his. His eyes glistened with the start of tears, and she threaded her fingers with his, thawing his frozen fingertips. He gave a half-hearted smile and continued speaking.

"Hawthorn was meant to disguise himself amongst the humans and gain their trust. But he disappeared before he completed his mission. He might know more about the plan. Nightshade doesn't know the shape he's taken. We need to find him before Nightshade's allies do. Perhaps he can tell us where to find the nymphs before they destroy humanity."

Rose's jaw dropped, and her eyes scanned his, searching for any hint of a joke, but there was none. The thought of everyone she knew dying overwhelmed her. She pictured April, her mother, and Gabriel on the floor, their chests unmoving, their eyes glassy.

The walls closed in around her. Her lungs constricted. Her breaths came in rasps. She grabbed at her throat, clawing at it with her fingernails, willing air to enter her lungs.

Gabriel's arms wrapped around her, and he mumbled something, but it came out muffled. She couldn't hear the words. The surrounding bookshelves swirled and blurred, and tears burned her throat.

Just focus on what you can still see. Take deep breaths, she thought to herself.

First her eyes caught on an oil lamp that lent soft light while reading, then to the comfortable lounge chairs. Some air entered her lungs, and she kept counting the images that weren't entirely blurred by tears. The books she loved to get lost in, and the chair Gabriel had sat in.

With each object, her breaths came more evenly. The blackness encroaching at the edges of her vision faded.

She could feel the steady thump of his heartbeat as he pressed against her. Her cheeks warmed when she looked down to see her chest was flush against his.

Gabriel's hands ran through her hair, and he mumbled. "You're going to be okay. Please be okay." *Were those the words he'd been saying before?* Rose lingered in his grasp for a little longer, wanting to believe that this could be more than a fantasy. But she'd only be setting him up for more heartbreak. There was a chance she wouldn't survive this, that they wouldn't survive this.

With a sigh, she pressed a hand against his chest, putting distance between them. "Thank you, Gabriel. I'm okay now."

"Are you certain?" His eyes warmed with concern.

She pressed away from Gabriel's grip. "I have to be. We have no time to waste. We need to get rid of those nymphs right now!" She held her head high despite her legs feeling like rubber.

"You've been through much. You're allowed to be upset. It doesn't make you weak."

Rose bit at her lip and muttered, "Perhaps you should take your own advice."

"Was that an insult or a sweet nothing?"

"Wouldn't you like to know?" she said with a grin and marched out of the room to face her mother before they left to fight the coming storm.

* * *

LAILAH WRUNG her hands and mumbled to herself as Rose approached. When she got close enough, she laid a hand on her mother's shoulder.

"Mother, we're going to leave soon. Please reconsider your decision. I don't want to worry about you being in danger from my father."

Lailah pursed her lips, but her voice was calm as she said, "If it makes you feel better, I'll continue to the next town, but I won't entrap you further by accompanying you on your journey."

Rose paused for a moment before she spoke. "I will respect your wishes if you promise you won't go back home."

Lailah touched a hand to Rose's cheek, "I've already promised you, but I will tell you once more. I will never go back to that wretched place, my child."

Clunky footsteps warned her of Gabriel's arrival, and when he was close enough, she reached a hand back, grabbing him by the arm. She looked up at him with tears pricking her eyes. "My stubborn mother doesn't have a place to stay, but she doesn't wish to accompany us on our journey."

Gabriel's frown curved up into a lazy half smile. "I suppose the apple doesn't fall far from the tree."

Rose glared at him. "I was requesting help, not unwarranted comments."

He took her hand in his and feathered a kiss on her fingertips. "But I love the faces you make when you're flustered." Her face flushed, and she turned away from him.

"Forget it. I don't want your help," Rose hissed. She placed a hand over her mouth, regretting the words the moment she'd spoken them.

He laughed. "Oh, but I think you do, even if you refuse to admit it."

Gabriel turned his attention to Lailah. "If you have no place to live, how can you guarantee Rose your safety? How can you promise not to go back to your husband's home?"

Her mother shifted uncomfortably before she spoke. "I'll find a job at a factory if I need to. I'll do piecework or toil away in the fields."

Gabriel clicked his tongue. "No. No. That won't do. If you want to stay behind, then I insist you use this house as your own. You shouldn't have to risk your safety or your pride. Leaving is hard enough."

Rose looked up at Gabriel, blinking as if to wake herself from a dream.

Her gaze drifted to her mother, whose mouth hung open in shock, but she whispered a silent, "Thank you."

With some trepidation, Lailah entered Gabriel's house, *her* house. Lailah was finally free.

CHAPTER 2

*I*t relieved Gabriel to be rid of the ghost house. A bonus was the radiant smile that lit Rose's face. When she leaned in and planted a kiss on his cheek, he flushed red and put a hand to his face.

If only she was this affectionate all the time. Half the time she was putting on this fake, tough act and at other times, he noticed her hesitating to touch him, comfort him. He didn't understand why, and it frustrated him. He wished she was more honest about her own feelings.

She's smart, kind, and cares deeply for other people. When she worked at the inn in Lullin, she'd made friends with April right away. Instead of fretting for her own safety, she saved her mother before running off to fight Nightshade's allies.

Now that he'd seen her father, Gabriel wondered if her upbringing was why she put on this unfriendly exterior. Growing up around a cruel man like him would've made him second guess anything that could be taken as a weakness.

As they packed their supplies into the buggy, his mind wandered back to their time in the room. He'd thought he'd seen Lara's ghost taunting Rose, but that had to be his imagination, right? He ran a hand through his hair and then grabbed the reins, urging the horse down the bumpy dirt road that led to Lullin. As trees encircled the cart, his thoughts drifted to how they would find this nymph in human clothing.

As they made their way to their first stop, Darkford, he could feel Rose's eyes boring into the back of his head. He faced forward, tightening his grip on the reins.

The questions would start any moment.

Right on cue, Rose asked, "What made you give your house to my mother? It was great of you to offer, but won't you miss your house being just *yours*?"

He pressed his lips together, and his shoulders tensed. "That place hasn't felt like home in a long time." It hadn't felt like home since Lara's death. It had become a shadow of its former self and a grim reminder of her. But he couldn't bring himself to say that.

Rose went silent for a few moments, and he was tempted to turn around and check on her when she finally spoke. "Is it because of the woman? The one that has a room with her belongings in it."

His breath hitched. "Yes, but I'd rather not speak of it just yet. Apart from my feelings toward the house, I didn't want her to go back to that horror of a husband. It wouldn't be right after everything we did to help her escape. She can't just march to her death."

Rose's arms wrapped around his waist so suddenly that she almost knocked him over. Her face buried into his back and tears wet the fabric of his shirt. "While I appreciate the hug, perhaps next time let's offer some warning so I don't fall off the mail cart," he said with a laugh.

He used his free hand to pry her hands loose, and she crawled forward to sit next to him. He turned to her and opened his mouth in mock shock. "No snide comeback. Are you sick?"

A slight smile lit up her face, brightening her scarlet eyes. "Not this time. Don't worry, I'll make it up for it later."

"Of that, I have no doubt."

Rose's eyelids fluttered closed, and she stretched her arms up as a yawn escaped her lips. "Sorry."

He waved her off. "It's okay. You should get some rest."

Rose yawned again and stretched out beside him. Her head leaned against his leg, and he stroked her hair until the tedious bumps of the cart lulled her to sleep. Long, dark hair covered her pale face. He tucked some stray strands behind her ear and slowed the horse from a trot to a walk so he could enjoy this moment longer.

When they arrived at the first town, night had settled in and stars dotted the sky. The town was lit by the gentle yellow-orange glow of lanterns lining the streets.

Handfuls of people coated with dirt and grime dragged their feet as they headed home, and businesses shuttered their shops for the day as they passed.

Gas lamps straddled the inn's front entrance. The outside of the hotel had dark grey columns and crimson red triangular tops. Tall rectangular windows hung open, letting in the crisp night air. Fresh crimson paint coated the building. A sign at the front proclaimed, "est. 1850."

Gabriel brushed hair from Rose's face and loosened his grip on the reins. The clink of metal on the floor of the mail cart made her stir. "Are we there yet?" she mumbled.

Gabriel smiled and shook out the pins and needles in his numb leg. "We're at our first stop. Let's go inside."

Rose rubbed her eyes and stretched. A delicate yawn escaped her mouth. She grumbled a bit and attempted to finger-comb her bedraggled hair, but she followed him without protest. As they approached the entrance, she pointed at the sign and glanced up at Gabriel. "What does est. 1850 mean?"

He forgot how much she still didn't know. When his lips curved up in a smile, she frowned. "What's so funny?"

"Nothing. Sometimes I just forget how much you have yet to see. The sign says it was built in 1850. EST is short for established. It's 55 years old."

She placed her fingers to her lips. "Wow, that's really old, but it looks so new."

"That's because they just painted it." Gabriel searched around for the hotel's stables and found one just about fifteen feet away. He used the reins to guide the horse and cart to the stables and searched for an open spot.

The place was nearly empty, and the stable hand had already turned in for the night, so when he found an open stall, he detached his horse from the cart and led it in. It whinnied, and he stroked its head. "Don't worry. We'll be back in the morning," he said.

He nodded to the cart. "Gather whatever you need, then we'll head inside."

Rose nodded and grabbed her small pack.

As they continued into the hotel, Rose trailed close behind. He peered back at her as she dragged her bags along. *She deserves a good night's sleep by herself.*

While he'd relish the company, they'd both needed sleep, and he didn't want to risk her seeing him hallucinate in case that happened again.

He ran a finger through his hair, mentally calculating how much of his savings he had left. The extra room would cost him, but she deserved some goodwill after everything she'd been through. With a sigh, he pushed open the heavy, wooden doors that led into the hotel lobby.

Sparkling chandeliers hung from the ceiling, the dim light of the candles, and a few stray bulbs illuminated the spacious room. A large spiral staircase descended into the center of the room, and vivid emerald green walls complemented the dark wooden floors. Scatterings of tables and chairs sat near the staircase.

A woman with mussed, brown hair awaited them at a dark wooden desk in the room's corner. With a perky smile plastered on her face, she chirped out, "Welcome," as they entered the building.

Gabriel walked over to the desk with Rose in tow and said, "I'd like to book two rooms for tonight."

The woman gave him a blank look. "You won't be rooming with your wife?"

Rose coughed beside him, and she clutched his arm in a vice grip as she got nose to nose with the woman. "His what? Surely you must be joking?"

She's definitely awake after that comment, he thought. Gabriel chuckled at Rose's shock. As his hand came to his mouth to cover his laughter, he saw the glint of his old, silver wedding band on his finger and slipped it in his pants pocket.

He must have put it on at some point absentmindedly. With a wave of his hand he said, "This lovely woman isn't my wife, but she's an excellent travel companion." He winked at Rose and relished the blush that colored her face.

The woman's brows knit together. "But you were just wearing a-"

He cut her off, holding up the hand without the ring. "I think you were mistaken, although she is rather stunning."

The woman blinked at his now bare ring finger. "Sorry. I must have been mistaken." She handed separate keys to Rose and Gabriel in a daze.

Rose's eyes widened. "Are you sure?" Gabriel waved her off with a smile.

"We leave early in the morning and you're...unpleasant when you haven't slept enough. You can thank me by getting a good night's rest."

She shoved his shoulder. "See. She's quite capable of stunning when angry."

Rose huffed and headed up the stairs just ahead of him. He thought that was the end of their conversation for the night, but once they were out of the innkeeper's prying gaze, she pulled him close. She planted a brief kiss on his lips and whispered "Thank you," before they went to their rooms.

The unexpected peck made his face flush.

His thoughts still whirled as he slipped into night clothes, but exhaustion made him drift off to sleep shortly after he sank into his bed.

When he awoke the next morning, it was to the chatter of various conversations and the clunk of footsteps as people moved about the hotel. The faintest sliver of sunlight filtered through the dark curtains, stinging his eyes. He placed a hand over his face, blocking out the sun, and groaned. "Shut up, sun," before getting up to close the curtains.

In the unforgiving mirror, Gabril spotted purple marks forming under his eyes and rubbed them as a yawn clawed from his throat. He rummaged through his pack on the bed, but didn't find a comb, so he ran his fingers through his hair a few times until he looked more presentable and flung open the door to head down for breakfast.

Rose already bounded down the hallway. When she caught Gabriel's gaze, she gave him a smile and waved.

His heart fluttered in his chest. A slight smile played across his lips when his gaze skimmed over her tangled hair and rumpled shirt, and he wanted to repay her for that stolen kiss from yesterday, but there were far too many prying gazes in the crowded corridor.

The urge to kiss her faded when she practically skipped to him, and his smile faltered. He wasn't sure he could handle a morning person just yet.

She peered up at him through hooded lids. "How did you sleep, sleeping beauty?"

He ran a hand over his face. "I'll let you know after I've had some coffee." He groaned.

"And you worried about me being grumpy in the morning," she said and linked her arm with his.

"It should be criminal to be this upbeat in the morning," he said as she towed him downstairs by the arm, but much like her kiss, her smile was contagious and by the time they arrived at the table to sit down, his jaw had unclenched and his gaze kept drifting to her lips.

Gabriel went ahead of her and pulled out a chair. In typical Rose fashion, she made an exaggerated gasp and placed a hand over her mouth. "Smiling and pulling out chairs before he's had breakfast. We'd better jot the date down in the history books."

His face heated. "I was just trying to be polite." He abandoned her chair and took a seat across from her.

"Sure you were." Her accompanying giggle coaxed out a laugh that shook his shoulders.

"Alright, you caught me. I was hoping to seduce you with my chair pulling skills. Is it working?"

Rose blinked and covered her face with the menu. "Perhaps you'll find out after breakfast."

He cleared his throat. "Let me grab the waiter." He raised an arm to flag down one of the staff to order coffee and food and turned back to Rose.

"So how did you sleep?"

She lowered the menu and blinked her lashes. "Better than you judging from the circles under your eyes." She took a sip of water.

"You're exhausting sometimes, but you're also gorgeous, so I'll forgive you." He winked.

She coughed and put down the water.

"Don't choke," he said, and she glared at him.

When she stopped coughing, she dabbed away water with the white napkin on the table. "Trying to kill me with compliments today?"

"Pardon. I'll wait until after you've finished your drink in the future."

Once the food arrived, they ate in relative silence and then headed back to their rooms to pack. The sun had just risen when they headed to their next destination.

* * *

ROSE HAD BEEN quiet as they'd packed up the mail cart. Every time he looked back at her she was frowning and staring out at the gravel and dirt road that led out of town.

As he tossed the last bag into the cart, she let out a long, drawn-out sigh, so he nudged her shoulder. "What's wrong?"

She gestured at the air with her hands. "What if we lose? What will happen to April and all the other people?"

Gabriel pinched the bridge of his nose. "We'll figure out a way to win this fight somehow, Rose."

She mulled over his response. "Somehow is far too vague. How can we defeat them when we know so little of their magic?"

His tongue ran along the roof of his mouth. "We know some things. Like the mirror I'd given you. It affected our mental states, and they communicated with it. Remember?" he noted, eager to change the subject.

"I suppose, but we still don't understand their weaknesses or motivations. Like why did Belladonna use her magic to create me? It makes little sense."

She stared down at her hands.

Gabriel placed a hand on her shoulder. "Cheer up. Once we get to the next town, I'll take you to the library and you can read whatever you want."

At that comment, she perked up. "The library might not be a bad idea. Maybe we can find out more about nymphs there."

He couldn't resist the smile that tugged at the corner of his mouth. He ruffled her hair and then secured the saddle to the horse. "That's the spirit. We'll go straight there when we arrive on Saturday. Now, let's get going."

She walked over to the entrance of the mail cart. When he saw the edge of her cream-colored skirt dragging on the ground as she walked, he offered her his hand. "Need some help?"

"Do you think I'm incapable?" Her forehead creased.

"Not in the slightest, but your attire doesn't appreciate being dragged through dirt," he said, pointing to her skirt.

She looked down and wrinkled her nose before picking up the edge of the skirt and taking his hand. "Thank you," she said and used his steadying grip to climb up into the cart.

He'd hoped for a quiet ride, but Rose kept saying "mmm" and "umm" several times until he let out a long sigh.

"If you don't stop mm and uming, I'll think you've turned into a cow. Is there something you wanted to ask me about?" he asked.

Her hand smacked against his shoulder. "What was that for?"

"Your rude comment. I wanted to know why that woman thought we were married. Care to explain?"

Gabriel's back stiffened. He'd been hoping she wouldn't ask about that. He brushed the question off with a laugh. "Maybe it's the way you're always mooning over me. You do seem to have a thing for me."

Rose huffed, and he knew he'd gotten her hook, line, and sinker. "You act like *I'm* the flirtatious one, but who's the one that stole my first kiss? Oh, right that was you."

Gabriel clicked his tongue. "But you were the one kissing me in the hallway. Anyone could've walked by and seen us. Shame on you."

The cart went silent. Her fingers tapped against the floor of the cart, and he imagined her blushing in embarrassment.

After an endless few minutes, he heard her shifting around in the mail cart. "Gabriel, can you tell me more about your family? You've said nothing about them. What do they do?"

Gabriel focused on the road ahead. His mental walls came up to block her out as a chill crawled up his bones. Images of his mother screaming as she got carted off to a "facility" for those with an illness of the brain flitted through his mind, but it also brought back warm memories of her tending to the small array of flowers he'd cared for long after her death.

He hunched over, his eyes staring out at the road ahead. *You can't run from your past forever. It's okay to share this with her*, he thought. "They aren't alive anymore."

There was a long pause, and she squeezed his arm. When he saw her in his peripheral vision, he placed an arm down, blocking her from sitting directly next to him.

Words toppled out, like water flowing from a destroyed dam. "They both died a long time ago. I was barely old enough to speak when my mother got very ill and died of a high fever that resulted in hysteria."

"I'm sorry to hear that," she whispered, and he felt her lean against his shoulder.

"My father went to war to gain this land from the Spanish. He'd always been kind. I don't remember my mother well, but he always talked so highly of her. The mirror you'd received was originally a gift for my mother. My father had gotten it from a friend."

Her arms wrapped around his waist, and she nuzzled at his arm. Tears stung his eyes, and when he spoke again, his voice cracked. "It wasn't always sad. We had a beautiful black dog we named Eve. You would've loved her. As a puppy, she liked to sit on my lap, and we never broke her of the habit when she became too big for it. She chewed on sticks, socks, and sometimes my shoes."

Rich laughter escaped her lips, and he ventured a look over at Rose, who smiled up at him. "She sounds like a handful, but you're right I think I would've liked her."

A hand left his waist, and she wiped away the fresh tears with her thumb. "I'd love to get a dog someday. Or perhaps learn to ride your horse."

The painful weight in his chest subsided when he saw her smile. Sadness and happiness warred within him, and the happiness won out when she kissed him on the cheek and placed her hand over his, interlacing their fingers.

* * *

As they continued on their journey, Rose kept sneaking glances at him through hooded lashes.

When he caught her, he threw her a beaming smile. Her face flushed, and she turned away. She didn't want to admit it, but she could get used to his attention.

She'd wanted to bring up the ring, but she'd changed her mind when her mention of the marriage comment from the inn had resulted in a snide remark. That was his common response when he wanted to avoid a topic of conversation.

While she was glad for the information he'd offered about his family, she wished he'd talk about the woman. It had to hurt keeping it to himself.

When he'd shed tears for that woman, the one with a room in his home, she'd hurt for him. But jealousy had taken hold as well. *Will he ever be over the mystery woman? He still refuses to talk about it and that ring looked like a wedding band. Meanwhile, I've endangered his life, and I know nothing about the outside world. Maybe he wants someone more experienced in life... someone a little more mature.*

Rose drew circles on the floor of the cart with her finger until the scent of smoke became strong enough to force her head up towards the scenery. On this part of the trail, only the stumps and twigs remained, like tree corpses.

Her heart dropped.

She'd been asleep on their first journey and hadn't noticed the streams filled with dirt and oil or the missing greenery. It almost made her long for the rich forests and farms of her hometown... almost.

The bustling markets and stalls of the city were stunning, but the thought of them coming at such a high cost left a sour taste in her mouth. She wondered if Gabriel felt the same way or if he was indifferent to the destruction.

Maybe this is why those nymphs want to destroy humans so much. We destroyed their homes.

Rose shoved the morbid thought away. She only hoped that when presented with a clean slate, those in the city would learn from their mistakes.

They grew nearer to Lullin with each passing hour. On the horizon, trees were replaced by factories and smokestacks tainted the air. By the time they'd gotten to the next inn, she wondered if she'd taken the right side in this battle.

CHAPTER 3

_T_hree days later, the salty hint of ocean and the choking aroma of factory fumes permeated her lungs, letting her know they'd reached their destination, Lullin.

Rose hiked her skirt up and eased out of the cart, being careful so her skirt wouldn't catch on its wooden edges. She plopped to the ground and dusted off her tan tunic.

As they entered the inn and strolled to the desk, a flash of blonde hair caught Rose's eye, and she smiled. Rose put her hands up to guard her face just in time to be wrapped in a crushing hug from April.

"I'd recognize those eyes anywhere. Long time no see," April said.

Rose returned the hug. "And I'd recognize your smile anywhere. It's good to see you again."

April pulled back a few inches and scanned Rose over. She gave a satisfied nod and said, "How long will you be staying for this time? A few weeks, months?" The words tumbled out of April's mouth so quickly Rose held a hand up and laughed.

"Slow down, April. We aren't leaving this second."

April batted her eyelashes. "Sorry. I'm just so excited. Maybe we can go to the market together and you can keep me company at the desk-"

Rose thought back to when April had taken her to the market and bought her Oyster's Rockefeller. Warmth settled in her stomach, but the happy memory gave way to annoyance when she thought back to the events leading up to the trip. April had told her she'd be right back and then left her alone at the desk for several hours. Rose crossed her arms over her chest. "You mean you're hoping to have someone to do your shift while you flirt with men at the inn."

April elbowed her and glanced at Gabriel. "Unlike you, some of us haven't been lucky enough to have a man fall into our lap."

Her cheeks heated. "He's not my man, and he hasn't fallen into my lap."

April rolled her eyes. "Sure. Whatever you need to tell yourself. Well, I hope you're able to stay longer this time. I'd love to go to the market together again."

Rose looked down at her feet. "We'll be staying here for a while, but we're not sure how long." A dark thought caught hold of her. *If they didn't defeat the nymphs, she might never see April again.*

April, oblivious to Rose's sudden change in mood, responded with her characteristic cheeriness. "Then we must make the best of the time we have together. Now for the real question. Will you be looking for separate rooms or will you share a bed?" She nudged Rose's shoulder.

Rose scoffed and opened her mouth to form a retort, but Gabriel interjected before Rose could respond.

"We'll be booking separate rooms."

"I guess you haven't made him yours yet?" she said with a teasing smile.

Rose's face burned. "April! That's improper."

April shrugged. "I'm still waiting for him to marry you. Perhaps I'll be waiting forever. I'll show you to your rooms." She gave Rose and Gabriel their own keys before sending them on their way.

Once they arrived at their rooms, they unpacked.

Her thoughts drifted back to the graveyard of a forest filled with tree stumps and air filled with black smog they'd seen on the way here. They were a stark contrast from the lush rolling fields and vibrant greenhouse of her home. Even the nymphs didn't deserve such poor treatment. Disgust and anger roiled through her stomach. She hoped she could talk to Gabriel about it when they got to the library.

Rose unpacked the meager belongings in her pack and then skipped downstairs. She found April leaning against the desk.

"So, where can I find the library?" Rose asked.

April said, "Oh, it's just around the corner. You go a little past the hospital and then look for the sign with the book on top. It's a massive building, so it should be easy to spot."

Rose smiled. "Thank you, April."

April shuddered. "Although, I don't know why you'd want to visit *that* place. All they have is books." She feigned a look of disgust.

Rose gave her a smack on the arm. "I like reading!" Her tone was defensive.

April wrinkled her nose in distaste. "Okay then. To each their own."

As she climbed the stairs and approached Gabriel's door, she heard him talking, but he'd been alone in the room. *Who could he be talking to?* she thought and inched over to the door, pressing her ear against the wooden surface to listen in on the conversation.

"Why are you here? I thought you were dead! Stop haunting me," he shrieked.

The roughness of his voice made fear constrict her throat. *Is something hurting him?* She threw open the door, ready to fight off an enemy, but she only found Gabriel shouting at the air.

His jaw hung open, but he tried to hide it with a sheepish smile. He looked like a cat who'd caught a canary. Then, he ran his fingers through his mussed hair. "So, did you find out where the library is?"

He was trying to change the subject, but how was she supposed to just let this go? Her eyes moved over to the vanity. Her thoughts drifted to the mirror. *Was he having the same problem she'd had back in the greenhouse? Was he slowly losing his mind?*

When her gaze lifted to his, the feverish side of Gabriel dissipated, leaving her wondering if she was the one imagining things.

"Let's go," he said and made it to the door in two long strides.

As they left the inn and strolled over to the library, it was like she was seeing the town for the first time.

Filth lingered in the air, choking out oxygen. The town's surroundings were more grey than green. Children dressed in tattered clothes and hunched over as they walked. Older men and young boys dragged their scuffed shoes along the dirt ground, the light in their eyes gone and their skin dull and smudged with dirt.

She again wondered if she was on the right side of this battle as she saw ornate houses next to filth-covered shacks.

As they drew closer to the library, the houses became more ornate and intricate. Many of them sported exteriors painted vibrant shades of ivy and cerulean. It was a stark contrast to the dirty and often plain looking buildings near the factories. Those had been a dull, lifeless grey. The factories sucked the life out of both the people and the buildings.

CHAPTER 4

As they walked to the library, Gabriel couldn't help but recall the haunting image he'd seen in his room. He'd dismissed the dreams as his imagination getting the better of him or perhaps fragments of Nightshade's memories.

But the twisted form of his beloved Lara that haunted him in the hotel. That was an illusion akin to the ones conjured by the mirror. Rose's reaction to the mirror had been similar when he'd returned to the greenhouse from Lullin. She'd thought he was an illusion.

It would make sense if the mirror were still intact.

As they left the inn, it took all his focus to keep his composure. He focused on Rose's red eyes and dark hair, trying to shake the illusion of Lara from his mind.

He wanted to comfort Rose, but it would be false reassurances that she would see through right away. So they continued to the library in deafening silence. He gazed at the floor the entire time, afraid of meeting her look of teary-eyed concern.

However, when they reached the small library with a sign sporting an open book, her expression brightened, and a half smile touched his lips. He took her by the hand, and his heart beat faster in his chest at the warmth of her palm against his. "I know you're excited, but be quiet once you're inside. Okay?"

Rose pulled Gabriel into the library with her.

A happy gasp escaped her lips when they pushed the doors open. Her eyes sparkled with wonder and excitement.

She called out, "I'll be over there...researching!" before she scampered off. She'd pointed in the general direction of the fiction section. A chorus of *shh's* accompanied her brief outburst.

Rose whispered a "Sorry," and her gaze flickered over to Gabriel.

He stifled a laugh and waved her off before she scampered off, deep into the bookshelves.

* * *

THE WONDERFUL SCENT of parchment and ink comforted her.

It reminded her of the many nights when she'd pored over endless pages. Her small book collection had been her only escape from her glass prison, and she'd read every book so many times that several pages had dark spots from the oil on her fingertips. But as she searched through the shelves, she regretted not asking Gabriel about how to find the mythology books.

She flitted from shelf to shelf like a bee to flowers, skimming her fingers along their spines, but she didn't spot a single mythology text.

Bookshelves lined every wall, and the endless books made her feel like she'd been thrust into a labyrinth.

Rose let out a sigh as she searched through a line of books on a dark wooden shelf that towered over her. It was like locating a needle in a haystack.

Her eyes lingered on the words *Manchineel, the Little Apple of Death* written in a fanciful mint green script. Her fingers itched to take the book, and she plucked it from the shelves, running a hand along the ornate cover with a picture of what looked like an apple tree. Her finger skimmed the deckled edges.

The feel of the paper against her skin made her thoughts shift to how many nymphs had to die so she could read this book, and she pursed her lips as her heart squeezed in her chest. "I'm sorry," she whispered and slid it into place among its companions.

Rose frowned and scanned the titles on the shelf. Herbs, poisons, and herbal remedies filled this section, but there was nothing about nymphs.

She methodically searched each line of shelves in the same way as the first, finding books on science, mathematics, and even animal medicine until she found a shelf lined with indigo and violet bindings. The placard for the section read *Mythology*.

The first book she picked up said *Stories of Olympus* on the cover. She carried the book to a plush chair near the window.

Fascinating pages about gods who could control lightning and thunder sucked her in, and she gasped at the vivid illustration of a three-headed dog with blood-red eyes and long, jagged teeth. Rose readily devoured the first several chapters before she flipped back to the table of contents and realized it wouldn't be of much use. It only had sections on Greek gods and goddesses.

With a sigh, she shut the book and placed it in its previous spot on the shelf. This time, she scoured the titles for the words "nymph" and "forest."

An ivy green cover and a worn binding got her attention first. The title read *Creatures of the Forest* and its age showed in the fragile yellowed pages.

She tucked the book under her arm along with one titled *The True Nature of Nymphs* and brought them over to a desk to read.

Creatures of the Forest contained hand-drawn pictures of massive monsters called Dryads that resembled oak trees. It said the creatures were a type of nymph. She flipped through a few more pages about sprites and fairies before coming upon a section that read *Nymph Environment and Temperament*.

This could be just what we need, she thought as she flipped to the next page.

Nymphs can be found in natural places like forests, springs, and moun-

tains. They are resilient creatures but are usually mild-mannered unless the nature they care for is threatened.

She huffed a bit at that. Nightshade had hardly been mild-mannered when he was alive.

When she flipped to the next page, the words nestled in the aging sheets made her jaw drop.

Nymphs can only die if the plant or natural feature that holds their spirit is destroyed.

She dropped the book to the floor like it had bitten her. *No. I must have read that wrong, right?*

She didn't want to touch the book again, but she needed to know if what she'd read was true. Rose took a few deep breaths and grabbed the book with shaky hands. "When I open this book again, I better not read what I thought I just read," she muttered to herself.

Still in a daze, she read the page again, hoping there was some exception or that she'd been mistaken. But it was clear as day. Nightshade was alive.

No, no, no. It can't be true. She flipped through the rest of the pages searching for anything that would tell her that Nightshade was still dead, that they'd destroyed him in their battle, but she found nothing.

Rose clutched the book to her chest. *He can't find this. Not in his current state.* She had to hide it, but where? She thought of the labyrinth of books. Perhaps putting it in another section would work.

The mathematics and science books seemed a perfect fit. *Hopefully, he doesn't check here.*

Rose pulled out the book with the shortest spine and hid the nymph book behind it. After she was confident she'd successfully hidden it away, she went back to her desk and cracked open the other book she'd grabbed, *The True Nature of Nymphs.*

The forest scene had a nymph on the cover that resembled Belladonna, and the author's last name was the same as Gabriel's, Messenger, but that had to be a coincidence.

In the table of contents, it organized the information into sections about the nymph's environments, weaknesses, temperaments, and physical characteristics.

Rose flipped right to the section on physical characteristics.

In their natural forms, their clothing blended into the forest. Several forms of nymphs have wings in sea greens, indigo, silvers, and violets. Rose touched a hand to her shoulder, remembering the shimmering silver of Belladonna's translucent wings.

She continued to skim through and saw a small section labeled *Nymphs in Human Form*. It read: *The nymphs can never truly rid themselves of their plant. It may manifest in gnarled hands, tree-like feet, and traits similar to albinism such as pale skin and red eyes. Some forms of nymphs have pupilless eyes the color of the midnight sky.*

She thought back to her previous encounters and remembered Nightshade's black, soulless eyes. She shivered.

Now, they just had to find their nymph in hiding.

Rose picked up the book, leaving her desk to search for Gabriel, but she quickly got lost among the shelves that surrounded her like trees in a forest.

"Gabriel" she called out despite the protests and leering gazes of the people in the library. "Gabriel" she said again, softer this time, as she peeked around corners.

His jagged, dirty blond hair peeked out from the shelves on plant life.

She came up from behind and wrapped her arms around him. He stiffened against her, and she whispered. "I think I found something."

He relaxed at the sound of her voice and she loosened her grip on him as she spun around to meet her gaze.

"What was it?" his eyes fell to the book.

"This book said that nymphs will still have something reminiscent of the plant they came from. It can be something in their eyes, hands, or even legs. We just have to check around town and see who it could be."

He reached out for the book, and she put it behind her back. "Can I take a look at it?"

She stood on her tiptoes so that their mouths were inches apart and batted her eyelashes. "You want this book? You'll have to earn it with a kiss in front of the entire library."

His gaze fell to her lips, and his cheeks flushed pink as he considered it. "Tempting, but I don't think I could manage just a kiss."

She blinked and her face heated. "Gabriel!" She smacked him with the book.

Other people in the library turned their eyes to them, and he placed a finger to her lips, a smile tugging at the corner of his mouth. "Sorry. I was only joking."

She blinked at him. "Were you?"

"Only time will tell, little Rose Bud."

She stammered, "F-fine. Don't tell me."

She cradled the book in front of her chest. "Who do you think might be the nymph in hiding?"

His brief laugh made her heart squeeze. "Changing the subject. Interesting. I was thinking someone in power would be the most likely candidate. Especially since they would need a person of authority to gain the humans' trust."

His gaze wandered to the ceiling. "Or it could be someone no one would suspect if they wished to monitor us."

"I think the second option sounds more likely."

Gabriel walked towards the exit and beckoned her to follow with a wave of his hand. "Good. We can search for our suspect first thing tomorrow."

"Why tomorrow?" Rose asked. Her gaze scanned the now mostly empty library. Librarians ushered crowds of people with books in hand out of the building. Her stomach rumbled again, demanding food.

Gabriel gestured to the view of the fading sunlight out the window. "It's almost night. Few people will be out and about."

On the way out of the library, Rose placed the book on one of the plush chairs she'd seen earlier.

As they made their way back to the inn, Rose thought about how they'd manage to find this nymph in hiding, and what they'd do when they did.

CHAPTER 4

When they arrived at the inn, they met in Gabriel's room. He shut and locked the door behind them. Gabriel opened his mouth to speak, but Rose raised a finger, silencing him as tilted her ear to the door and listened for possible eavesdroppers.

"Sorry. I just wanted to be cautious. We don't know if the infiltrator is here."

"Fair point." He settled into a chair next to the small fireplace. "Tomorrow, I'll check the hospital since I spent a lot of time near the doctor. Do you think April could be a suspect? You spent a lot of time with her."

Rose shook her head. "Doubtful, considering the style of clothing she wears, but I'll still check. It could've also been a guest at the inn."

Gabriel smiled. "Just try not to be too obvious."

Rose crossed her arms over her chest, "Okay. Okay. I'll do my best to be secretive." She nudged his arm. "But, in exchange, I want you to be more honest with me. Tell me if you have another *situation* like earlier today."

When Gabriel said nothing, Rose cleared her throat. "Well? Are you going to be more honest with me or not?"

He couldn't meet her gaze when he spoke. "There's nothing to worry about. I'm fine, honestly."

"I trust that as much as I trust April when she says she'll be right back. Promise me you'll tell me if you get worse."

He met her eyes. "I promise."

The lie burned his tongue. He wouldn't keep the promise if it meant endangering her.

If the hallucinations got worse, he wouldn't risk becoming a liability in the battle. Nightshade's smug expression when he'd handed him the ax for the Manchineel tree played through his mind. It was like he'd known something bad would happen.

She eyed him warily. "That promise sounded uncertain. If I find out you lied to me, I'll make you regret it. I know where you live," she said with a tight-lipped smile.

"Oh, sounds promising." A flicker of humor touched his eyes, and she shook her head.

"A-anyway. I'll see you in the morning." Rose spun on her heel and ran out of the room, slamming the door behind her.

* * *

WHEN THEY HEADED out the next morning, Gabriel went straight to the hospital. However, as he approached the building, the scent of char and ether burned his nose, and he placed a hand over his nose and mouth.

The hospital was silent. No line of patients waited near the front door.

Gabriel approached the entrance and there was a sign that simply said, "The hospital is currently closed for repairs. If you need medical attention, please seek the hospital in the next town over."

He peeked through one of the glass windows. No doctors or medical staff milled about. Strange. Gabriel paced in front of the hospital. *Maybe the post office will have some leads,* he thought and walked over in that direction.

His mind cycled through different theories about the hospital's sudden shut down. *Was it a fire? A standard repair?*

When he pushed open the front door of the post office, his thoughts were interrupted by jeers and jests from his former coworkers.

They whispered amongst themselves., "What is he doing back here?"

"Didn't he leave without warning?"

"It's Mr. Disappearing Act."

A shrill voice rose above the rest. "Hey, look, it's the messenger boy who fled town. What are you doing here?" Gabriel's eyes snapped over to the source of the sound, a small man with greasy skin and red cheeks.

He approached Gabriel with a swagger and a toothy smile that revealed yellow teeth.

In the corner of the mailroom, his former boss busied himself with a small stack of letters. He sighed and pushed his glasses up his nose, but he made no move to stop the angry man.

The short man's rounded face and ruddy cheeks betrayed the anger glimmering in his glassy blue eyes. Gabriel noticed the large dark pupils within the glassy blue depths. The man's rolled-up sleeves and pant legs meant he wasn't the nymph in hiding.

Although, he was mean enough to be one of their kind.

Gabriel shot the man a beaming smile. "I was just looking for some temporary work since I'll only be here a short while."

The unexpected cheeriness in Gabriel's tone made the man jerk back, eyes wide, but he quickly regained his composure.

His icy gaze stared up at Gabriel. "And why would our boss offer you a job again after what you did?"

Gabriel looked down at the man. "Gee, I wonder. Maybe because I'd delivered mail flawlessly before I left. Had I not?" His gaze turned to the old man who shrugged.

"Gabriel has a point, even if he is rather smug about it."

Gabriel ran a hand through his hair. "Regardless, it's none of your business. Now go back to doing your job, whatever that is." Gabriel waved his hand dismissively.

The man curled his lips back in a snarl. But before he could launch another retort, a young man bolted from the sorting room and grabbed the blue-eyed man by the shoulder. "There you are, Edward. You're needed in the sorting room, now."

Gabriel snickered. *After making all this fuss, he's just a mail sorter. Unbelievable.*

"So long, *Edward*. Off you go now," Gabriel said with a laugh and shooed him off like a small child.

Edward's face flushed bright red, and he followed the other man to the sorting room.

Gabriel strode over to his former boss's desk, head held high. The old man looked up over his half-rimmed reading glasses, meeting Gabriel's eyes. "Well, I wasn't expecting to see you again anytime soon. You know some warning would've been nice before you left. We were short-handed because of you, Gabriel." The man's tone was scolding, but the corner of his mouth quirked up in a half-smile.

Gabriel rustled his hair and turned his face away as he spoke. "I'm sorry about that. You were very gracious for allowing me to work for you before. Even when I was horribly injured. Would you mind allowing me to take on a few small jobs while I'm here this time? They don't have to be consistent. Anything will do."

The old man's gaze scanned him over from head to toe. "I'll give you some work, but if you leave without warning again, I'm sticking you on mail sorting duty next time. Understand?" The man pointed a thumb in the direction of the sorting room.

"Yes, sir." Gabriel said.

"Gabriel, you can just call me by my name, Frank. I'm not a fan of that *sir* stuff." Frank pinched the bridge of his nose.

"Okay, Frank. Please let me know what I can do to help."

* * *

In the morning, Rose went up to April and tapped her on the shoulder as she was scurrying about setting up breakfast. April spun and put a hand over her heart. Plates wobbled in her hand, and she hurried to straighten them. "Oh, it's just you. You gave me a fright. Did you need advice on the ways of men, Rose?"

Rose flushed red all the way to her ears. "No!"

"Sorry. I couldn't resist. What can I help you with?"

Rose ran her fingers along the bobby pins in her hair. "I was wondering if I could help with some odd jobs here and there."

April's eyes lit up, and her grin widened. "Of course. I missed having you around. You were such wonderful help and you're rather fun to tease." She gave Rose's shoulder a playful shove.

"Thank you. I appreciate this, April."

"It's my pleasure. I already have something you can do."

Rose eyed April warily as she adjusted the stack of dirty plates in her hands and shoved them into Rose's arms.

"You can start by helping me with breakfast."

Rose sighed. "Giving me your least favorite job. I wouldn't expect anything less from you, April."

She shrugged. "I wasn't about to look a gift horse in the mouth and seeing as you generously offered your help…" Her voice trailed off.

"Alright. Alright. I'll take care of it." Rose's gaze scanned over April as she walked away. While her overly perky personality wasn't normal, she wasn't a nymph either. Her wide doe eyes had large pupils at their center. And the clothing she wore… Well, there was no way she had anything to hide.

Instead, she focused her efforts on checking for deceivers amongst the guests, especially if they'd been there previously.

Women wearing pearl necklaces and pale hats clutched the arms of men wearing checkered suits and top hats. They laughed at everything the men said even if it wasn't particularly funny to Rose, and she wondered if any of them had jobs.

As she passed by the jewel-toned group, she shouted an "Oops" and forced herself to trip, dropping several towels to the floor. As she bent down to pick them up, she glanced at the women's ankles, attempting to find anything that would signal her as a nymph, but she found nothing apart from stockings and the swish of a skirt.

The woman's face flushed red, and she yelled, "Were you looking up my skirt?"

Rose stammered. "No I-"

April rushed over, cutting off Rose's protests. Her hands waved around frantically. "Of course not, ma'am. Our employees would never disrespect someone of your status like that."

The woman puffed out her chest and huffed. "You're absolutely right." She strutted away with the man in tow.

After the woman was out of earshot, April hissed in Rose's ear, "Be careful. Those wealthy clients can be a little testy, but they pay most of our bills."

Rose nodded. "Understood. I'll be more cautious."

After that, she avoided any strange behavior near the wealthier clients and instead focused on quietly observing people she'd seen before.

The men in emerald and indigo clothing were still at the hotel, but when she'd gone to serve them lunch, she hadn't seen any sign of wooden appendages or nymph-like eyes and didn't dare drop a plate or spill water to search them too closely.

Shortly after lunch, a courier rushed in carrying letters, with his brow coated in sweat and fingers tipped in ink. "Mail for the Lullin Inn," he shouted. April plopped the lunch plates she'd just cleared onto an empty table and rushed over to the courier.

Rose kept an ear tuned into April's conversation as she moved to scoop up April's discarded plates.

"I'll take the mail," she chimed.

"Sign here, April."

April giggled and twirled a strand of hair around her finger. "Of course. Here you go."

He handed over the letter and their fingers brushed. April flushed, but neither of them pulled their hands away. The courier stood there for several breaths before the clock chimed.

"Sorry, April. I have to get to my next delivery." He slipped his mail carrier back over his shoulder and scrambled through the front door to finish his deliveries for the day.

Did she like him? That felt oddly intimate even from here, Rose thought as she carried the plates towards the kitchen. Too late, she noticed a woman in a tan dress. She back pedaled too quickly, and the plates in her hand wobbled.

She hissed out a "damnit" as one of the lunch plates she'd been clearing fell from the stack and clattered to the floor before she could grab it. Shards of the plate shattered near the woman's feet. "I'm so sorry," Rose said, and put the plates down on a nearby table. "I'll go get something to clean that up." When she looked up, her eyes met a woman her age with a heart-shaped face and warm chestnut eyes. Her face heated, and she bit her lip.

The woman gave a cheerful smile. "I'm the one who's sorry. I should have been more careful. Here, let me help you with that." She reached down to pick up shards of the shattered porcelain plate.

Rose blinked. "Uh. Thank you."

When the woman had bent down, she'd glimpsed her ankles and saw what appeared to be lumps. This woman wasn't going to like what she did next.

As the woman moved to walk away, Rose walked a little too fast and "accidentally" stepped on the heel of the woman's shoe, revealing the socks underneath.

Rose sighed in relief as she took in the bark colored socks with the striped pattern. *It was just the socks, not wood or vines.*

The woman turned around to face Rose. "Are you alright?" she asked.

Rose nodded. "I'm fine. Are you okay?"

The woman waved off Rose's concern. "Don't worry, dear. Shoes are replaceable. But you seem to be having a tough time today."

April rushed over, stepping in. "Sorry, ma'am. I'll help her with the rest of these dishes, and you can have dinner on the house."

April took the stack of plates from the table and let out an exasperated sigh. " Why don't you take laundry duty for the rest of the day? If you break too many plates, you'll get my mother's full wrath. "

* * *

BY THE END of the work day, her arms felt like lead weights, and her fingers pruned from hand washing clothing for the last four hours. With a huff, she snatched a pin and attached the final item of clothing on the clothesline.

A half a work day searching had yielded nothing except April's annoyance. Earlier she'd smiled at Rose, but the last two times April had come in to check on the washing, she'd rubbed at her temples like she was trying to ward off a Rose sized headache.

She wasn't sure if the day had passed quickly because of the whirlwind of activity or her own anxiety.

After April came to dismiss her from work, she couldn't sit still. Rose paced back and forth in the hallway on the second floor.

When Gabriel approached her, his own gaze was hollow.

Rose brushed April off and approached Gabriel, clearing her throat to get his attention. His head jerked up at the noise, and he let out a soft sigh. "How did the search go, Gabriel?"

He frowned. "I didn't find anything. Did you have any better luck?"

She shook her head.

Rose's stomach grumbled, and he covered his mouth, trying to hide the forming smile. "I think your stomach is telling us it's time for dinner. I just saw them bringing in a tree a few moments ago, so I think you'll like this."

He took her by the hand, and his sudden touch made warmth bloom low in her stomach. As they left the hallway, a flood of light made her squint. Her embarrassment turned to awe as they descended the spiral staircase.

Scents of cinnamon and pine wafted through the air. A large evergreen tree sat in the center of the lobby, and staff members attached blue and green glass orbs to its branches. Tinsel was being hung to the rafters by a young woman standing on a ladder.

What is the large tree in the center of the hotel for? She knew this had to be a special occasion because they'd turned on the expensive electric lights in the dining hall.

She tugged on Gabriel's sleeve. "Gabriel, why are there so many decorations? And a tree in the center of the lobby?"

He smiled. "It's almost Christmas, Rose. The decorations are part of the festivities. We also have a big feast and exchange gifts."

Rose's mouth watered at the thought of a feast. "That sounds like a lovely holiday. Will we get to celebrate it together?"

His gaze glued to her lips. "Sure. It would be a good excuse to curl up around a fire. Can my present be my presence?"

Rose's heart thumped in her chest. "Or you can stick with some hot cocoa and a nice meal so you don't end up with bruised skin and a bruised ego."

He smiled, and it lit up his bright green eyes. His hand went over his chest dramatically. "Oh. You wound me."

"You brought that on yourself." She rolled her eyes and let him lead her over to the dinner table.

Dinner consisted of a golden-brown chicken carried out along with a plate of fresh bread.

Rose cleared her throat as Gabriel cut the chicken into thin strips. "So. Were you able to find any potential nymphs at the hospital?"

Gabriel shook his head and placed the forks down. His eyes clouded over. "The hospital was a ghost town. There was a sign on the door noting that it was closed. I didn't find anything."

Rose dropped a piece of bread halfway to her mouth. "Really? Why do you think the hospital would close like that?"

Gabriel ran a hand through his hair. "I'm not sure, but it smelled like smoke near the entrance."

Rose's eyes widened. "Oh no. I wonder if there was a fire. Hopefully, they open again soon so we can find out what happened."

Gabriel moved food around with his fork, but ate nothing. "Hopefully."

When they finally finished dinner, they left her polished off plate and his half full one at the table before ascending the stairs.

Once they were away from the prying gaze of the other patrons, she took his hand. He leaned down and feathered a brief kiss on her lips. "To repay you for that lovely kiss the other night." The words were a breathy whisper that sent shivers down her spine.

He turned to go towards his room with his head down and his eyes shadowed. Her heart squeezed.

Rose grabbed his arm, stopping him. "Tell me if something's wrong. Alright?" She bit her lips, blinking back the start of tears.

"Of course," he said flatly with a false smile that did nothing to ease her concerns. He gave her hand a small squeeze before slinking into his room and shutting the door in her face, leaving her alone in the dimly lit hallway.

* * *

GABRIEL SANK INTO BED. His eyelids drooped, but his mind refused to cease. Theories about the hospital's closure raced through his mind like horses in an open field. *Why would there have been a fire in the hospital? Was this an accidental fire or was it the nymphs at work?*

Even sleep offered him no reprieve. A flicker of auburn hair and pale skin caught his eye. *Not again*, he thought. Unable to look away, he watched as his dead wife slowly took shape before him. It wasn't exactly his Lara. This was some sick, twisted form of her. Her hair stuck up at odd angles, and her eyes burned with fever and maybe fury. Her skin was paper white and translucent.

She lifted her bony finger and pointed it at Gabriel, causing the breath to freeze in his chest.

"Murderer," she whispered. The apparition took a halting step forward. "Charlatan. Your *gift* was my undoing. My death was your fault."

Gabriel swallowed hard, working up the nerve to speak back. "What do you mean, imposter? What did I give you that could've possibly killed you?"

"It was the mirror, you imbecile," she spat and then lunged for his neck. He screamed, but the sound came out strangled. This had to be a dream. He had to wake up. Trying to push towards consciousness was like wading through a thick sludge.

How could the mirror have killed her? he thought as her hands gripped harder at his throat.

Someone shook him, and a feminine voice said, "Gabriel, Gabriel, wake up." The musical sound called out to him like the sound of birds chirping.

It sounded like Lara. He didn't dare open his eyes.

It's just part of the dream, he thought, but the shaking continued.

She shook him again, calling out for him in *her* voice. "Gabriel, come on. Wake up,"

He opened his eyes hesitantly and rubbed at them. He had to be hallucinating or dreaming. The person sitting beside him looked exactly like Lara before the sickness took her.

He pulled her into a crushing hug, and she stiffened against him. He lightly stroked her beautiful, auburn curls, but the hair he touched felt smooth.

"Lara. You're okay," he said as tears streamed down his face. "I missed you more than I can say."

She shoved him away and peered at him with confusion in her eyes. Eyes that flashed from grey to red.

When he squinted, auburn curls became pin straight red-black hair. A taller frame shrank to a shorter one. It was Rose, not Lara, staring back at him.

Gabriel shook his head, trying to rid himself of the illusion clouding his mind.

Rose's breath warmed his face. She pushed damp hair from his forehead. "Gabriel, are you okay? You were screaming in your sleep."

"Sorry to worry you. I had a night terror that refused to cease. It persisted after opening my eyes."

She pulled her hand back, cradling it against her chest. Several moments passed in silence before she spoke again. Her voice was a whisper, "When you were holding me, you mentioned Lara. Is she the woman with the room in your home?" Her eyes shone with unshed tears.

Gabriel looked down at the floor, unable to meet her gaze. Lara was gone. She'd been dead for almost two years now. Guilt burned his throat. He'd avoided talking about Lara long enough.

He focused his gaze on the bed as he spoke. "Yes. The room you stayed in was hers after she became sick. She is...*was*...my wife." His heart clenched, and the ring weighed down his pocket.

He held the silver band up to the yellow candlelight. "This was the real reason the woman at the hotel thought we were married."

She placed a hand over his. "I had a feeling, but I didn't want to press you about it."

He tucked his legs underneath him. "Thank you. The way she went was... terrifying. Shortly after our marriage, she became ill with a fever and hysteria. At one point she had such an awful nightmare that she lashed out at me in her sleep."

Gabriel swallowed over a lump forming in his throat. "That was when they attempted to send her to an asylum. I refused and kept her home but in a separate room. She died shortly after. That was the same room you'd stayed in. When I opened my eyes a few moments ago, you sounded and looked like her."

Rose's forehead creased in worry. She pulled Gabriel into an embrace. Tears streamed from her face, soaking his shirt as she held him. "I'm so sorry. Before, I kept asking you about the room despite your protests."

He wrapped his arms around her. His hands rested on the small of her back.

Belladonna's warning about the Manchineel tree replayed in his mind. *Don't breathe in the air near the Manchineel tree.* Perhaps that was why Nightshade had so readily given him that axe. He'd been his own worst enemy.

* * *

R

OSE PULLED BACK from Gabriel's embrace. "How long have the terrors and hallucinations been going on?"

Her eyes scanned his room. Clothing littered the floor and bed.

Gabriel shoved his hands in his pockets. "The hallucinations started recently, but the night terrors have happened almost every night since the battle with Nightshade."

She struggled to form words around the thickness in her throat. "Why didn't you tell me sooner?"

His gaze drifted to the pale pink scars on her hands. "I didn't want you to worry. To be distracted by my problems."

Her knees pressed against his. "It's far too late for that. I worried the first time I overheard you talking to yourself. If the hallucinations are worsening, you must see a doctor."

Gabriel's chin tremored. "Going to a doctor now is a one-way ticket to the asylum. That's what they'd attempted to do with Lara."

"Well, I can't let you be like this alone. Let me help," Rose whispered.

"How do you plan to help?" Gabriel asked.

Rose gripped his bed sheets so hard her knuckles went white. "I'm going to find you a cure no matter the cost."

Her mouth formed an *O*, and she placed a hand over her mouth. The silence stretched on until his stare made her fidget and the tick of the beside clock made her itch for conversation. "For today, get dressed. We're going to the hospital to find out why it closed and to check the staff for nymphs."

With one last lingering look back, she strode to the door and exited his room, but she stayed just outside, pacing as she waited for him. *What am I going to do if he's incapacitated*, she thought. *Should he even come with me on this journey? It'll be dangerous in his state.*

When he didn't come out of his room after ten minutes, her hand hovered over the doorknob. Worry creased her brow. *He's taking too long*, crossed her mind just as he called out. "Okay, Rose. I'm ready now."

Rose shoulders sagged as the handle turned, revealing Gabriel in his usual tan breeches and off-white top, his honeyed hair combed into submission.

They went downstairs for breakfast, but their small meal of bread and fresh fruit tasted like sawdust in her mouth. Hopefully, the hospital would have answers.

CHAPTER 5

When they arrived at the hospital, a tinge of char tainted the air. The usual crowd of factory workers and soot-stained children lined up outside the hospital. If it weren't for the scent in the air and Gabriel's mention of the sign, she wouldn't have believed it had closed at all.

Rose pushed open the door to find that the doctors wore the most concealing attire. Many wore long pants and long sleeve shirts. Several wore butcher aprons stained with blood.

Here it would be easy to hide wooden skin.

The most suspicious figure milled about with thick tinted glasses obscuring his eyes. He kept on his gloves even as he filled out paperwork.

It was the same doctor who'd offered Gabriel a job last time.

He caught Gabriel's gaze and approached them. Her back stiffened, and she tugged on Gabriel's sleeve. "Gabriel, I think he's-"

The words froze on her tongue when the doctor's gaze flitted to hers. His lips curled back in a grin that sent a shiver down her spine.

Gabriel, blissfully unaware of the potential enemy, flung himself into conversation with the doctor. She caught a few words about "deliveries" and "broken limbs," but her attention focused on his gloved hands and covered eyes as the two conversed.

She needed to find out if he was Hawthorn. *Maybe I can get the gloves off of him?* she thought.

Rose pretended to mindlessly fiddle with her skirt and tripped herself so she would fall just close enough to the doctor where he'd be able to catch her.

Instead of the doctor stopping her fall, he moved out of the way. Gabriel caught her instead.

His brow furrowed as he pulled her upright. "Lose a battle to your skirt?" A smile tugged at the corner of his lips.

She forced a giggle. "I'm just ever so clumsy. My mistake. I'll be more careful."

He squinted at her. "Uh huh." Rather than question her further, he returned to his conversation with the doctor.

"So what happened to this place? I came here yesterday, but the building was closed."

The doctor's gaze flickered up to the ceiling briefly before he spoke. "We had a small fire. A new employee wasn't very careful with the chloroform and a few rooms went up in flames," his voice cracked when he spoke.

"I'm sorry to hear that," Gabriel said in a soothing tone.

He was lying about the hospital fire. Why else would he hesitate like that?

"Doctor, what is the patient here for?" Rose pointed at the man laying in a bed down the hallway. Bandages wrapped up the rest of his right arm.

The doctor pointed over at the new arrival, moving his gloved hand out of reach, and she hissed out a breath.

"Oh, that was from a factory accident. It's fairly common for the factory workers to injure their arms or have difficulty breathing."

Gabriel forced her finger down. "Anyway. We should get going now. We have some business to attend to while we're here."

"I'm glad to see you're well, Gabriel. Please come by anytime." The doctor smiled, and they approached the exit.

As she brushed past him, she bumped into his shoulder and something clattered to the floor. Her gaze snapped up to his eyes. His red, pupilless eyes. The doctor's back stiffened, and he bent over to snatch the glasses from the floor and place them on his face.

He moved to walk away, but she wrapped her hand around his wrist. "Doctor, I need to speak with you. Alone."

Rose beckoned for Gabriel to follow her.

Gabriel frowned at her, and she mouthed *nymph.* His mouth opened to an "O" and he followed her down the hallway.

She followed the lingering scent of char to an abandoned room with scorch marks and shut the door behind them.

When they were all out of sight of the other doctors and nurses, she pushed Hawthorn against the wall. "Tell me what you know about Nightshade's plan."

He looked stunned at first, eyes wide. "Who is Nightsha—" he started to say, but she tightened her grip on his wrist.

"You aren't fooling me, Hawthorn."

Hawthorn shrugged. "So, I suppose you saw through my guise. What do you want, and how do you know my old enemy Nightshade?"

Her voice rose an octave. "Enemy?"

His flat gaze bored into hers. "We broke ties, or were you unaware of that, little halfling?"

She released her hand from his wrist. "I'm sorry. I don't wish to hurt you."

Hawthorn rubbed at his wrist. "You could've fooled me. Who attacks someone that might be an ally?"

Her gaze flickered to Gabriel. "The nymph has a point."

Rose didn't meet Hawthorn's gaze when she spoke. "I'm sorry. I believed you were Nightshade's ally."

Hawthorn laughed, but it was a hollow sound. "Perhaps in the future, you should think before attacking. Trust that when the time comes for me to pick a side in this war, I won't forget your actions today, nymph girl."

Nymph girl. The impact of his words hit her all at once, like a stampede of elephants, and she blinked in surprise. *How could he tell she was part nymph?*

As if knowing her thoughts, he said, "Your eyes give you away."

She hadn't considered that, but it had been clear in the book they used to find Hawthorn. It clearly marked her as a nymph.

He grinned. "I'm not entirely fond of you, but I detest Nightshade even more. What do you want to know about his plan?"

Rose trailed her fingers along the fabric where her bustle hid under the skirt, and Gabriel spoke up instead. "Where can we find the nymphs who wish to poison the humans' water supply?"

The doctor, Hawthorn, eyed Rose with curiosity. "The half nymph serving as your travel partner should be able to sense a nymph when it's near... unless she hasn't fully accepted her powers yet."

Rose shook her head. "I wasn't aware I had powers until now."

He clicked his tongue. "How...disappointing. But to answer your lover's question, the nymphs plan to destroy a city north of here somewhere in Pennsylvania. That was the last I heard before I cut ties."

Rose's face flushed. "Was your story about the hospital a lie? I noticed your hesitation earlier."

He clamped his lips together. "Shortly after Gabriel left with you before, Nightshade sent nymphs to burn down the hospital with me inside. Although, the part about the chloroform being the cause was true. That's why I'm covering my hands. They've refused to take human shape since the fire, so I've had to adjust."

He inched up his glove enough to reveal charred grey wood in several places along his hand.

"They'll probably target the city with the most people. Up there, they're known for their coal mines and factories, so a large accident is unlikely to rouse much suspicion. As for Gabriel, it might be best if you leave him beh—" He meant to say behind but stopped short when Rose leveled a glare at him.

When he'd left her in the greenhouse for too long, she'd lost her mind. She'd bring him with her regardless of the consequences.

Gabriel's golden brown hair passed through her peripheral vision as he approached Hawthorn. "Why do you want me to stay behind?"

"With no powers, you'll be a liability, a hindrance."

Gabriel's hand balled up at his side. "You're probably right, but her traveling alone would arouse suspicion. I won't stay behind."

Gabriel ran a hand through his hair and then exited the room.

As she turned to follow him, Hawthorn grabbed her wrist. "Keep a close eye on him. I can see in his eyes he's losing his connection to reality."

Hawthorn's gaze searched for Gabriel, his ears turned to the ceiling listening for him. "Does he know that Nightshade still lives?"

She shook her head.

"Good. Keep it that way for as long as you can and leave this town soon. It isn't safe here."

A pit formed in her stomach as she removed her wrist from his grip and went after Gabriel. She found him in the waiting room, and Hawthorn's words swirled through her mind as they went back to the hotel. They knew where the nymphs were.

Now, they just needed to form a plan.

CHAPTER 6

Gabriel's sleep logged mind struggled to focus as Rose dragged him down the street toward the hotel.

When the doctor mentioned leaving him behind, he'd imagined what would happen to her if his mind wandered in the middle of a battle. Last time, they'd narrowly escaped with their lives and that was when he wasn't hallucinating his dead wife.

Even with Rose tugging on his hand, guiding him to the inn, he felt like he was floating. He couldn't string together words to question her about why she'd taken so long to follow after him. *Had the doctor said something to her after he'd left the room?*

His thoughts were interrupted when someone thumped into him and released a string of curses. He fell to the floor and plates crashed around him, scattering shards of ceramic. Gabriel blinked and looked up to see a pink faced April.

He rubbed a hand over his face. "I'm so sorry, April. I should've been watching where I was going."

The brief grimace that crossed April's face was quickly replaced with a tight smile. "Don't worry about it. I'll go ahead and clean this up. Have a good day."

Gabriel's face flushed red. He muttered, "Thank you," then rushed up the stairs, leaving Rose behind without a single word.

He didn't stop until he'd closed and locked the door to his room. Finally, his breathing calmed. He slumped to the floor, leaning against the chilled wood. *Perhaps the doctor is right. Maybe I should stay behind,* he thought as he rubbed his temples.

He could use his remaining savings to fund her travels and stay at the inn until she returned, but he didn't relish the thought of her traveling alone. Perhaps Hawthorn might know of someone else willing to travel with her. *It might be safer for both of us this way,* he thought.

The tumbler of amber liquid called to him from the nightstand. Draining the glass warmed his body and helped numb the sting of being left behind. Having that conversation with Rose wouldn't be pleasant. With a sigh, he picked up the empty glass and brought it downstairs for cleaning. He'd have to get some more without arousing Rose's suspicion.

He ran a comb through his hair. As he fixed the starched collar on his shirt, he noted wrinkles in his shirt and pants. Blotchy, yellow stains covered them.

He sighed and grabbed some fresh clothes from his pack. With somewhat steady hands, he took off his soiled shirt and pants, then tossed them on the floor. He'd have to bring them downstairs too, so the inn could put them with the rest of the washing.

Carrying the pile of clothes in one arm and a glass with the lingering scent of alcohol in the other, Gabriel walked downstairs. He peered over his mound of clothing to check for passersby.

When he reached the bottom of the stairs, he stumbled two steps forward on his way to April.

He placed the tumbler and the pile of clothing on the desk. "Hey April. I wanted to return this glass."

"Sure, Summer can you grab it please?" She beckoned over a timid girl with dull grey-brown hair to take his dirty clothing over to the washing area. He gave the glass to April, who sniffed it and wrinkled her nose before placing it on the counter.

"Does Rose know you've been drinking?"

He glanced down at his nails, pressing the skin of the nail beds. "No. I don't want to concern her."

April snapped. "Look at me."

He lifted his gaze to hers. Her lips pressed into a thin line. "You'd better not hurt her. She's rather fond of you."

"Yes ma'am," Gabriel said with a lowered head.

"Good. Now go. She's waiting for you to join her for dinner." She shooed him off to the dining area.

Some small, square glasses covered Rose's striking red eyes, but he picked her waist length, red- black hair from the crowd. When he spotted her, she sat at a table with her hands folded in her lap, but her gaze darted to each platter of food being brought out.

Gabriel crept up behind her and placed his hands on the back of her chair. "Fancy seeing you here. Care to have dinner with me?"

Rose glanced up at him and smiled. "Why of course." She held out her hand and let out a slight giggle when he feathered a kiss near her fingertips before taking a seat across from her.

At least for now, we can try to forget what the coming morning will bring, Gabriel thought.

"So, Rose, what big mysterious nymph secrets did Hawthorn reveal to you after I left the room?"

A frown flickered across her face, but it fled so quickly that he wondered if he'd imagined it. "That I'm the most powerful nymph of all." She pretended to flex her thin arm. He covered a snorting laugh with his hand.

"Says the girl who can't even wrangle a horse."

"He was too squirmy." She stuck out her lip in a pout.

"Sorry. I was just teasing you."

When he placed a hand over hers, she bit her lip, and he had a strong desire to feel the softness of those lips against his, to tangle his fingers in her silky black hair.

But he couldn't do that. He couldn't remain by her side. The doctor was right, he would only be a burden, a liability in the upcoming battle.

She smiled when she caught his gaze on her. "We should get going soon now that we know where the nymphs are. I'm just glad this time neither of us will have to be alone." She gave his hand a squeeze. "When do you think we should leave, Gabriel? I was thinking maybe the day after tomorrow. That would give us time to research, pack, and say our goodbyes."

Gabriel's words froze on his tongue. *I'm the one who needs to say my goodbyes, but I don't know if I can,* he thought.

Her elbows came up onto the table as she leaned in. "Cat got your tongue? You're being unusually quiet." When he stayed silent and ran a hand through his hair, her smile fell. "Gabriel, what do you think?" Her voice wavered.

He pulled his hand from hers. "Rose, I don't think I should go with you. Maybe you can find a more suitable travel partner, like a nymph ally? Someone strong enough to aid you in battle." Tears wet his cheeks and dripped onto his hand. He swiped at them and chanced a look at Rose.

Her hand gripped the tablecloth. Silky black hair brushed the table and fell over her face. "Hawthorn is a fool. We're not getting separated. Not again. You have to come with me!" She slammed her fist on the table and several people turned to stare at the spectacle.

When she rose from her seat with the tablecloth still in hand, glasses toppled over and a plate shattered. She released her grip and the fabric fluttered to the floor. With tears filling her eyes, she ran out of the room and into the dark night.

I knew she wouldn't be happy, but I hadn't expected her to react like this. I have to go after her. He got up from the table, skirting around the broken glass and followed Rose's form until he lost sight of her. He had a feeling he knew where she was heading.

* * *

ROSE DIDN'T KNOW where her legs would carry her. All that she knew was she needed to run. She had to get away from the pain, the pain he'd caused. Earlier he'd told Hawthorn he'd stay by her side. *What changed? Why was he now siding with Hawthorn?* A sob burned her throat as she ran, and a scream escaped her. "You idiot. I don't want you to leave." She shouted into the night. The thought of him alone, not knowing what was real or imagined made her heart squeeze.

It reminded her of the way the mirror had made her feel, but the mirror couldn't be doing this. it was in pieces. She couldn't leave him here, not like this. His condition would deteriorate even quicker without someone to ground him and Hawthorn warned her that it wasn't safe here.

The shadowy outline of a wooden sign with a book at its center came into view. Without thinking, she'd run to the library even though it was closed. Rose leaned against the closed door and slumped down to the ground. Sobs wracked her body, tears spilling out as she cried. "What am I going to do? I don't know how to ride a horse. I've never even lived on my own. How am I supposed to do this without him?"

She'd hoped that Gabriel would stay with her, that he'd help her, but now she felt lost. Part of her wanted to give up, but the back of her mind chastised her. *Pull yourself together. How can you help anyone else if you can't even help yourself?* "Compose yourself." She smacked her forehead with her open palm.

Hawthorn's term for her came to mind. *Nymph child.* Maybe she could show Gabriel that they could do this together, that she could become strong enough for the both of them. She'd show him her magic, but first she'd have to learn how to access it.

Determined, she crossed her legs and closed her eyes, counting backward to calm her mind like she did when panic took control of her. "I'm only giving myself until then to cry; after that I need to pull it together. I must learn to do this myself. I have to be strong enough to protect us both," she repeated to herself.

Ten, nine... As she counted, her breathing became less ragged and the shaking in her hands subsided. The ghost of Belladonna's voice whispered, *You can do this, my child.*

She thought back to the weapons Belladonna and Nightshade had used. She pictured it in her mind and closed her eyes.

Energy coursed through her, raising the hairs on her arms. But when she looked at her palm, there was no weapon. She sighed and tried again. This time she focused on her hand. She pictured grey purple flowers of a Belladonna and the green stems they sprouted from.

When she opened her eyes, her nails were green. Not quite what she'd been hoping for, but it was a start.

She imagined the small hairs on a Belladonna flower and a tingling sensation shot through her fingers.

With her other hand, she stroked the top of her hand, now silky like the flower's petals. Closer.

Each attempt made her breaths more labored, but she was no closer to using her magic. *What am I doing wrong? It should be Belladonna magic, right?*

A whispering voice rang through her mind. *We are alike, but you aren't me, little Rose Bud.*

Her head whipped around searching for the source of the noise, but no one else was there. *You're probably just imagining her voice,* she thought, but the strange whispers had made a valid point.

Maybe she needed rose magic. This time, instead of imagining herself like Belladonna or Nightshade, she thought about her name-sake, the rose.

She imagined a short rose staff covered in thorns. Something thin but strong enough to be used as a weapon. Something bloomed, growing in her palm. When pain pricked her skin, she looked down and saw a small, thin whip about half a foot long and covered in thorns.

Red blood dripped from her palm, and she dropped the whip to the ground, but it didn't dissipate. Instead of gripping it with her entire hand, she reached down and grabbed one of the few spots that held no thorns, but the weapon swung back and forth and scraped her skirt.

Rose smiled. Even if it wasn't as easy to handle as Belladonna's or Nightshade's weapons, she'd been able to create a nymph weapon. She really did have nymph magic flowing through her veins.

Feeling satisfied with her handiwork, she decided to head back.

She wondered if Gabriel had gone looking for her. Not long after the thought, she saw him, wild-eyed and running towards her.

She moved the vine whip behind her so he wouldn't impale himself just before he crushed her in a hug. "I was worried about you when you ran off. Please don't scare me like that again."

Her face flushed. *Maybe this decision weighed heavily on him as well.* She let his embrace warm her chilled skin until one of the thorns on the staff pricked her thumb, making her wince.

She wriggled in his grip. "Gabriel. I have something to show you."

He pulled back from her, gazing into her eyes expectantly. The furrow forming in his brow made her hesitate. She shifted from foot to foot.

"What did you want to show me?"

She pressed her lips together. "Hawthorn said I had nymph magic, and I thought if I could master some magic maybe I could be strong enough for both of us. Strong enough to convince you to go with me and..." She moved the thorny weapon into view. "I know it's not much, but I made this."

His eyes widened in surprise when he saw the weapon, and he smiled. He placed a hand to her cheek. "That's impressive that you learned so quickly. See? You'll do fine without me."

She shook her head. "That's not true at all. It was because of you that I learned this so quickly." A blush crept onto her face, making her ears pink at the edges. She stammered as she tried to get the next words out. "I-I want to protect you because you're precious to me. Please don't stay behind."

Gabriel paused, choosing his next words carefully. "You're precious to me too...but I don't know if I'm comfortable with you taking that risk for me."

She moved away from his touch. "It's not your decision whether or not I take this risk. It's mine and mine alone. I want you to come with me." Her voice shook and her grip around the whip tightened, the thorns digging into her skin.

Gabriel sighed and ran a hand through his hair. "Okay, Rose. I'll go with you, but under one condition: if I get too ill to continue or put you in danger, you're to bring me back at once. Understood?" His gaze was stern, and she knew there was no bargaining with him on this.

She pressed her lips together and dropped the thorn covered whip to the grass. "Okay," she said.

He offered her his hand, and they walked back to the inn hand in hand.

* * *

GABRIEL COULDN'T KEEP his eyes off her as they approached the inn. He'd almost lost her. Again. He squeezed her hand to get her attention, and she turned towards him. "Rose, I'm sorry I upset you earlier. I don't want you to continue without me. But what Hawthorn said got in my head. If you got hurt on account of me, I'd never forgive myself."

She squeezed his hand back. "And I couldn't live with myself if something happened to you. You've almost died once trying to save me. I refuse to allow that a second time."

"I would do it a second, third, and even fourth time."

Her eyes widened. "Why? Are you daft or do you just have a death wish?"

He laughed. "Maybe I just value your life more than my own."

"You're the one that deserves a long, happy life, not me." The words came out a barely audible whisper.

He kissed her hand. "That's not even remotely true, and I'll spend as long as it takes to make you believe that."

A dazed look lit her eyes, and he got lost in their rose red depths. Not caring who saw, he pulled her into his chest until their lips were just inches apart.

She leaned into his touch, brushing her lips against his, and he tangled his hands in her hair. Her mouth opened, and he explored her with his tongue, causing a low moan to escape her lips.

Her arms wrapped around the back of his neck, and her teeth grazed his lower lip. He gasped and pressed into her so that their chests molded together. He wanted more of her, all of her, but it couldn't be here or now.

Reluctantly, he pulled away from her kiss. Her lips were swollen and red. Her hair was tangled, and her cheeks flushed as they both gasped.

Turning his head up to the crisp night air, he took a few deep breaths to calm his racing heart. She finger combed her hair as she kept stealing glances at him.

He smiled at her, and she stared down at the ground. She reached out for his hand wordlessly, and they walked together to her door. She stood up on her tiptoes and gave him a quick kiss on the cheek before squeaking out "Goodnight" and darting into her room. She slammed the door shut behind her.

Before he went to bed, he ventured downstairs and ordered a beer, carrying it up to his bed. Perhaps the stuff would chase the nightmares away.

As he lay in his own bed sipping at the alcohol, he wondered if he should've agreed to go with her.

Probably not. But he couldn't bear the thought of being away from her. He just hoped he wouldn't end up being the death of her. That was his last thought as he surrendered to the comfort of sleep.

CHAPTER 7

*R*ose awoke to sunlight streaming through the small window in her room. She pushed back the curtains and then got dressed. No sound came from Gabriel's room next door.

As she slipped on her skirt, she thought about what types of new animals they might encounter on their journey. *Maybe I'll learn about some fantastical creatures. Something kinder than nymphs*, she thought.

She took one last glance in the mirror and moved a few stray hairs from her face before walking to Gabriel's room. Apprehension crept into her step, so instead of her usual loud banging, she gave just a slight knock on the door.

It was enough to wake Gabriel, who answered with a grumble and mussed hair that stuck straight up in random places. "Rose, is it time for breakfast already?" he mumbled, his voice still gravelly from sleep.

Rose nodded. He held his hand up to stop her from coming into the room. "Okay, wait there for a few moments while I get changed, then I'll be right out." He closed the door, and she heard rustling sounds.

After a thump and a banging noise, he muttered, "Damn."

He must have hurt himself in his rush to get ready, she thought and giggled a little at his clumsiness. After waiting a few moments, he emerged in a fresh outfit and his hair combed neatly to the side. Now, when the sunlight hit it, little golden strands shone through.

He cradled his hand which was red at the knuckles and several fingertips. "What happened to you? Get injured getting dressed?" she teased.

He rolled his eyes. "As a matter of fact, yes, I did."

He held out his injured hand. "I jammed my fingers in the dresser trying to close it. I must be tired." He gave a sheepish grin.

Rose grabbed his hand and feathered a kiss on it. "There's a kiss to make it better. Now, let's go. We're losing time we could spend at the library."

She smiled up at him before marching down the spiral stairway.

* * *

GABRIEL DRAGGED his feet to breakfast. They grabbed a table together and sat down to have some canned peaches and oatmeal with sugar and dried fruit atop it. And of course, he had his life's blood: coffee.

He inhaled the rich, nutty smell. As he sipped at the bitter beverage, he wrapped his hands around the mug and let the steam curling up from his cup warm his face and soothe his hands.

He savored the warmth as it thawed his frozen fingertips. The occasional breeze coming through the inn's front door sent a shiver down his spine as it chilled his skin. Even this far south it got too cold for his liking.

Rose gazed at the steaming mug with wide eyes, and he realized that she'd probably never had coffee before.

Her face lingered near the steam, and she sniffed it and sighed. "You're always drinking that. Does that taste as delicious as it smells? It's like roasted nuts!"

A lazy smile curled his lips. Gabriel turned to her with a finger on his lips and whispered, "You might not like it. It's-"

Too late. She'd already grabbed the steaming mug and was tilting it to her mouth. As she gulped it down, her nose wrinkled and she shoved it across the table. "It's so bitter. Why do you drink this?"

He chuckled a bit at that. "I didn't ask you to try it. It's an acquired taste."

She curled her upper lip up and shoved the mug back over to him. "Perhaps the reason it's an acquired taste is that it's telling you the taste isn't worth acquiring."

The comment left him scrambling to cover his mouth to avoid spitting out his coffee. "I don't drink it for the taste. I drink it because it gives me energy to deal with you this early in the morning."

She rolled her eyes at him. "Well, you're no pleasure to deal with in the morning either." She turned up her nose at him, but a small grin tugged at her lips.

After breakfast, they headed to the library. They arrived just as the doors were being propped open. Rose ignored the exasperated sighs of the librarians at the entrance as she pushed her way past them and into the building.

She immediately left his side, wandering from shelf to shelf like a child browsing a sweets shop.

Gabriel walked over to her and tugged on her sleeve to stop her aimless searching. "Do you know about the organizational system for the library?"

She cocked her head to one side. "There's an organizational system?"

He slid a palm down his face. *Of course there's an organizational system*, he thought.

It was painfully evident now that she'd spent most of her life trapped in a greenhouse. "Yes, Rose, there is. Here. Let me show you."

He directed her over to a section that was all about geography. It had information on plants and animals in different regions from the north. He plucked a book off the shelf called *Pennsylvania Environments and Wildlife* and deposited it into Rose's waiting palm.

She stared up at him with bright eyes and then padded over to a nearby desk so she could start reading it. Before walking away, she placed a hand on his shoulder and whispered "Thank you."

Once she'd plopped down in a chair to read, he moved on to his favorite section of the library- science and mathematics.

A math book jutting out from the shelf captured his interest first, so he slid it off the shelf only to hear the smack of another book falling to the floor. He cringed as a chorus of "Shh" was directed at him and picked up the fallen text.

The cover held a picture of a nymph. *How'd that get there?* he thought and brought them both to the table.

He sat on a plush lounge chair with both books and cracked open the math book first. It was about using different geometric shapes in architecture to offer stability and style. Not exactly what he'd been hoping for, but he skimmed the first several chapters before the pull to read the misplaced book called out to him with so much fervor, he couldn't ignore it any longer.

His fingers leafed through the mythology book until he found the chapter on nymphs.

There were several pages dedicated to eating habits, natural enemies, and even courting, but a line from the section on weaknesses sent a shiver down his spine.

A nymph can only die if the plant or natural feature which holds its spirit is destroyed. He slammed the book shut and his palms started sweating. *Nightshade might still be out there.*

Images of Rose playing keep away with that book yesterday flashed through his mind. *Had Rose hidden this from him?*

The betrayal stung.

I agreed to travel with her despite my better judgement, and she can't even trust me with simple information? As Gabriel replaced the book, another thought crossed his mind.

He'd already suffered night terrors and hallucinations. *Maybe she's trying to protect me?* That was a thought he liked much better, but he couldn't be sure without asking her. He was afraid to know the answer.

* * *

TUCKED AWAY in a quiet corner of the library, Rose flipped through the pages of the book Gabriel had given her. In it were pictures of trees whose leaves changed colors in fall. It was fascinating. She'd only ever seen it once in Florida as a child and only for a few days, but the colors hadn't been fiery reds, vibrant oranges, and sunflower yellow. They had just been dull shades of brown.

But the most interesting photos showed the ground blanketed in white snow.

It rarely got cold enough for snow. It only happened once every one or two generations, if you were lucky.

Once her curiosity was sated, she got up from her velvety perch and searched through rows upon rows of books for Gabriel.

She had no luck in any of the non-fiction sections, but when she walked through the mythology section, she froze.

Gabriel's broad shoulders hunched over, and his eyes filled with tears. His hand clutched a book with frayed edges and an ivy green cover. The same book she'd hidden yesterday.

Her heart beat faster, and her breaths came in jagged gasps. Her feet froze to the spot. *Should I be honest with him or pretend I didn't hide the book? What if he hates me for hiding that from him?*

When he turned in her direction, she ducked behind a bookshelf.

He started walking back to where she'd been reading. Rose scrambled over to the area Gabriel had pointed out to her, the geography section, trying to make it there before he did.

He can't know I was spying on him, and how did he even find that book...unless he's interested in the math and science books?

Not long after she'd half sat, half fallen into her chair and opened her book, Gabriel's hand tapped her on the shoulder.

"So, how did the research go?" He smiled, but it didn't reach his eyes.

Her heart lodged in her throat. Her own grin faltered when she responded, "It went well...I'm really excited to go there now!"

If you'll still agree to go with me. She thought. His expression was closed off, revealing nothing.

"Good., then let's go. We should take plenty of time to pack before we head on our journey." His tone was flat.

Then he held up a finger. "Actually...On second thought, wait here for a moment. I have to let the post office know I'm leaving...again." He turned on his heel and headed out of the library without another word, leaving her alone with her thoughts.

CHAPTER 8

*H*e shouldn't have bothered telling his former boss he was back. *At least I didn't ask for any full-time work,* he thought as he ran to the entrance and pushed open the front door to find chaos.

People rushed around in a flurry of activity. The postmaster was on the floor sorting mail and delivering packages. *This might make things a bit more difficult.* When he spotted Frank looking over the addresses on envelopes, his eyes squinted underneath thick glasses.

Gabriel ran a hand through his hair. "Sir, I have something I need to tell you."

Frank's head snapped up, and his wild gaze stared at him through glasses that sat crooked on Frank's face. "I'm glad you're here. I know you usually go to the hospital, so can you deliver this to Doctor Thorn for me?" He deposited a letter into Gabriel's palm.

Gabriel searched around for any available workers, but he found none. "Sir, I can deliver this for you, but I'm leaving town today."

Frank's gaze flicked over to the men sorting mail and then back at Gabriel. "Okay," He said through ground teeth and then rushed off.

Gabriel turned the letter over in his hand. It had a vine pattern on the outside. The full name on the letter was Dr. Nathaniel Thorn. *It must be for Hawthorn*, he thought. He went over to the hospital to deliver the letter.

He itched with curiosity, and his mind wandered, thinking of the possible contents of the letter. *Maybe it was orders from one of the other nymphs. Or a call to action.*

When he didn't see Hawthorn right away, he went up to the main desk.

"Can I speak to Doctor Thorn?" he asked.

"Of course, but it'll be a moment. He's with a patient. Do you have a letter for him?" The man gestured to the letter in his hand.

"Yes, I do, but I'd also like to speak to the doctor in person."

The man paused for a moment and said, "Very well. Wait here." After that, he hurried off, and Gabriel was left in the main hall to watch the rush of incoming and outgoing patients.

Some of the people who walked out cradled an injured arm or leg. Others wore makeshift masks made of filthy cloth.

Gabriel tapped his foot as he waited. His eyes kept glancing at the ticking clock on the wall. Ten minutes passed, and he debated leaving with his questions unanswered.

Maybe I should've just delivered the letter, but what if it's important news? When Hawthorn finally appeared, he sighed in relief.

Doctor Thorn handed medication over to an injured man.

Hawthorn's head turned when the receptionist called out, "Dr. Thorn. There's a letter here for you," before pointing to Gabriel.

Gabriel held out the letter. "I came because I have a delivery for you, Hawthorn."

Hawthorn put a finger to his lips and hissed out a "shhh." His voice dropped to a whisper. "Don't use that name in public again or I'll have to reconsider our tenuous truce."

Hawthorne's eyes caught on the letter, and his skin paled.

Gabriel whispered, "Sorry, I don't mean to pry, but who's the letter from?"

Hawthorn sputtered, "I-It's from Nightshade's army. They've

found me." Hawthorn turned a solemn gaze to Gabriel. "You should leave. Now."

Gabriel nodded and turned on his heel. He needed to get Rose.

ose had just gotten to the climax of a book where a knight faced off against a dragon when Gabriel shook her shoulder.

"We need to leave. Now." Sweat plastered his hair to his face and his gaze darted around the library when he spoke.

She didn't like being interrupted in the middle of a good book, but urgency was written all over his face.

Rose grumbled, "And it was just getting good." She sighed and closed the book, putting it on a nearby cart for the librarians.

Once she'd gotten rid of the book, Gabriel took her by the hand, and led her back to the inn. She shuffled after him, tripping over pebbles as she tried to keep up.

"Can you slow down?"

"Nightshade's army just sent Hawthorn a warning in the mail. We need to leave as soon as possible."

Rose half-jogged the rest of the way there.

The second they burst through the front door, he turned to her. "Pack everything but be fast."

She raced back to her room and stuffed dirty and clean skirts and blouses together in her pack. She tucked wayward sleeves and skirt hems into the bag before tying it shut. It was sloppy but packed.

Then she hurried over to Gabriel's room, but her hand hesitated halfway to the door.

What if he isn't himself again? She ran a hand through her hair, pushing the thought aside before giving a few quiet raps on the door.

"Come in, Rose," he said.

Rose pressed a hand to her chest. She swung open the door to find him neatly folding and packing his clean clothes. *Thank goodness*, she thought.

His hands moved painfully slow as they creased fabric, and placed a shirt into his pack. She tapped her foot. "Do you need any help packing?" Rose asked with a tight-lipped smile. *Please don't say yes.*

The need to leave was an itch invading her skin. She wanted to go now, and he was taking too long. Especially since *he'd* been the one telling her to rush.

Gabriel turned to her and eyed her bag with suspicion. "No, thank you, Rose. How did you pack so fast?"

She turned up her nose. "Unlike you, I have a sense of urgency."

She snatched the pack from his grasp. "Just put the clothes in like this. We need to go now. You can organize late-"

Her words cut off when Gabriel's mouth dropped open, and he swatted at the air. "Leave me alone." She followed his gaze, but he was shouting at nothing.

Rose tiptoed closer, and grabbed onto his hand, but he shook her off. "I don't trust myself like this, Rose. Stay back."

She shuffled backwards until she bumped into the wall. Gabriel took several deep breaths and sat down on the bed, but his gaze stared at nothing.

"Gabriel if the hallucinations are getting worse, you must see a doctor. Perhaps they can help you."

The muscles in Gabriel's jaw worked, and he turned to her and spoke with a clipped voice. "I'd rather take my chances being haunted by these false images."

Rose crossed her arms over her chest. "If you believe that's the best plan, then your judgement can't be trusted."

"You wouldn't say that if you saw the inside of an asylum."

Rose frowned. "I won't let that happen to you."

Gabriel's shoulders slumped, and he sighed. "You aren't my parents or my wife. You wouldn't have a choice."

Rose pursed her lips, and the silence stretched between them. She reached out to touch his hand, but he pulled away. "Why did you hide the nymph book from me?"

She cringed. She'd hoped he wouldn't bring that up. "I was worried it would upset you and…"

"Make my condition worse?" he offered.

Her thumb ran along the fabric of her skirt. "Yes."

"Next time be honest with me."

Rose blinked at him in disbelief. "I'll be more honest when I see honesty from you."

He glared at her. "Fine. Are you ready to leave?"

Rose clutched her room key tighter. "We could've already left if someone had packed faster."

She slung her bag over her shoulder and turned on her heel to walk to the door, but the scent of smoke tinged the air. "Do you smell smoke?" she said, a hint of a waver in her voice.

Gabriel's face blanched. "You can smell that too? I thought it was part of the hallucination."

Rose raced towards the stairs. The smoke was thicker there. Orange and yellow flames licked the ground floor and crawled up the spiral stairs. "We have to get out of here."

Gabriel threw up his hands. "How do you propose we do that? We're on the second floor. Unless you can grow wings and fly."

She knew it was a joke, but the thought of sprouting nymph wings popped into her mind before she dismissed it with a shake of her head.

She'd barely been able to conjure a weapon. Risking her life on the off chance that she could actually fly wasn't a great idea.

She thought back to the covers on the hotel beds. Climbing might be an option. "Follow me. I think I have an idea." Rose ran back into the room and shut the door behind them.

She snatched the sheets from the bed and created knots along the thicker duvet, then let it fall down the side of the window. It wasn't long enough.

"Gabriel. If we're going to make it out of here alive, I need your help. Secure this to something sturdy and I'll grab the covers from my room." Once Gabriel was working at attaching the sheet to something sturdy, she ran from the room.

Heat burned her cheeks as she flung open the door. The fire licked at the upper part of the staircase now. A loud crack sounded as a flaming piece of wood from the first floor fell to the front desk with a thunderous crash and the flames spread. Thick plumes of smoke burned her nose and throat, making her cough.

Rose pursed her chapped lips. They didn't have much time left.

She rushed to her bed and grabbed the covers before carrying them back to the room. The flames were close enough now that the end of the duvet nearly caught fire. She yanked it away from the creeping flames before shutting the door.

"Gabe-" a coughing fit racked her body.

The coughing made his gaze flicker to her. "Are you okay?"

"I'm just fine. Not like we're trapped in a burning building or anything."

She inspected the surprisingly well-fastened rope. She grabbed the end of the first sheet and started to tie them together, but he knocked her hand away. "Let me. The knot needs to be sturdy."

In a dizzying series of loops, he attached the two quilts together and gestured at the makeshift rope. "Ladies first."

Rose touched his cheek with the back of her hand. "Make sure you come right after me. Okay?"

He took her hand and kissed it. "I will do my best. Now, go."

The flames licked at the door now, setting it aflame. She tossed the rope out the window, tugging on it to make sure it was sturdy before shimmying down, being careful not to touch the fire that now seeped from several windows.

When her feet touched the floor, she tugged the rope and shouted. "Gabriel. Go!"

At first, nothing happened and tears burned in the back of Rose's eyes. Her breath caught in her throat.

When he heaved himself over the ledge, her heart leapt into her throat.

The rope strained at his weight, and she dug her nails into her palm. "Hurry."

The flames grew closer, licking at the top of the rope. The rope snapped, just before he reached the ground, and she scurried underneath the rope to break his fall. His body crashed into her, knocking them both to the ground.

"Gabriel, thank the heavens." She sighed and wrapped her arms around him.

Now that they were safe from the fire, her thoughts shifted to April.

Is April okay or still in the building? Rose skimmed the crowd, but she only saw April's mother.

She tapped Gabriel on the shoulder. "I need to make sure April's alright."

Gabriel loosened his grip on her. "Of course. I'll see if I can spot her."

Rose pushed herself up and dusted off her skirt with her hands before approaching April's mother. "Where is April? Is she okay?"

April's mother's gaze darted to the building and then back to Rose. "She went back in there looking for you when she didn't see you leave the building with everyone else."

A shiver went down her spine. Rose ran towards the entrance, but something tugged her back. She whirled around to see Gabriel's hand wrapped around her wrist. "Let me go. I have to help her. If she dies it'll be my fault."

His grip didn't loosen, and his breath brushed her ear. "It's not your fault. You weren't the one who set the flames. Fire is a nymph's weakness. What do you think will happen to you in there?"

Rose's lips pinched together. "I don't care what happens to me. I need to help her."

Gabriel spoke through clenched teeth. "I couldn't live with myself if you died in there, and there are people counting on you to protect them from Nightshade's nymphs. Don't be so impulsive. You have a brilliant mind, so use it."

Rose shook her hand free. "There's no time to mull this over. That building could collapse any second."

She moved towards the building, but he blocked her way. "You don't have a choice. I'm not letting you go back in there." Gabriel turned to April's mother.

"Do you have some cloth and maybe a little water?" Gabriel asked.

The woman ripped off a piece of her skirt. "You may take this cloth, but I have no water. There is a well towards the back of the inn where we wash our clothing, but it doesn't have enough water to stop the fire."

Gabriel took the cloth. "That's okay. I only need enough water to douse the cloth. Guide me to the well—quickly."

The woman hiked her skirt and ran towards the back of the hotel. Another piece of burning wood broke off and crashed to the ground. Rose jumped back.

A few painfully long moments later, Gabriel returned with the drenched cloth. "Stay here. I'm going in to help her." He placed the cloth over his nose and mouth and headed into the inferno.

* * *

WHEN GABRIEL WALKED into the building, flames heated his skin, and he ducked to the side as a burst of fire hurtled towards him. The smoke scraped at his lungs even through the wet cloth. "April! Where are you?" he shouted.

Fire crackled and the snap of wood breaking filled his ears. A shriek sounded from the stairs. April dangled from the banister. The steps had collapsed beneath her.

Gabriel approached April, but the area under her legs was surrounded by flames.

"April. Rose is safe, but we need to get out now."

April's rasped. "You need to leave before the building collapses. Go." She coughed and her entire body shook.

"Not without you. I need you to let go off the rafter. I'll be there to catch you."

Gabriel hovered under her, getting as close as he could without touching the flames. Heat beat at his skin. When she let go of the railing, he held out his hands, and winced as her entire weight crashed into his arms.

He yanked her away from the fire and placed her down beside him.

April let out another hacking cough, and he handed her the damp cloth. "Here. Put this over your nose and mouth. It will help with the smoke."

"Thank you," she said in a pained whisper before placing it over her mouth with shaking hands.

He guided them both to the door, but there was another large snap. Gabriel pushed April back just before a piece of wood fell in front of the door's entrance. It went up in flames, blocking the exit.

He eyed April's too pale skin. "I'll move the wood and you run."

She cocked her head to one side. Her gaze flitted from him to the wood and back again. "Are you mad? Do you want to burn your hands to a crisp?" The words sent her into another coughing fit.

"I'll be fine. Just go." Gabriel slipped his shirt off and tore it, wrapping it around his hands like a cast. He grabbed the wood that wasn't aflame yet and tossed it out of the way.

April still hadn't moved. "Go!" he shouted again. He grabbed her with one hand and pushed her through the door. A cough tore through his lungs as smoke invaded the room.

She stumbled out of the building, and he followed after her. A burst of heat warmed his back as he ran through the exit with her staggering just ahead of him.

They'd just cleared the building when he heard a deafening groan and a crunch. He turned around to see the scorched building collapsing in on itself.

* * *

ROSE LET out a sigh of relief when Gabriel and April exited the building… until she saw the condition they were in. Patches of skin on Gabriel's back and chest were pink. His shirt was gone, but he had blackened rags on his hand.

April breathed heavily. Her face was paper white, and her gaze darted wildly around her, but she was alive.

Rose rushed over to April and Gabriel, but her gaze caught on April who was lowering herself to the ground with shaky arms. Rose knelt down beside her. "I was so worried about you."

April's face looked too pale, but when she saw Rose she smiled. Her hand clutched a damp cloth. She coughed into it so loudly that Rose could hear her lungs rattle. "I'm glad you made it. When you didn't escape, I had to go back for you."

Gabriel's eyes darkened, and he turned to Rose. "She got the brunt of the smoke."

Rose placed a hand over April's. "I'm alright. But what about you?" April's eyes were shot through with red.

"I'm okay, but you look blurry." She rubbed her eyes.

Rose struggled to take in air. She looked to Gabriel, and a muscle twitched in his jaw. "We need to take her to the doctor."

"Why? What's wrong with her?" Her grip on April's hand tightened.

"She breathed in a lot of smoke, Rose." She didn't feel the hand resting on her shoulder, and his words sounded muffled.

Tears stung her eyes. "April it's just some ash in your eyes, right?"

April's voice cracked. "No. I can't see you. What's happening?"

Her grip on Rose's hand tightened. "Everything's gone dark. Mom?"

Another violent coughing fit wracked April's body and her hand went limp in Rose's. April's body slumped, and Rose caught her before her head hit the floor. Her gaze flickered over to Gabriel.

"What's going to happen to her? "

His gaze darkened. "I'll carry her to the hospital."

He didn't answer her question, and her heart beat faster in her chest as Gabriel scooped April up in his arms.

When they arrived at the entrance, Rose pushed her way through the crowd until she reached the inside of the building. Once there, she tapped the closest doctor on the shoulder.

"Where can I find Dr. Hawthorn?" she asked.

The man's eyes scanned her appearance and then darted to April. She grabbed his shirt collar. "Please, we need his help. Now."

The man pried her hands from his collar. "Doctor Thorn is seeing another patient, but we can assign you to another doct-"

She cut him off. "This is an urgent matter, and he's the most renowned doctor for miles. We need to see him. Tell him it's Rose."

He shuffled back a step. "I'll see if he can meet. For now, take a seat over there," he pointed to some chairs in the corner of the room.

Gabriel carried April over to the man. "This can't wait. It's urgent. There was a fire, and she inhaled a lot of smoke."

April's chest rose and fell in shallow movements. She didn't speak, and she'd drifted off.

He gave April a once over and gestured at Gabriel. "Come with me."

Gabriel turned to Rose who was pacing through the halls, her hands bunching the fabric of her skirt. "Are you coming with us?" he asked.

"No. I need to speak to Dr. Thorn."

"Do you want to say goodbye?"

Her lip quivered, and her voice cracked. "Don't ask me that. She's going to live. She has to. I just need to find Dr. Thorn."

"Are you sure?" he repeated as the doctor guided Gabriel away.

The hitch in his voice made her throat burn with unshed tears. She ran after them. "Wait."

Rose squeezed April's hand. "Please stay alive for just a little longer."

April's clammy hand offered Rose little comfort.

Each second dragged on as she waited for Dr. Thorn. When he finally burst through the doors, she rushed over to him. Getting close enough that she could see his dark pupilless eyes. "What took you so long?"

"I came as fast as I could. I heard there was an urgent matter."

He glanced around the room. "Where is the patient?"

When his gaze wandered down to the scorch marks on the bottom of her skirt, he sucked in a breath. "What happened to you?"

"Nymphs set fire to the inn...Did you know this would happen?" she snarled.

His gaze drifted to the floor, and he didn't speak.

"I'll take that as a yes. If April dies, know that you have made an enemy out of me."

Hawthorn's gaze flitted to hers. "You did a successful job of alienating me as an ally. This was a result of your folly, not mine. I will not apologize for guarding my own life."

She ran up to him and pressed a finger to his chest. "Your cowardice destroyed dozens. Just know that."

His face paled, but then his lip curled back in a snarl. His human finger pointed at Rose. "I wasn't the reason he set that fire. You can blame yourself. When word spread that you would travel to Pennsylvania, Nightshade decided to have his allies send you a warning."

Rose's jaw clenched. "And if I were to chance a guess, you're the reason they knew where to find us."

The doctor frowned but did not speak. Before she could hear his excuse, she rushed off to search for Gabriel and April.

Blood pounded in her ears. "It can't be my fault," she thought as she strode down the corridor.

She flung open several doors looking for April. One held a man with a gaping wound in his leg. Another was missing a leg, and the sight of the blood churned the contents of her stomach.

When she walked into the next room, a lumpy sheet covered the bed at its center. Gabriel slumped in a chair, his hand in his hands. When the door creaked open, he turned towards her. Tears made wet tracks on his soot-stained face.

Rose placed a hand on Gabriel's arm. "What happened?"

"The doctor said she'd inhaled too much smoke. They tried caffeine and morphine, but nothing helped. We were too late. I'm sorry."

Rose's grip tightened on his arm. "No. No. No. It can't be." She ripped the sheet off the bed.

April's pale face was frozen in a slight smile. Her eyes gazed far off into the distance.

Her hands gripped the covers tighter. "She can't leave. Not like this. It's my fault. I was the one trapped in the building and she came back to save me."

Rose felt a hand on her back. "It's not your fault, Rose."

Her throat burned. "It should've been me. One of Nightshade's allies set the fire as a warning. They don't wish for us to go to Pennsylvania."

Gabriel's hand tightened on her shoulder.

"Then we should hurry and get the cart packed before they can come and hurt anyone else," Gabriel said and got up from the chair to leave.

Rose leaned closer to April's motionless form. She placed her forehead against April's cold skin and whispered, "Goodbye, friend." She kissed April's icy hand before pulling the sheet back over her face and leaving her behind.

Silent tears streamed down Rose's face, and she gulped back sobs as they trudged back towards the inn. The air tasted like ash and death.

I can't face April's mother. Her daughter is dead because of me. She grabbed Gabriel's sleeve. "Can we just go straight to the mail cart?"

Gabriel's eyes searched hers. "Shouldn't we tell her?"

A cry escaped her lips, and she couldn't stop the sobs. "I can't. Hawthorn said it was my fault. That they were after me."

His arm wrapped around her shoulder, pulling her into his chest, and his hand rubbed soothing circles on her back. "It wasn't you, Rose. They were the ones that set fire to the inn."

She pressed her head against his bare chest. "They'll pay. Every last one of them." Her voice cracked on the words.

Gabriel's back stiffened, and his hand stilled on her back. She looked up into his eyes. "We'll stop them together, but no one else is getting killed."

"We might not have a choice, Gabriel. This is a war."

He stroked her hair. "If it comes down to that, I'd rather be the one to get my hands dirty."

She pushed her hand against his chest. "No. This is my battle, not yours."

He pushed her away, putting distance between them.

A chill charged the air between them as they skirted the destroyed inn and went straight to the stables, which had been far enough from the fire to remain untouched by the flames.

Rose hurried to get the horse before April's mother could come looking for them, but the horse whinnied and shook his head when she moved too suddenly.

Gabriel held up his hands in a placating gesture. "Easy boy. It's just us." He stroked the horse's mane as he attached the reins, and Rose stashed the rest of their meager belongings into the mail cart. Gabriel slid on a fresh shirt and then climbed up into the mail cart.

With heavy hearts and a light carriage, they set off east towards the ocean. After twenty minutes of riding, metal tracks came into view.

"We're here," Gabriel said and brought the horse to a stop.

A wooden building with people lining up outside appeared before them. A large metal beast shone like a kitchen pan and steamed like boiling water.

She tucked her head in the mail cart and whispered, "Gabriel...what *is* that thing? It looks like a beast." She pointed at the metal monstrosity.

Gabriel narrowed his eyes as he peered at her and then what she was pointing at. After a pause, his forehead smoothed, and his lips tilted up in a grin. "Rose, that's no beast. That's the train! It can take us places, like the horse. With all that reading you've done, you've never read about trains?"

Rose shook her head and crouched down further into the cart. "So...it won't hurt us?"

Gabriel covered his mouth as full-blown laughter shook his chest and stomach. "I'm sorry. I just—" his words cut off as another laugh caused his eyes to water, and he tilted his head up to the sky.

She deflated at his laughter and glared at him. "Don't make fun of me. I didn't know." She looked down at the tattered hem of her skirt. *I'll have to make sure I look up more about transportation next time.*

When he didn't stop laughing, she shoved his shoulder. "You know I spent my entire life in a greenhouse, right? It's not my fault I'm like this."

His laughter slowed, and he wiped tears from his eyes. "Sorry. It just surprised me that's all. I didn't mean to upset you."

She crossed her arms over her chest. "Well, you did."

"And you upset me by insisting on getting your hands dirty in this battle, so we'll call it even."

She pouted, "I suppose that's fair."

They made their way to the train station's entrance with the horse and buggy in tow. When they got to the back of the line, a man with a blue hat appeared and gestured to the horse. "Will you be buying a ticket for today's train?"

Gabriel nodded and grabbed their things from the mail cart before the man led the horse away.

Rose wanted to ask Gabriel what the man was doing with their horse, but the ticket counter drew her eye away from the animal's retreating form.

A man stood in a booth handing out slips of paper from behind metal bars. *He looks like he's in jail.* She wanted to ask Gabriel about it, but was unwilling to risk him laughing at her again, so instead she scanned the outfits of the other people in line.

Women wore lifted shoes. Their skirts had embroidered edges and the fabrics were bright ceruleans and emeralds. Rose glanced down at her plain tan skirt with a grimace. The guest room in Gabriel's home had held dresses in soft blues and bright yellows reminiscent of the clothes here. She hunched her shoulders, hoping no one would notice her drab attire.

Gabriel's gaze flickered to hers. "Sorry. I know we didn't have time for you to change clothes."

She rubbed the singed fabric between her thumb and forefinger. "It's not that. Though I'm in desperate want of a bath."

He cocked his head to one side. "What is it then?"

Her gaze fell from his. "It's just... I feel rather out of place."

Gabriel took in those around them as if for the first time. "These are the wealthier passengers. Don't worry. Not everyone will be dressed like this."

A small sigh escaped her lips, and she placed a hand over her chest. "That's a relief. I feel rather plain in comparison."

He smiled and tucked crimson-tinged strands of hair behind her ear. "One could hardly call you plain. You could put them to shame in a potato sack."

Rose blinked and hid her face behind her hair. "I don't care for false flattery, you know."

"Who said it was false?"

Her lips parted, but one look into his warm green eyes halted any protests. No humor danced in their depths. He was serious, and his gaze kept traveling to her lips and scanning the rest of her body in a way that made her squirm.

The man behind the counter said, "Next," and they moved up in line, pulling them out of the moment. She fanned her face with a hand as Gabriel approached the ticket counter.

"Two tickets for Pennsylvania," Gabriel said and her jaw dropped when he handed the man eighty dollars for their tickets.

Gabriel held a slip of paper out for her. "Don't lose it."

She gulped and took the ticket. "I'll make sure to pay you back for the ticket. Somehow."

He waved her off. "Don't worry about it. It was worth the cost to save my back from such a long ride by mail cart."

Then his lip curved up in a wicked grin. "Although I could think of something else I'd accept as payment."

She smacked his arm.

"Ow. That's going to bruise."

"Good! Maybe it'll teach you to be less vulgar."

"I just meant a kiss." He whined.

She rolled her eyes. "Somehow I don't believe you."

He ruffled his hair with a hand, and his face flushed pink. "Let's get you into the train before you make a scene."

"I wasn't the one making the scene," she grumbled, but when he held out his arm for her, she took it.

As they approached their car, they passed by the women in jewel-toned skirts and dresses again, but as they continued down the line, she saw groups of workers in tan and beige work clothes that mirrored their own.

When they got to the front of the line, a man held out his hand. When she didn't move, he said, "Ticket please."

Gabriel handed over his ticket, and Rose followed his lead.

Once they entered the train, Gabriel explained that the number on their ticket told them their car and where to sit.

Gabriel pointed towards the car behind them. "If you keep going that way, you can get to the expensive seating areas and a dining car. We'll get some food there once we've settled in."

"It smells amazing." The scent of pepper and sage tickled her nose, but she knew they needed to find their seats first.

After passing through a few cars, he pointed at a plush bench seat and gestured for her to sit down. "Wait...what about your horse?" she asked, gripping the back of the bench.

Gabriel laughed. "You weren't paying attention? I handed it over to someone before we got in line for our tickets. The horse is safe and coming with us."

"That's good." She slid into the seat and placed her small pack at her feet.

Once they'd dropped their belongings in their chair, he turned to her. "Want to clean up and visit the dining car?" he asked.

Rose's stomach rumbled at the mention of a hot meal, and she nodded.

Just as she got up to follow Gabriel, a loud whistling noise rang out. She covered her ears. "All aboard," was shouted throughout the cabin, and then the ground moved beneath her.

Rose reached for the edge of the bench, but she lost her footing and fell backward into Gabriel's lap.

Gabriel whispered in her ear. "While I'm rather enjoying the view, a kiss would have sufficed."

Her face flushed and she scrambled upright. "That wasn't intentional. I just lost my balance."

"Then I'll have to offer my thanks to the conductor."

"I'll make sure to repay you for your behavior later." She jeered, but as she got up her stomach did little flips and she swayed on her feet. He grabbed her elbow, keeping her upright.

"Easy now. Let's grab your pack so you can wash and change before dinner."

Rose gave a slight nod as she forced down bile. *If I can manage to stomach food,* she thought.

Even with Gabriel's support, she swayed and stumbled at first, but after a few minutes of walking through the cabins she regained her balance and the train ride became smoother.

She released her vice grip on Gabriel and grabbed onto the backs of benches to steady herself. A man shot her a disdainful glare when she accidentally elbowed him. "Sorry," she muttered as they approached the washroom.

A sickening smell hit her as they came near the washroom, and she pinched the bridge of her nose before swinging the door open. The claustrophobic room held a small wash bowl and a hole in the ground that served as the toilet.

Rose locked the door behind her and grabbed one of the few clean changes of clothes she'd packed. She slipped out of the slightly singed skirt. She had to contort her body to raise her legs enough to change into her clean clothes without getting too close to the stinking hole in the room.

Using the wash bowl, she did her best to clean up the grit on her face and arms. With a final glimpse in the mirror, she opened the door to see Gabriel in new clothes and with his hair slightly damp.

As they walked towards the dining car, they passed back through the cars with the couch-like seating. The people there were drinking and eating, and they were dressed in fancy clothes. When he saw her gawking at the people, he nudged her shoulder.

"If you go even further back, past the dining car, there are also sleeping quarters for passengers going on particularly long journeys."

She nodded, but her attention was diverted when the scent of lemon, meat, and salt reached her nose. It made her mouth water.

When they brushed through the next door, she saw a full dining room. People passed by the tables with metal trays piled high with meat, vegetables, and a ton of seafood. She even saw potatoes that were so hot steam rose from them.

She tugged Gabriel's sleeve and said, "Can I get whatever I want?"

He smiled. "Yes, of course you can. But let's wait for our table first."

They walked over to a stand by a person dressed in black pants and a white, buttoned-up, collared shirt.

He turned to them and asked, "Table for two?"

Gabriel replied, "Yes."

The man said, "This way, sir," and led them to a table with a white cloth covering it. Two empty wine glasses rested on the cloth's surface. The waiter pulled out a chair for Rose and Gabriel.

He skimmed Rose up and down before swapping their wine glasses for water glasses and pouring them both some water.

He handed them both menus. "Would you like some time to decide?" he said.

Gabriel took one look at Rose staring down at the menu with wide eyes before saying. "Yes, I think we'll need some time." The man gave a slight nod and walked away.

Rose was so hungry she had a hard time deciding on just one thing. There was prime rib and several different types of seafood, including oysters and Seafood Newburg. She eyed the oysters on the menu, but she wanted to try something different. Then, she remembered the steaming potato and decided that had to be part of her meal.

Rose pointed out her order on the menu, the potatoes and prime rib, and Gabriel's face paled, but he said, "Okay."

When the waiter came back, she ordered her dinner. Gabriel asked for some rolls with butter for the table, and he got himself Chicken Francaise.

As they waited, Rose fidgeted with the fork. When the silence stretched on for too long, she asked, "Gabriel, have you ever traveled north? Does it snow a lot there? What kinds of food do they have?"

When he didn't answer for several seconds, she looked up to see him staring right through her. She waved a hand in his face. "Gabriel. You fall asleep sitting up?"

For a moment, he didn't respond, and she worried she'd lost him again. Then he shook his head and said, "Sorry, my mind wandered off. What were you asking about?"

Rose sighed. He hadn't heard anything she'd said. She started with just one question. "Have you ever been to the north?"

He stared up at the ceiling. "Hmm. I didn't go as far north as Pennsylvania, but I went to Georgia for a delivery once. They had beautiful trees filled with peaches. The land there was covered in lakes with crystalline waters."

She closed her eyes and tried to imagine such a place in her mind. A place untouched by the industry that ravaged their land. It sounded nice.

"As a matter of fact, one of our first stops will be in Georgia. You can see some of it out the window when we get there tomorrow morning. You can sleep and I'll wake you when we get there."

Her back straightened. "Really?"

A warm smile lit his green eyes. "Of course. Especially if it makes you happy."

She flushed and opened her mouth to speak, but the steam wafting from a metal tray and the scent of butter made her lose her train of thought.

As the server placed the food on the table, she gripped her fork tighter. *Make sure to eat slowly,* she reminded herself as he slid the prime rib in front of her. She covered her skirt with her napkin, hoping to busy her hands until the server was finished.

The smoky aroma of the prime rib tickled her nostrils. The scents of salt and pepper and something else a little spicy made her salivate. The meat had a rich, brown crust on the outside, but as she sliced off a piece to eat, she saw it was pink in the middle.

I have to take small bites, so I don't draw attention to myself. She thought as she guided a piece of the meat onto her fork and placed it in her mouth. She had to suppress a groan of delight. The tender meat melted in her mouth. *Amazing.*

The basket of warm bread in the center of the table called her name, and the butter smelled sweet. She snatched a roll from the center of the table and, using her knife, spread butter on the bread. Then she deposited a piece of bread in her mouth. A contented moan slipped out as she ate it, and she covered her mouth with a hand as Gabriel let out a slight laugh. "Enjoying your food, I take it?"

"It's amazing." The delicious fragrance of lemon and cream and the canary-yellow sauce coating Gabriel's meal drew her eye.

She batted her eyelashes at him. "But yours look even more amazing. Can I try some?"

He shook his head. "You're such a glutton, but sure. Clear some space on your plate."

Rose moved her food to one side so there was enough space for the chicken. Gabriel sliced off a generous piece and placed it on her plate next to the prime rib. Then he scooped up a small bit of his noodles and placed them on top of the chicken.

She gave him a megawatt smile and then took a forkful of the chicken and plopped it into her mouth. The sour tang of lemon balanced the richness of cream. When she bit into the chicken it felt velvety on her tongue. She could get used to eating like this.

"Thank you." She picked up a piece of prime rib and deposited it on his plate.

They ate in silence for the rest of the meal. When they were finally done, she felt as though her stomach might explode at any moment.

She'd eaten way too much, but she was content. She rubbed her swollen belly.

Gabriel said, "I'd ask if you enjoyed the food, but that would be a silly question considering you devoured it like a stray dog inhales scraps. Are you going to lick the plate clean?" There wasn't a single crumb left. She'd even scraped up most of the sauce.

Rose's thoughts went back to her time in the market with April. She'd drooled over the oysters at the market and April offered to buy her food with a bright laugh and an offer of *You can pay me back later*, but she'd never paid her back and now she never would. Tears filled her eyes, and her gaze drifted to the floor. "April would've loved this. I never got to pay her back for that treat she bought me from the market."

Gabriel placed his hand over Rose's. "I know. You haven't had time to properly grieve, and I wish I could give you the time and space for that, but we have to stop the nymphs before they kill anyone else."

Rose wiped tears from her eyes. "I suppose you're right."

"Of course I am." Gabriel removed his hand from hers and beckoned the waiter over. "Why don't you return to your seat? I'm going to order a coffee and then I'll join you."

Something in his smile gave her pause, but when her eyelids drooped, and a yawn escaped her lips, she pushed up from her chair and walked towards the exit.

Rose didn't hear the conversation, but when she looked back he handed the waiter six dollars. *Either our meal was more expensive than I thought or he just lied to me,* she thought.

When she made it to the plush bench, Rose curled up and shut her eyes.

A few minutes later, Gabriel sat down beside her with a cup in his hand that smelled of rotten yeast, and that was the last thing she remembered before she drifted off to sleep.

Light streamed through the windows. She groaned and turned away from the light. *Is it morning already? It feels like I just fell asleep.*

Gabriel shook her shoulder. "Rose. Rose, wake up or you're going to miss it."

When she realized he wasn't going to stop anytime soon, she cracked open an eye. "Miss what, Gabriel?" she grumbled.

"We just arrived in Georgia. You wanted to see it, remember?"

Her eyes popped open and she pressed her face to the window, eager to see the beautiful place he'd described, but her stomach dropped. Smokestacks belched smoke in the distance, and the trees' branches were barren in the cold of winter. Tree stumps and buildings surrounded the forest like invaders.

She pursed her lips together as she tried to focus on the good. There were still huge swaths of trees as far as the eye could see.

Another silvery machine turned her head. A device resembling a carriage passed by her window, traveling south. It carried people inside and moved without the aid of horses.

But she wrinkled her nose in distaste when the vehicle passed by, coughing up black smoke.

When her face fell, he placed a hand on her shoulder. "I thought you were excited to see this place."

She turned to him and said, "I was, but they destroyed it."

He looked around at the scenery. "What did they destroy?"

"The trees and probably the rivers. It's all machines and smoke now."

Gabriel rested his head on his hands. "I suppose I don't think of it that way. The technology is beautiful in its own way. There are vaccines and medicines that doctors use to save lives."

She hadn't thought of it that way. She supposed the elegance and vivid colors of some of the buildings were beautiful.

When the train started up again, she tried to see the industry through his eyes, and the weight on her heart eased slightly.

One more day and they'd be at their destination and would have to find the nymphs before the nymphs found them.

"Gabriel, where do you think we should check first when we get to

Pennsylvania?" she asked. She didn't know anything about the area and wondered how they'd ever find them.

Gabriel shrugged. "Your guess is as good as mine. But my first priority before searching for them is checking in at the inn. I want to sleep when we get there. These seats are comfortable but they're no bed."

She hadn't thought about that. She'd slept like the dead, but she could sleep just about anywhere. What she looked forward to was a bath whenever they arrived at their destination.

She desperately needed to use the bathroom, but she dreaded using the one she'd seen earlier and she didn't quite remember where it was. She tugged on Gabriel's sleeve. "Where was the bathroom again?"

"It's just down the hall. I'll show you." He grabbed her hand and led her down the hallway. After passing through a few cars, they came upon a small room. He opened the door. Inside was the foul-smelling toilet and the small wash bowl.

"Here you are," Gabriel said and then gave her a gentle push into the small space.

CHAPTER 10

Gabriel was second guessing his decision to accompany Rose on this journey.

He'd already gone one sleepless night on the train, and he didn't think he could manage another. It was difficult to pretend everything was fine when he was falling apart at the seams.

Once he'd ushered Rose into the tiny bathroom, he slumped to the floor. A blurry image of his mother screamed, *"You'll be the death of her just like your father was the death of me."*

What do you mean? He did everything he could to save you, he thought, but he didn't dare speak those thoughts aloud. It felt like someone had poisoned his mind.

The word poison reverberated through his head, making him remember something Belladonna had told him. *"Don't breathe the air of the Manchineel tree."*

When he'd harvested the antidote for Rose, he'd forgotten to protect himself from its poisonous air. *Can the tree's poison cause hallucinations? Perhaps a nymph or an herbalist in Pennsylvania will know.* He raked his fingers through his hair.

But if I tell Rose that I've been poisoned now, she'll want to head home, and we don't have time to go back now, not with nymphs on the loose. Stop-

ping them has to come first. Damn the consequences. Gabriel steadied himself with several deep breaths when he heard the whoosh of water coming from the bathroom.

Pull yourself together, Gabriel. He pressed his fingers into his eye sockets in an attempt to banish the mockery of his mother.

The door creaked open only moments after he'd pieced his facade back together.

Her gaze lingered on his mussed hair before she spoke. "How much longer until we get there?"

Gabriel smiled. "We should be there by tomorrow evening, so why don't we settle into our seats and take a rest?"

He stuck his hand in his pocket and wiped his sweaty palms on his handkerchief. Then, he took Rose by the hand and guided them back to their seats.

Outside the windows, the scenery had grown dark and many of the passengers had curled up in their seats, asleep. His body begged for sleep, but the threat of waking screaming from a night terror and disturbing the other passengers on board urged him not to give in to his drooping eyelids and constant yawns.

When he leaned into the chair, his body won out, and his eyes closed.

An eerily familiar voice clawed its way into his sleeping mind.

"You couldn't help me or your mother. Can you really help her?" Lara's face appeared before him. Her lips curled up in a wicked grin, and her hips swayed as she approached him.

This is a dream. She's dead. It can't be her.

Her finger curled under his chin. *"There is no waking up from this dream darling."*

She brandished a knife this time and put it to his neck. He bit his lip to keep from crying out as a sting raked across his bare flesh.

When blood dripped down his neck, he jolted awake.

A cold sweat drenched his clothing and skin, and several onlookers were staring at him. He must have been making noises in his sleep. He shook his head and smacked his cheeks to stay awake.

When he glanced over at the clock, it read 8:00PM. The dining car would still be open, and he couldn't risk nodding off again. A more serious outburst would get him locked up in an asylum for sure. He shuddered at the thought of being put into one of those prisons with bars on the windows and people monitoring his every move.

No. We'll find an antidote before it comes to that. Before I lose myself.

His heart squeezed at the thought of lying to Rose, but he knew she'd worry if he told her what was happening to him.

Rose still dozed beside him, so he eased up from his seat, being careful not to disturb her and went to the dining car to order a cup of coffee. Apart from a few business men, the car was empty.

He stretched his arms up, and a yawn clawed at his throat. It wasn't just the lack of sleep affecting him. Rose was perceptive, and if his act of being well wasn't convincing, she'd corner him and find out the truth.

As he gripped the gold colored handles of the flowery tea cup, a man approached him. Steel grey hair was combed neatly atop his head and he was dressed in a sleek business suit. It was so perfectly smooth that even sleeping on a train hadn't wrinkled it.

He held out a hand to Gabriel. "My name's Jim."

Gabriel sipped at his coffee, eyeing Jim's outstretched hand with disdain. Jim dropped his hand but didn't take the hint, choosing to settle into the chair across from him.

Why did someone have to come bother me right now of all times, Gabriel thought. He smiled through gritted teeth as Jim spoke. "Where are you heading?"

Gabriel shifted in his seat, but the old man seemed harmless enough. "We're traveling to Pennsylvania, sir."

Gabriel hoped that would be the end of the conversation, but instead the old man smiled and rubbed his beard at the word *we*. "Ah, you've got a traveling partner. Who are you traveling with? Friend, family...or lover?"

Gabriel coughed as he choked on his coffee. "I'm traveling with a friend. She's sleeping now, but my mind wouldn't rest." His eyelids drooped closed, betraying his words.

Maybe another coffee wouldn't hurt. He inhaled the rich caramel scent that coated his tongue and took another sip of the bitter beverage before flagging down the waiter.

The man laughed. "I'm guessing you haven't had many late nights before, so here's some advice. Don't stay sitting for too long or sleep will come and snatch you up."

Jim took a sip from his cup. "I almost forgot to ask- what's your name?"

He bit out. "It's Gabriel."

"I can see you aren't interested in talking, so perhaps I should go." Jim got up to walk away.

Maybe I shouldn't have been so harsh. Gabriel called after him, "Sir, have you ever been to Pennsylvania?"

The man turned back to Gabriel and nodded for him to follow. "Suddenly interested in chatting? I'll tell you all about Pennsylvania, but let's walk and talk. My feet don't like to stay still for long."

He followed the man and started asking him questions in hushed whispers as they entered the cabins. "Are there any big factories there?"

"There are several, but the state is more well-known for coal mining," Jim replied.

Gabriel nodded. If there were factories, they might be the nymphs' target. They wanted to destroy as many people as possible.

"What part of Pennsylvania has the most people, the most industry?"

The man shrugged. "Probably Philadelphia. If you're looking for work, they have plenty of factories and a few mines. If I were you, I wouldn't stay too long there. All that smoke will give ya one heck of a cough."

That would be even more reason to suspect that city, he thought.

"Are there any other famous buildings nearby? I'm going to do some sightseeing in my spare time."

Jim thought about it for a moment. "You can try Houston Hall. Plenty of people like to take pictures of that building. The trolley will take you there."

"Are there any parts of the city that are dangerous? Places that we should stay away from?"

"Maybe Centralia and Philadelphia. Their mines collapse or catch fire fairly often. Are you looking to work there?"

Gabriel rubbed the back of his neck. "Yes. Should I avoid working the mines?"

Jim's raised a finger. "If you value your life and your health, then yes."

A woman hissed a "shh." They both fell silent.

As they walked through the cars, their shoes thudded against the floor. Several business men glared at them in the dimly lit cabin.

They continued in silence until they reached the cars closest to the smoke. Instead of continuing into the segregated cars, they turned around.

Jim turned to Gabriel. "So what brings you and your traveling companion so far from home? You look like you're from a small town, so how'd you afford the trip out?"

Gabriel thought about it for a moment and figured a half-truth would do. "My father went into battle fighting against the Spanish for control of La Florida. He died in the battle, so I was left with some compensation." He hoped that would be enough to make the man shy away from asking any more questions.

Jim's expression fell into a frown. He made a show of faking a small yawn and stretching his arms up. "I'm sorry to hear that. Well, I wish you the best of luck on your journey. I'm going to hit the hay. Goodnight." Jim waved at Gabriel and walked towards the back of the train.

Gabriel was left alone with his thoughts once again. Thankfully, pink and grey light already peeked through the window, and once Rose was awake, he'd have someone to keep his mind occupied.

When he sat down next to her, she shivered, and he grabbed a shirt from his pack and placed it over her sleeping form. She wrapped the shirt around her like a blanket in her sleep and snuggled into his side.

He wrapped an arm around her and gazed out the window as the sun rose. He just needed to make it a few more hours.

* * *

ROSE DIDN'T STIR until the chill of the car made her shiver, and the bench creaked as Gabriel sat beside her. She was unwilling to open her eyes despite the faint light seeping through the curtained windows.

Gabriel placed something over her, and she pulled it tightly around her, desperate for the warmth. She scooted towards him, nuzzling into his side. He placed an arm around her, and she drifted back into a peaceful sleep until the morning light became strong enough to force her eyes open.

It's morning already? she thought as she groaned and stretched. Forgetting where she'd slept, she nearly hit her arm into Gabriel. Her face flushed when she looked down to see her hands on his chest and her body pressed flush against his.

She scrambled backwards. "Sorry. I must've been cold." Looking down at her lap, she realized the thing she'd clung to earlier was his shirt.

"Well, good morning, Sleeping Beauty. I would have woken you, but you looked rather...comfortable," he said with a lazy smile as he ran a hand along her arm. Light purple circles darkened the area underneath his eyes, but he was as mouthy as ever.

She bit her lip. "I was comfortable. Thank you for the shirt."

He cocked his head at her. "Who are you and what have you done with Rose?"

Her hand crumpled the shirt, and she tossed it at him. "I was being polite. Perhaps you can try it sometime."

"Ah there's the Rose I know."

"Hmph. Silly for me to think you'd know how to accept a thank you."

He pulled her to him and bent his head to her ear. "I don't know I rather liked that kiss you offered as a thank you. I'd graciously accept another."

"Keep dreaming." She pushed away from his chest and turned to stare at the window.

Snow dusted the ground, and the buildings cropped together like trees in the forest. They were fewer and farther between this far north, standing like lone survivors of a long and brutal war.

A nagging feeling settled in her gut at the landscape. All of this destruction made her wonder if she'd chosen the right side in this battle.

She couldn't side against Gabriel, who had saved her life, but she couldn't help the nymphs after they'd taken away April. April had been Rose's first friend outside of Gabriel. Her cheery disposition and mischievous antics had been a bright spot in the chaos of her life. Rose bunched the fabric of her skirt with her hand. Tears fell from her eyes and dripped onto her skirt, and she wiped them away.

No. These nymphs will pay for their treachery.

Gabriel tapped Rose's shoulder, breaking her out of her thoughts. "So, are you excited? We should get to town tonight."

When she turned to face him, he cupped her cheek, wiping away a stray tear. "Did I say something to upset you?"

Rose shook her head. "No. I was just thinking about April. I really miss her." Her voice cracked.

He opened his arms, and she sank into his chest. His hand stroked her hair. "I know. I'm sorry. Is there anything I can do?"

Her head tilted up towards his. "Any chance you can make me forget? Forget what happened, and what I have to do here?"

Folding her into his chest, he sighed. "I have one idea, but you'd hit me for it. I'll gladly let you cry it out while I hold you instead."

"Thank you." She nuzzled into his chest as tears fell down her face and wet his shirt. He held her tightly against him until the blade cutting into her heart had dulled and the train slowed down, the brakes screeching as it brought the metal monster to a stop.

Her legs felt stiff. The stale cabin left her lungs yearning for fresh air.

"I'm ready to get off this train," Rose mumbled into his chest.

Gabriel pulled away enough for her to look up at him. "We'll be able to exit in just a few moments. You can talk to me until then. Ask me anything?"

The dark circles under his eyes drew her gaze. "How did you sleep?"

Gabriel's back stiffened. "I slept fine. What about you?" he said too quickly, and his voice cracked, belying his words.

"I slept well. Thank you for asking," she responded flatly.

She thought back to the obscene amount of money he'd spent on the food and the train. *How is he affording all this on a Courier's salary?*

"Gabriel, where did you get the money to pay for this trip? I thought we didn't have a lot?" she asked.

There was a long pause, and Gabriel ran a hand through his hair. "I may not have been entirely honest about my financial situation before...I earned a large sum of money from my father when he died." His tone said he was holding back something.

"And?" Rose prodded.

Gabriel stuffed his hands in his pockets. He looked at the floor when he spoke. "There's a little more. After he died, I invested some of the money in the stock market. It went rather well. That's how I've paid for most of our trip." He looked back up at Rose with some hesitation, worried she'd be mad, but she was more curious than angry.

"What's the stock market?"

CHAPTER 11

Gabriel held back a laugh, knowing it would only upset her. Instead, he just smiled.

"It's a way of investing money in a company you're interested in. If they make money, so do you. If they lose money, then you do as well."

After a few breaths, she said, "Okay," with no further questioning.

They'd been sitting in silence for a while when Rose said, "What are some of your hobbies?"

Gabriel lets out a long "hmmm" as he mulled over his answer. "I've always had an interest in math and science. I was never one for fiction books. Most of the ones you saw at my house were Lara's." He trailed off at the mention of Lara's name, and his eyes watered.

Rose reached up and wiped a tear away with her thumb.

She put her hand on his shoulder and gave it a light squeeze. Then she leaned over and kissed him on the cheek. A determined look shone in her eyes. "I won't leave you alone again. I promise. I'll protect you no matter what."

Gabriel placed a hand to his cheek, shell-shocked from the declaration and the feathered kiss. When she went to move away, he pulled her back in.

"Maybe we can help each other forget?" A smile played on his lips.

Rose answered by moving her mouth to his. The softness of her lips and the feel of her arms around his neck made thoughts of Lara melt away.

He inhaled the smell of her like roses after a rainstorm. He deepened the kiss and tangled his fingers in her hair. Gasps sounded from the people in the car.

A woman exclaimed, "How improper."

Rose let out a longing sigh and wrapped her arms around his neck, oblivious to the commotion. He wanted to be closer to her, to have all of her, but that would have to wait.

Reluctantly, he removed his mouth from hers and gave her a last kiss on the forehead.

The woman from before was beside them now. "What are you two doing? Are you even married?"

Gabriel slid the ring from his pocket and onto his finger before holding the band up for the woman to see.

Her face reddened, and she huffed. "Regardless. You should still find a more appropriate place for such... behavior." She waved her hand at them.

The woman's arm looped through her husband's as they strode away. Her nose was still turned up as she exited the train car.

Rose pulled at the collar of her blouse. "Are we not meant to kiss like that?"

Gabriel laughed. "Not in public."

The tips of her ears turned pink. "I didn't realize. Sorry."

He placed a kiss on her hand. "Don't be sorry. It was lovely."

He couldn't leave her alone. She didn't deserve to go through the same pain and suffering he'd felt. He'd find a cure for the poison taking over his mind. He had to.

He squeezed her hand. "I'll stay by your side no matter what."

Her eyelids fluttered, and her face flushed. He was awestruck by the unique beauty of her red eyes, eyes filled with glints of wit and wonder.

They got up and exited the train.

Gabriel sneezed as they exited the train car. Smokestacks crowded the horizon, and he could see a large college building in the background. On the street there were horse-drawn carriages. The occasional car passed down the wide streets, status symbols, no doubt.

Smog tainted the air. As they gathered their belongings and got off the train, Rose wrinkled her nose in disgust. He didn't exactly disagree with her reaction. There were few trees, and the air scratched at his throat and nose.

They grabbed their luggage from one of the attendants and Gabriel went around to get his horse and buggy.

They pulled his horse along until they were out of the train station.

Everyone moved about without a care. It was like the smog didn't bother them. Maybe they were just used to this sort of environment, but he couldn't stand it.

As they wandered through the town looking for an inn, Gabriel started to notice there were far more people here than there had been in his hometown. The mass of bodies pressing around them felt suffocating. Houses crowded every corner like they were trying to cram as many people as possible into one space. There were factories, a streetcar, and even a library.

However, just beyond the city limits there were also less pleasant things like a coal mine. Gabriel recognized those leaving the coal mine by the soot covering their skin and clothes.

This is the reality of a city, he thought. He hoped his town would never become like this.

They walked together and took in their new surroundings. Rose pointed at the mine in the distance. "Could that place endanger the water supply if the nymphs targeted it?"

Gabriel glanced over at the mine. "Perhaps, the runoff from the mining process can pollute the water, but it's rather far from the river."

Her brow furrowed in thought. "We should keep an eye on it regardless."

They continued through town as the sun set. "Aren't there places to stay here?" Rose asked.

Good question, he thought. His feet felt like lead, and his body protested each step.

"I'm sure there's something nearby," he said.

The streetlights were coming on, and he'd almost given up when they spotted a large building with a sign that read *Hotel.*

The emerald green exterior and bright electric lights peeking through the massive window panes screamed expensive, but they needed a place to sleep.

A post sat near the entrance, so he tied up his horse before entering the massive double doors. The women inside were dressed in fiery reds, deep violets, and vivid greens, and wore dresses with delicate lace around the collar and corsets that forced them upright. Their silky skirts shimmered in the light. The men wore grey and green buttoned up tailcoats and suits.

He cringed as he glanced at those in the surrounding area. He'd already spent a fifth of the money he'd brought, and they'd need about another hundred dollars to get home. The thought of spending even more of his life savings on this trip made him hesitant to reach for the thinning wallet in his pocket, but it would be dark in a few minutes, so they didn't have much choice.

As they walked over to the desk, several heads turned to follow them, and the man at the front desk gave them a once over and then said with an exasperated sigh, "Are you booking a room for the night?"

Gabriel shifted from one foot to the other, staring down at his plain tan attire self-consciously. *Maybe he doesn't think I can afford to stay here? I suppose he's half-right.* He tried to sound as confident as possible when he said, "I'm looking for two rooms, please."

The man looked him straight in the eye and wrinkled his nose at Gabriel. "We don't have room for someone of your status, sir. Our rooms are $3 a day or $10 for a week."

His jaw nearly dropped, and he had to force himself to remember that confidence would be key here. It was double the price of the inn. But they had seen no other places to stay, so he supposed he didn't have much choice. He took out twenty dollars from his pocket and slapped it on the table.

The man eyed him suspiciously for a moment but took the cash. When he saw Gabriel's fierce glare, he bowed his head. "I'm sorry, sir, but you look as though you escaped from the mines. I didn't realize someone of your status would travel in clothing such as that." He gestured to their clothing.

"We've had a hard journey, so we'd just like to get some rest."

"Of course, sir. My name is Charles. I'll get your keys." He grabbed two keys from cubby holes behind him and handed them both to Gabriel.

Gabriel snatched them up, and his lip curled up in a venomous smile. "Perhaps this can be a learning experience for you. My horse is outside. Do you have a stable?"

The man's eyes widened. " My apologies, sir. I'll go ahead and have the horse moved right away." He waved a man over. Once he was at the desk, Charles said, "Please see to it that this man's horse is stabled this moment."

"But Charles he's-"

Charles raised a hand, cutting the employee off, "A paying customer. Now go. The horse is..." he trailed off and looked to Gabriel.

"He's tied to the post in front of the hotel."

"You heard the man. Go take care of it." The man went outside to move his horse.

Hopefully, we'll have some time in the next couple of days to look for different accommodations. I'm sure Rose is feeling uncomfortable too. Maybe if they ventured outside the city, it wouldn't cost so much. He didn't even want to think about how much this place probably charged for food.

Charles handed one key over to Rose and one to him, and they headed to their rooms. He was relieved to sink into his bed until he glimpsed the number 314 on her key. Looking down at his own key, he stifled a sigh. He was number 316. They'd be right next to each other.

If something goes wrong, she'll be close, but if I get too sick, she'll know. When he turned back to Rose, she gaped at the scenery. Her eyes sparkled with wonder.

She pointed to the lightbulbs. "How do they afford so many of those? I thought they were expensive."

Gabriel put his finger to her lips as several patrons stared at her.

He whispered, "This is an expensive hotel. It's far more expensive than the inn, and the people here will be rude if they think we're of a lower class, so try to pretend this is normal for you."

Rose clapped a hand to her mouth, and her cheeks turned pink. She didn't blurt anything else out, but she had such a wide-eyed, eager expression that he couldn't help but smile and roll his eyes. *She just can't help herself.*

On the way to their room, they passed by walls covered with beautiful oil paintings. He even recognized one or two by famous artists. They had darker shading and an unusual combination of colors. It really stuck out on the plain, cream-colored walls. He wondered why they'd picked such a dull color for the wallpaper.

Rose's jaw dropped as the door to her room opened. She spun in a slow circle, marveling at the large, four-poster bed, and to the right of the door was a switch which Gabriel flipped. Light from the bulb in a metal cone bathed the room in soft light. In the corner was a plush, cream-colored lounge chair. A full-length mirror was embedded in the closet's door.

The small fireplace in the room would help heat the room in the cold of winter—a relief, as they'd mostly packed light clothing.

Not too far from the fireplace was a door. "What's in there?" Rose grabbed onto the door and turned the handle.

When she opened it to reveal a private bathroom, she squealed in delight. It had a cast iron clawfoot tub, a white and black tiled shower stall, and even a flushing toilet sitting atop a marble slab. *Well, at least this is making her happy, even if it's costing a fortune,* he thought.

Rose ran from the bathroom and enveloped him in a hug so suddenly that she nearly knocked him over. "I love this room!" Rose said.

Gabriel grinned. "I'm glad you like it. Get settled in. I'll see you at dinner. I'll be right next door." He gestured to the room to the right of hers and pried her off him. If he stayed with her much longer, he'd commandeer her bed.

Once inside his own room, Gabriel sank onto the bed, his pack in hand. He let out a long yawn and barely resisted the urge to curl up under the sheets. *Just unpack and then you can sleep.*

His head bobbed, and he swayed on his feet as he unpacked, folded, and put away his clothes.

Knowing Rose, she'll probably live out of her pack until we switch hotels again, he thought with a smile as he placed the last of his clothes into the dresser.

He must have passed out from exhaustion soon after putting his clothes away because the next thing he knew, the image of an entire forest aflame engulfed him. Rose screamed, chains holding her to a burning tree.

"It's not real," he said to himself and dug his fingernails into his right wrist, but he couldn't feel the pain.

He pressed his hands into his eyes. The scene blurred but didn't go away. He took deep breaths, trying to make the images dissipate. Tears streamed down Rose's face, and her voice cracked out a meek *"Help."*

His heart dropped into his stomach, and he reached out for her, but a leaf fluttered onto his arm and burnt his skin. He looked up to see green apples. She was tied to a Manchineel tree.

Nightshade laughed as he stoked the fire. His limbs refused to move as Rose cried for help that would never come.

He woke to the sound of running water, and he cracked open one eye hesitantly. Relief flooded him as the afterimages of the dream blurred and then disappeared.

Gabriel wiped the tears from his face and looked out the window to see stars dotting the inky black sky. Once the water stopped, he pushed himself out of bed and went to Rose's room next door. "Are you ready for food?" he called.

Galloping footsteps and a thud sounded from her room as she

rushed to the door. She cracked it open and poked her head out. "Are we going to get food now?"

Gabriel nodded. "One moment, please." When Rose slammed the door shut, he jerked his head back just in time to avoid being hit.

There was a lot of rustling, but soon she emerged in a simple, tan skirt and a pale pink blouse. She'd also cleaned her face and her damp hair clung to her skin. *Maybe she feels self-conscious about the other people here too,* he thought.

"You look nice," he said with a smile.

A blush colored her cheeks. "Thank you."

She grabbed Gabriel by the hand, and they walked down the stairs for dinner.

Just like the dinners they'd had on the train, the food downstairs smelled heavily of sage, lemon, and pepper.

The server carried large portions of meat, plates of pasta with creamy sauces, and even unusually large portions of chicken that smelled of lemon and cream to tables.

They were so enamored by their meals that they didn't speak a word during dinner, but they agreed to meet in the morning to search for places that may attract the nymphs. When Rose got up to go to her room, she turned back to him.

"Aren't you joining me?"

"You want me to join you in your private room?" He clicked his tongue. "If that's what you want, I will, gladly."

Rose huffed. "Fine. Keep your secrets, but I'm going to get some sleep. Goodnight."

Once she'd stomped away, Gabriel stayed behind to pay the bill and order a glass of whiskey to banish the nightmares. He bit his lip as he forked over the $13 for the meal and drink.

If these hallucinations continue, my cash might be depleted before we ever leave Pennsylvania.

Lara's lilting voice invaded his ears. *Then I guess you'll go broke, murderer.*

He sipped at the drink on the way to his room, ignoring Lara as best as he could.

When Gabriel was finally in his room, the exhaustion hit him all at once. He placed the half-full tumbler on the nightstand and collapsed to the bed.

Nightmares of his loved ones being harmed tortured him in his sleep, but there was one that chilled the blood in his veins.

Rose's eyes were wild as Nightshade gripped her by the throat. *"You tried to bring that weakling into battle and now look at what happened. Lucky for you, I'm merciful. I'll let you die with your lover."*

Next to Nightshade, his own body laid unmoving with skin a sickly mottled white and grey.

Gabriel bolted upright in bed. Sweat beaded his forehead. He knew it was just a dream, but it felt so real.

He must have cried out because someone knocked on the door. When he opened it, he was surprised to see Rose there with her hair unkempt.

Rose knocked on the door. "Is everything okay? I heard screaming."

Gabriel opened the door to reveal Rose in a long nightgown with lace along the sleeves and a bow at the center of her chest. His eyes fell to the bow as she rubbed her eyes from sleep, and gave a soft yawn.

She caught him staring, and narrowed her eyes at him. "You'd better move that gaze unless you want to be not okay very soon."

His gaze skimmed downward until he reached her exposed ankles, the white fabric hanging from her body loosely covered her lower legs.

The swishing fabric got closer, and a hand waved in front of his face. "Did you not hear me?"

"I heard you quite well. You said to move my gaze, but you didn't specify where," he said as his lip curled up in a lopsided smile.

She sighed. "My eyes. Keep your gaze up here on my eyes."

"Ah yes, your lovely eyes that get even more gorgeous when you're frustrated with me."

She rubbed at her temple. "I'll go get changed so you aren't...distracted and we'll have an early breakfast before we scope out some of the factories."

"I much prefer the distraction, but all good things must come to an end."

She spun on her heel and exited the room to get changed. She kept glancing over her shoulder at Gabriel on the way out, like she wasn't sure if she should leave him alone.

After she left, he shut the door and locked it. *I can't believe that worked. At least now I know how to distract her from the truth.* She hadn't even noticed the alcohol on the nightstand.

Once he'd switched into fresh clothes, he gathered Rose and they grabbed breakfast before they exited the hotel for the day.

Gabriel's gaze kept drifting down to Rose's lips even as she speared scrambled eggs and deposited them into her mouth. His cheeks flushed red and he looked down at his food. He wanted to talk about the kiss from the other day. The one that had made his blood run hot and his heart race so quickly that he'd forgotten everything else around him.

"So…about that kiss on the train."

Rose paused and placed her fork down. "What about it?"

He hesitated. He wanted to say that he wanted to kiss her again. That he wanted to do more than kiss, but he couldn't tell her that, not now. If he got locked in an asylum or killed in battle, it would only make the loss harder on Rose. "It was…nice."

Rose sighed and gave him a small smile. "Yes…it was."

He knew that wasn't what she'd hoped he'd say.

* * *

AFTER BREAKFAST, they went to a store to get some clothing suitable for the winter's chill.

On the walk there she'd refused his hand and jacket despite the shivers that made her teeth chatter, but she skimmed the lush fabrics of the rows upon rows of clothing reverently.

Her eyes caught on a black coat with silver buttons running along the front, and Gabriel held it up for her. "Do you want to try this on?"

"It's beautiful, but it looks expensive. Are you sure?"

"I insist. A beautiful coat for a beautiful woman."

"I'll forgive the shameless flirtations this time because this truly is a beautiful coat, and I'm freezing." She snatched the coat from him, but her cold hands fumbled as she tried to slide her arm into the sleeves.

"Here, let me help you with that." He held out his hand, and he slipped the jacket over her thin shirt. They both flushed when he lowered down to fasten the bottom buttons of the jacket. His hand lingered on the last button until she pushed at his forehead.

"Okay, it's on. You can move away now."

"Sorry." He stood up and appraised her.

"Can you turn around for me?"

She crossed her arms over her chest. "I won't indulge your fancies, if that's what you're hoping for."

He blinked, and his cheeks heated. "I wanted to make sure it fits properly. Although you look striking in that coat."

"Fine, I'll turn, but only because you said I look striking." She flipped her hair over her shoulder and then gave a quick turn. His breath caught in his throat. The coat emphasized each of her curves and it made her crimson eyes blaze like a fire. She looked like she'd escaped from a fairytale.

"It fits perfectly. Do you like it?"

She pulled the coat tighter around her. "I love it."

"In that case, we'll get it."

She jumped up and down which drew his attention to her scuffed flats. She'd need some warm shoes as well.

This trip was going to cost him. "It looks like you'll need some new shoes to match your coat. What size shoe do you wear?"

Rose rocked on her feet. "Well...I'm not sure."

"Give me one of your shoes then. We need to find you some winter boots."

She sat on a nearby bench and pulled off a shoe for him. "Just make sure it's comfortable," she added.

"Get the most uncomfortable boots? Of course, Rose."

Rose hid her face in her hand, "Ugh. And I thought I was sarcastic."

He pressed a fist to his mouth, stifling a laugh and searched through the boots while she waited. A pair of black lace-ups that appeared to be her size caught his eye first.

When he got back to the bench, she swung her legs and whistled. Her gaze quickly fell to the boots in his hand.

"They look perfect. Can I try them on?"

"No. I got them just to torture you."

"Very funny," she said and held out her hand to take the boots.

She slipped them onto her feet but struggled with the laces.

"Need help?"

"Perhaps a little," she admitted with a nervous smile.

He laced them up as she watched intently.

Rose tested the fit, swinging her legs around, and then getting up and walking around the shop. "They fit perfectly." She beamed.

"Do you like them?" Gabriel asked.

Rose stared down at them dreamily. "Yes. They're as beautiful as the coat."

"Are they comfortable?"

She nodded. "They're so soft it feels almost as nice as going barefoot."

"Great. Let's pay then."

Her head tilted to one side. "Don't you need a coat?"

"Oh, right." He skimmed the racks and plucked the first one he could find in his size.

"There. Now we're ready to go."

When they paid at the front desk, she let out a high-pitched squeal. "Thank you!" She wrapped her arms around him, crushing him in a hug.

Now he wished he'd told her what he'd really wanted to say when he'd seen her in that coat…*I like you. I want to be with you.* It was still on the tip of his tongue, but he couldn't form the words.

Instead, he smiled. "You're welcome. You deserve it."

He'd ended up spending more on the clothing than he had on the hotel; the coat alone had been about $35, a sizable chunk of his savings. *At least it made her happy,* he thought.

* * *

AFTER THE SHOPS, they visited the coal mines. Gabriel rubbed his numb arms to keep the cold out of his thin, black, wool sweater. He stayed closer to Rose so that their shoulders nearly brushed, and the closeness warmed his freezing skin.

They sat and watched the people come and go for work. Although many of the workers were glassy eyed and appeared devoid of happiness, none of them had any markings that made Rose or Gabriel suspect one of them could be a nymph.

At first, when they looked around, they didn't see the potential for harm. The worst-case scenario would be the mine collapsing, but that would still only affect the people in the mine, not the water.

But he thought of the soot and the cleaning of the ores. The mining process could taint the water as easily as the factory's dye. *And a fire could take out half the town and all the miners*, he thought.

"I'll work here, see what I can find out," he said. "It doesn't look like they have many women working the mines. Plus, I don't want you putting yourself in so much danger."

Rose nodded in agreement, and they went to look for other potential hiding places for the nymphs.

As they went deeper into the city, they saw a factory which coughed smoke into the air, making it hard to breathe. Textile production created plenty of toxins that could poison water.

They watched some people come and go but didn't see any nymphs. Most of the workers were women.

Gabriel turned to Rose. "I think we may have found another potential hiding place."

She nodded in agreement. "I was just thinking the same thing. We'll both apply for jobs and meet back up tonight?"

"Sounds like a plan." He gave her hand a slight squeeze and left for the mines.

CHAPTER 12

hen Rose set off on her own, she had no idea what to expect. Before she entered the factory, she placed her tinted glasses on her face and pushed them up her nose with a pointer finger.

A wave of warmth heated her skin as she entered the textile factory, and she slid off her jacket. She skidded to the side at the sound of, "Excuse me, ma'am," just in time to avoid a young boy that looked to be ten years old hefting a roll of fabric that was taller than he was.

One girl's fingers had small pinprick-sized scars all along her fingertips, and she worked on an automated sewing machine that emanated heat.

Another girl passed by, her posture hunched. Rose tapped the young girl's grime-coated shoulder, and she turned to face Rose with a hand shielding her face. "Excuse me. Where can I find the boss?" The girl looked up with a vacant stare and pointed to a man who wore dark glasses inside. *Strange. I'll have to keep an eye on him.* She walked over to his table and asked, "Do you have any jobs available?"

He looked straight into her eyes, and she pushed the glasses up her

117

nose, making sure they were still in place. "What's your name?" he asked.

She straightened her back at the question. "It's Rose."

"Do you know how to sew?"

She tucked a strand of hair behind her ear. "Yes, but I haven't sewn recently."

The man nodded, and beckoned the hunched over girl. "You'll start today on the floor above this one with the slower workers. The pay is per piece, so the more pieces you make, the more money you make."

He nodded to the young girl beside her. "Jane will show you the way to the upstairs room." He pointed to rickety looking stairs in the corner.

Rose adjusted the part of the glasses that looped over her ears. *Does he see my eyes? What if they realize I'm a nymph?* She gulped at the thought.

The young girl pulled her along by the arm. "I'll show you how to get upstairs."

The girl tugged Rose along to the back of the building. Rust coated parts of the stairs.

As they ascended, her breaths came in short gasps and she avoided looking down as her stomach lurched into her throat.

The top of the stairs revealed frowning faces and dusty clothes of countless women and children. A flash of red passed through her peripheral vision, but when she followed it with her gaze, it disappeared. *Was that a nymph or am I imagining things?* she thought as she was led to long rows of people sewing in robotic motions.

None of the workers laughed or talked. They only sewed, their eyes fixed on the machine or their needle and thread.

The dusty air scraped her throat, and the urge to run, to escape the stuffy room windowless room surged through her.The air weighed down on her, clogging her lungs like too many rocks in a stream of water.

Her gaze wandered to the workers beside her as she tried and failed to imitate their movements while working with wool. She gazed longingly at the machines until the girl's clothes got caught in a machine and she had to rip part of her skirt off to yank free.

If it can do that to the skirt, I don't want to know what it would do to my hair and skin. She stared back down at the sloppily constructed hat forming beneath her fingers. She wasn't sure anyone would purchase what she'd made.

How am I supposed to find and defeat the nymphs if I can't even figure out how to make a simple wool hat? She curled the wool yarn around one needle and made a loop on the other. Every time she tried to pull the yarn through the loop, her fingers slipped.

By the end of the day she'd only made about six of the wool hats, and only half of them looked fit for use. Striking red eyes that mirrored hers appeared in her peripheral vision again, and this time she whirled to see a girl approaching her. She had the stature of a child, but her eyes held a cool, calculated glint to them.

The girl pulled her aside and whispered into Rose's ear, "Have you never sewn before?"

Rose shook her head. "No. I thought I could figure it out, but..." She held up the sloppy attempt at a hat. "Obviously I was wrong."

The girl's gaze darted around the room, and when Rose opened her mouth to speak, the red-eyed girl placed a finger to her lips. "The bosses aren't watching, so I'll help you this time, but you're going to have to learn or you won't last long here."

The girl wrinkled her nose at Rose's pitiful pile. "Six pieces will net you almost nothing. Tomorrow, I'll teach you how to sew, but for now take a few of my pieces. No one deserves the ire of the managers here." A shiver slid down her spine.

The girl slinked away and returned with an armful of hats. There had to have been at least twenty or thirty. She dumped them in front of Rose and held out her hands with callused fingers and flashed a toothy grin. "My name's Elizabeth. What's yours?"

Rose took her hand and shook it. "It's Rose. Thank you for the help." Elizabeth's turned over Rose's smooth, uncalloused hand.

"I can tell you don't work much, but don't worry, your body will adjust...eventually."

A thud sounded through the room, and her gaze darted to the doorway.

"I'll speak to you later. You don't want *them* catching you talking during work hours." She snuck back to her seat and a couple seconds later a brick wall of a man with tinted glasses entered the room.

He walked around surveying the workers, and when he saw Rose's small stack of hats, he approached her. "That's all you managed in a day? Pathetic." He spat on the floor, and Rose wrinkled her nose in disgust.

"If you want to earn more than a few pennies, you'll have to be faster than this."

And if you want to keep your tongue you'll learn some manners, swine. That's what she wanted to say, but she'd be outnumbered in a place like this.

He grabbed one of Rose's wool hats and turned to leave. On the way out, he said, "Come and turn in your pieces to receive your pay," before exiting the musty room. Rose let out a sigh.

She was glad she'd found some help from a young nymph, of all things. If it hadn't been for Elizabeth, she might have received even harsher punishment. *Perhaps not all nymphs are rotten,* she thought.

She wondered if Elizabeth even knew she was a nymph. She'd have to find a way to discuss it with her later.

Rose peered over her pile of hats as she tiptoed down the rusty stairs. She plopped them down in front of the rude manager from earlier. When they'd finished counting, he held out a measly $0.20.

As she left the factory, she had to stumble along in near darkness. Only the electric lights that dotted the streets led her to her hotel.

Rose's skin felt grimy from the air in the factory. Even her coat had a thin layer of dust adhering to it, and she wished she'd dropped it off at the hotel first as she swiped at the soiled fabric.

A cough racked her body with such force that her entire body shook. *We'd better find the information we need before I get sick from whatever toxins are in the air here.*

She clomped along in exhaustion as she walked in the hotel's direction, but a familiar voice turned her head. "You aren't planning on walking, are you? Where are you staying?"

Rose's head turned to see Elizabeth standing before a miniature version of the train. "I'm staying at the hotel. Why?"

Elizabeth's brow furrowed. "I'm not sure how you're affording *that* place, but the streetcar goes past there."

Rose shrugged. "My travel companion and I didn't know where else to go when we got into town. Do you know of a safe, clean place to stay?"

I might have an idea, but the streetcar is about to leave. Get on."

Rose followed Elizabeth and the other women onto the streetcar. It wasn't as fancy as the train, but it was better than walking. She followed Elizabeth's lead and paid the $0.05 fare, wiping out a sizable chunk of what she'd earned today. *Now I know how Gabriel feels whenever he has to pay for food or the hotel.*

She plopped down in an empty seat next to Elizabeth before the train filled to the brim with women and children.

She sank back into the chair, her eyes fluttering closed as the weight of exhaustion hit her like a punch to the gut.

After what must have been a few minutes later, Elizabeth tapped her on the shoulder rousing her. "This is your stop. Better get out now if you don't want to end up stuck in a strange place across town."

Rose said a quick "Thank you. See you tomorrow," before hopping off the streetcar and stumbling to the hotel.

She rubbed at her arms, longing to scrub herself clean and get some rest.

When she entered the hotel, several people gawked at her ragged appearance. *Afraid if you mix with a commoner that you'll catch poor?* she thought as she glared back at the onlookers.

A staff member approached her. "I'm sorry, but I think you might be lost. This isn't an inn for common folk."

Rose waved the key in front of the man's face, "Are you certain about that?"

He cleared his throat, "Pardon my prying, but it appears as though you've worked in a factory all day. Surely you can't afford it on a factory salary."

She crossed her arms over her chest. "My traveling partner, Gabriel, purchased the rooms. He's new money, and he still enjoys working on occasion, as do I. Will that be a problem?"

"No ma'am, but will he be coming back like...that?" He said gesturing at her filthy clothing.

"It's a possibility. He is working at the coal mines right now."

The man placed a hand over his chest. "The coal mines. Oh, this won't do. You stay right here," he said before storming off.

A few moments later, he returned with a man with salt and pepper hair, wearing a finely pressed suit. The older man looked her up and down and then turned to his employee. "What seems to be the problem?"

He gestured at Rose's clothes. "I mean look at her. She's disrupting the guests looking like that."

The older man frowned. "I came because I heard you were traveling with a man named Gabriel. Is that correct?"

Rose blinked. "Yes. Do you know him?"

The older man smiled. "Yes. He was excellent company on the train and had a penchant for coffee."

She cracked a smile. "That sounds like him."

"In that case, it's nice to meet you. If this man or anyone else gives you trouble, have them call for Jim, okay?" He held out his hand, and she shook it.

"Thank you. I'll let Gabriel know when he returns from work."

The staff member turned up his nose at her. "Well, you should at least wash up. I'll take your coat to be cleaned, and you'll need a towel."

He shuffled over to the desk and retrieved a small, white towel from a rack and handed it to her along with a bar of soap. "Here you go, Ma'am."

Teeth pressed together in a grin, she muttered, "Thank you," before running up to her room, waltzing into the bathing area, and shutting the door behind her.

She peeled the filthy clothes off and hopped into the shower stall. She hadn't seen a shower before, but she saw a knob that looked like a spigot. She tried pulling it, but no water came out. Then she pushed the knob in—still no water. That only left one more option. She turned the knob and water poured over her face. She jumped back out of the spray when it burned her skin. *How the heck do I make it cooler?*

She moved to the side and spotted a second knob. She turned it first to the left and then to the right. When she turned it to the right, the water went from steamy to warm. Rose went back under the warm water. It flowed over her skin and removed some grime. She grabbed the bar of soap she'd been given and scrubbed the remaining dirt away.

Once she felt clean, she went over to the large bathing tub and filled it to the brim with water. She sank into the bath, letting the soothing warmth take away some of her aches and pains.

AFTER HE'D parted ways with Rose, Gabriel had spent the entire day breathing in fumes as he toiled away in the mines, but he failed to find out anything useful. None of the people he worked with appeared abnormal in any way. He wished Rose was with him. She was always the observant one.

With every dig of his pick into the rocky wall of the mine, his back and shoulders ached. He could still feel each swing reverberating through his body. He'd never spent so much time working. It was criminal having people work such long hours. They'd received a short break to eat and get water halfway through the day, but it had been far too short.

The stars peeked through the night sky when he emerged from the cave. He coughed from the sudden change in the air, and attempted to brush off the layer of soot and coal dust coating his body.

His sore legs dragged along the dirt road as he headed back to the hotel. Cars and horse-drawn carriages passed by, and he cursed himself for not having the foresight to keep them with him.

After arriving at the inn, it took all of his energy to make it up to his room, but he needed to get cleaned up. He went to his bedroom and clomped into the bathroom.

After using the newfangled shower system, he changed and went downstairs to hand over his dirty clothes for washing and then went to bed. His empty stomach rumbled in protest and he eyed the closed dining hall. He'd just have to have a big breakfast.

Talking to Rose will have to wait until tomorrow, he thought as he sank into the comfortable mattress and fell asleep.

* * *

THE NEXT MORNING, the sound of Rose's door slamming closed woke him. Greyish light peeked through the window, and his heart leapt into his throat as he dared to turn to his clock. It was half past four. *If it weren't for Rose, you would've been late on your second day. How did you forget your alarm?* He tugged on clothes and pulled the door open to his room.

He stopped short when she passed right in front of his nose. "Sorry, Rose."

She smirked at him. "You're running late. If you don't hurry, you'll have to go to work without your precious coffee," she said in a sing-song tone.

Gabriel was going to comment that she'd just gotten up too, but her hair was pinned back in a neat bun that told him otherwise.

"See you at breakfast, slowpoke. I'll order you that bitter drink that you love so dearly...if I'm feeling generous." She winked and walked away.

After she'd left, he realized he'd forgotten to ask her if she'd found anything.

Gabriel rushed back into his room and hastily dressed before racing down the stairs. He glanced at the clock on the wall. Breakfast might have to wait or else he was going to be late. Just as the thought crossed his mind, someone tapped him on the shoulder. Red eyes appeared in his peripheral vision.

He whirled around to see Rose. "I thought you might want to eat something before heading into work." She imitated his usual mischievous smile and handed over an orange and a steaming mug.

"You're enjoying this, aren't you?"

She smiled and said, "It's nice seeing you flustered for a change." Then she kissed him on the cheek and started walking towards the door.

"Oh and I found one," she said with no further context.

Wait, red eyes. She isn't wearing her glasses.

"Rose, wait you forgot your-" but he was too late. The front door to the hotel shut behind her and worry hitched in his chest. *Be careful, Rose.*

* * *

As she swung open the hotel's front door, she thought she heard Gabriel's voice behind her, but she quickly brushed it off as the streetcar approached. Whatever it was, it could wait until later.

She needed to find a moment to speak to Elizabeth. Maybe she could make a powerful ally or even teach her about nymph magic.

The possibilities whirled through her mind as she entered the streetcar with a large group of women. After a few stops, Rose glimpsed Elizabeth's red eyes as she hopped onto the streetcar.

Elizabeth smiled and grabbed onto a handle, standing next to Rose. "Back for another beating I see," she nodded at the small white markings on her fingers. Most of the cuts had already closed.

Elizabeth glimpsed Rose's eyes and her mouth dropped open. "Your eyes."

The girl leaned down to Rose's ear. "You're a nymph too?" Her voice came out a whisper.

Rose reached to her face and didn't feel the frames of her glasses. *I guess that's why Gabriel had called after me. I didn't imagine his voice.*

Elizabeth's gaze skimmed her hair, and her lower lip quivered. "That's how you healed so fast. You're the one they were looking for. Black hair and red eyes." Elizabeth twirled a strand of hair. "Born to a human because of Belladonna's fertility magic. Your Belladonna's only surviving heir, Rose."

Elizabeth flinched when the doors of the streetcar slid open. "I'm sorry, but I have to go." She turned to walk away, but Rose grabbed her arm with a firmer grip than she'd expected.

"Wait. You helped me yesterday. Maybe I can help you?" Rose asked.

Elizabeth shook her head. ""If they know I've helped you, they'll kill me. I can't be seen with you."

Rose tightened her grip, and Elizabeth yelped. "I didn't know who you were until now, so I haven't told them anything, but the nymphs here will kill you if they know you're here. Please, let me go."

The fear in Elizabeth's eyes made Rose loosen her grip. She took a deep breath. "I'm sorry. I didn't intend to hurt you, but I couldn't let you escape when you know what I am. The last nymph that knew who I was got my friend killed and put me and my traveling companion in danger."

Her gaze flickered to the floor. "I don't want to hurt you, but they might make me."

Rose placed a hand on Elizabeth's shoulder. "I don't want to hurt you either, but I need to know you won't betray me. If you agree to help me, we can destroy Nightshade's reign together."

And if you betray me or get Gabriel killed, I won't show you any mercy, she thought.

Elizabeth bit her lip, and she gazed around the train. Her gaze hardened as she looked back at Rose. "I'll help you if you promise to help the others," Elizabeth said.

Rose pursed her lips. "What others?"

Elizabeth sucked her teeth. "There are others like me that were threatened. They worked for Nightshade out of fear, not loyalty. Will you show them mercy?"

The tension in Rose's shoulders eased. "I will give them a chance, but if they attempt to hurt me or my comrade, I will put our safety before theirs. Understand?"

Elizabeth bit her lip. "I understand. I would do the same."

"Good. Let's meet tonight to discuss what Nightshade is planning and then we're going to stop it together. If you know anyone trustworthy who can help us, bring them with you."

Elizabeth ran her nails along her arm. "I do know one nymph who will side with me. He doesn't fear Nightshade like the others. I will see if he can join us."

Rose bit the inside of her cheek. "I'm sorry, but I have one more favor to ask you. My powers activated recently, and I'm still learning to use them. Can you train me to use nymph magic?"

Elizabeth leaned in, and her voice came out a hissing whisper. "You don't know how to use your magic?"

Rose scratched her head. "I can form a rudimentary weapon, but I can't manage much else. Belladonna may have given me her powers to help in the battle with Nightshade, they didn't come with instructions."

Elizabeth sighed. "I'll do my best, but I'm no teacher."

Rose placed a hand on Elizabeth's. "Thank you. When this is over, I'll make sure you never have to work in a horrid factory like this again."

Elizabeth's smile returned, and she grasped Rose's hand. "Tonight, I'll tell you about their plan. The bosses called us disposable and weak when our backs were turned. We'll show them."

Just then, the doors to the streetcar hissed open, and she rushed to exit the streetcar with the others. "Come on," she called when Rose didn't follow right behind her.

Now we're getting somewhere, she thought with a smirk and followed after Elzabeth and the other workers.

The factory coughed black smoke as they approached.

Today, they moved her to nets, but thankfully she still worked alongside Elizabeth.

After a bit, Elizabeth came and crouched beside her. "I recommended moving you here. These are easier to make."

She held a half finished net in her hands. "Here. Look." Elizabeth's hands move like a blur. When she caught Rose's awed stare, she slowed her feverish pace and handed Rose an unfinished net and said, "Listen and copy what I do."

At first, Rose could only copy with clumsy motions, but after some basic instructions and a few fumbles, she found her rhythm. Without thinking about the steps, her hands just knew. She could copy Elizabeth's movements, although with much less mastery.

After half a day, she'd made twenty nets.

Elizabeth checked back in at the end of the day. "Still not great, but better than yesterday, amateur."

Elizabeth scooted towards Rose and dropped her voice to a whisper. "I'll follow you back on the streetcar tonight," she said before going back to her work as though nothing had happened.

When they left the factory, Rose was still exhausted, but she had far fewer cuts than she'd had the day before.

They got onto the streetcar without incident, and, just as promised, Elizabeth didn't get off at her usual stop. She waited for Rose's stop and got off with her.

Once they'd exited the streetcar, Rose guided them both towards the hotel.

Before they entered the building, Elizabeth grabbed Rose by the arm. "Before I go in there, I need to know. Can your companion be trusted?"

Rose hesitated. Her mouth opened, but no words escaped. *He isn't stable, but I don't think he could ever be dangerous. Could he?*

Elizabeth took Rose's hesitation as a *no*. "In that case, I think it's better if I only tell you the plan."

She looked around for potential eavesdroppers and kept her voice a whisper even though the clearing appeared empty. "They plan to poison the water. Nightshade is still bitter about people contaminating the water in his forest, so he wants to destroy them the same way."

Rose stared at the girl in confusion."I know that, but how do they plan to poison the water?" Rose asked.

Elizabeth's gaze darted around again before she spoke. Her voice came out a whisper. "They plan to use the poisons the factories already produce and mix them with a little extra something from the forest. They're going to dump it all into the river that supplies the city's drinking water."

Realization hit Rose like a punch in the gut. Perhaps that was why this place felt toxic to her. Maybe they'd already started their attack.

But before she could open her mouth to ask any more questions, Elizabeth took in her panicked expression and added, "They haven't started their attack yet. The factories are this toxic on their own."

Elizabeth lowered her gaze and mumbled, "They care for certain parts of nature, but destroy others. I don't understand the humans, but I want to."

Rose had to agree with that sentiment. "People are complicated. My friend died trying to save me from a fire that Nightshade's allies set. However, my father was as cruel as Nightshade himself."

Elizabeth shuddered. "I'm sorry to hear that you lost your friend."

Rose straightened her back. "That's why we have to stop them. If the water gets poisoned, countless people would die. It could spell all out war."

It felt like neither side was ever going to win. The nymphs were vengeful and lacked compassion, while the humans were self-destructive and didn't respect their environment or each other. But that was something to deal with another time. Now, they had to stop the nymphs before they did something they couldn't come back from: mass genocide.

When Rose said nothing more, Elizabeth placed a hand on her shoulder. "Then we'll find a way to stop them together."

CHAPTER 13

Gabriel's limbs ached. His lungs felt as hard as lumps of coal. As he made his way back to the hotel, his thoughts drifted to where they would stay once their week was up. *Maybe I can visit the next town over, but how will I have the time while I'm working for the mine from dawn to dusk?* He ran a hand through his hair and walked towards the hotel, but the sound of Rose's voice quieted his thoughts.

His feet froze when his eyes caught on the person beside her, and he ducked behind a nearby building. The girl had red eyes; a nymph, and a young one at that. She barely reached Rose's nose.

Rose and the girl huddled together, whispering. He pressed his back against the wall as he sank to the dirt. He only heard part of what the girl said, "—companion be trusted?"

He'd missed part of the sentence, but since the girl was asking about Rose's companion, he guessed that she meant him.

He could understand why the girl might not trust humans, and they needed to win over the girl to get information. Frankly, he wouldn't blame the girl for not trusting his kind because he didn't trust that nymph either.

What shocked him most was Rose's hesitation. *Did she really not trust him?*

He thought back to how she'd hid the book from him in the library. Tears welled up in his eyes, and he placed a hand over his mouth, choking back a sob. If she caught him eavesdropping, there was no telling what the nymph girl would do.

The girl glanced around, and he held his breath as he pressed into the wall, hoping she wouldn't spot him. Once he heard them speaking again, he hissed out a breath.

It was difficult for him to hear the girl's whispers, so he could only make out Rose, who still spoke at full volume. "How do they plan to poison the water?"

He clapped a hand over his mouth, muffling a gasp. They were discussing the nymph's plans without him.

The forest is important to the nymph's health too. If the poisoned water runs through the forest, what will become of the water nymphs and the plants near the water? Why were they desperate enough to agree to such a plan?

He longed to confront them and ask these questions, but he stayed rooted to his hiding spot, a silent observer instead of a participant. The chatter stopped, and he turned to see Rose and the girl walking toward the hotel.

Damn. They're probably going there to meet with me, but if I follow right behind them, it will look too suspicious. He sat on the dirty ground, his back leaned against the building's wall, thinking about what he would do about Rose's distrust of him.

She didn't have a pleasant childhood. Maybe she just isn't trusting in general? He shook his head. She'd trusted April and now this nymph girl she barely knew.

Maybe she's worried about how I'll react because of the hallucinations? As if on cue, his vision blurred, and his head felt heavy. His mind played Rose's hesitation on repeat, and a faint figure appeared. A man with dark hair and green eyes like his own.

"What's stopping her from taking the nymph's side if she doesn't even trust you?" he said with teeth bared like fangs.

"Shut up. It isn't true, and you aren't real," he spat, but his heart dipped into his stomach. Anger and confusion swarmed through his chest when he caught sight of auburn curls and grey eyes. The angry Lara and his father circled him, mocking him for his weakness.

"She can't trust you because you're too weak. She'd be better off without you," fake Lara snarled.

Gabriel covered his ears in a futile attempt to block them out. "Stop it. You're wrong." His throat burned. He held his ears, shaking and sobbing.

Lara stared at him with glassy grey eyes. "Don't cry. You'll be joining me in hell soon enough." A few breaths later, the hallucinations faded.

He sat there with his knees to his chest, and his head rested on his hands as he stared into the darkness of the night. "She hid this for a reason. There has to be a reason," he whispered.

After wiping away tears from his face and taking a few deep breaths to steady himself, he pushed himself up and approached the hotel. He had a nymph to meet.

* * *

GABRIEL SLOUCHED like an old man as he entered the hotel. His smile was as fragmented as a broken mirror, and the thick layer of soot that coated his body was absent just underneath his eyes.

Had he been crying? she thought.

Before she could ask any questions, he leaned in so that his breath brushed her ear, "Is this the nymph you mentioned this morning?"

"Yes," she whispered.

Gabriel extended his hand for Elizabeth, but she only stared at it with narrowed eyes and then wrinkled her nose.

With a forced smile, he let his arm drop to his side. "Hi, it's nice to meet you. Perhaps we should have this conversation somewhere a bit more... private?"

Her lip quirked up in a smile that didn't quite reach her eyes. "Yes. I think that would be best. Lead the way." She gestured towards the stairs, and he led them up to their rooms as the judging eyes of the guests in the hotel followed every step.

Rose glared back at them, and a few people had the decency to turn their gazes to the floor.

He stopped in front of the door to Rose's room and stood aside for her to open the door.

Once they'd shut the door behind them, Gabriel said, "As Rose might have told you, I've been having hallucinations. I've been waiting to share this information, but the nightmares and images are getting worse."

Rose's jaw dropped. "How much worse?"

His gaze dropped to the floor, and he picked at his nails but didn't answer the question.

Elizabeth broke the silence. "You're suffering from hallucinations?"

His face flushed. "Sorry. I thought Rose had told you. They started shortly after I came into contact with the Manchineel tree. I think it's poison is affecting my mind."

Rose grabbed his arm. "Why didn't you tell me?"

"The same reason you had a private conversation with Elizabeth outside the hotel."

Elizabeth gulped. "You heard our conversation?"

He narrowed his eyes at Rose. "Only the part where Rose hesitated when you asked her if I could be trusted."

She reached out to touch his shoulder. "I'm sorry. I do trust you, but not as you are now."

"You mean because of the curse?"

Her chin fell to her chest. "Because you thought I was Lara."

Elizabeth stood between them. "You can sort out your personal problems later, but right now I need to know, did Manchineel take her human form?"

Gabriel cocked his head to one side. "She's a nymph?"

Elizabeth's back stiffened. "Did she not take human form to curse you?"

He gazed up at the ceiling, thinking back on the encounter. "No, but Nightshade gave me the ax to cut the antidote from her branches. He was rather smug about it."

"I didn't expect them to be working together. I'm going to be on the most wanted list for *HIM*. I'm dead. Dead!" Her hands shook, and she covered her face.

Rose placed a hand on her shoulder. "Maybe they aren't working together. Wouldn't an ax on her plant hurt? That doesn't seem like the action of allies."

Elizabeth bit her lip. "He's made his allies do worse."

Rose's voice came out sounding far more confident than she felt. "You will not die because we're going to protect you, but if we're going to help, we need to know more about Manchineel and about the curse or poison affecting him."

Elizabeth gave a hollow laugh. "Even with Belladonna's magic, you don't stand a chance if they're working together."

Rose smiled. "Maybe I don't, but we do. Together. But I need you to tell me what you know."

Elizabeth hissed out a breath. "Fine. Manchineel was Nightshade's lover before Belladonna. If it's poison, then there's a chance we can find an antidote..." her voice trailed off, and she looked up at Rose.

"And if it's a curse?" she prompted.

"If it's a curse, then you'll need to destroy her magic or force her to break the curse. Curses must be broken by the magic of the nymph who formed them."

Elizabeth turned to Gabriel. "If she truly didn't take human form when you were so close to her tree, then perhaps we still have a chance. It may mean she can't change forms for the time being."

Rose cocked her head to one side. "What could keep her from changing forms?"

Elizabeth traced the embroidery on her skirt. "The only reasons that would happen would be if there had been some severe damage to her body or to her tree."

"Does that mean Nightshade can't transform either? We destroyed his body."

"It would render him immobile, perhaps for a few days or weeks. The level of damage would determine the length of time."

Rose pursed her lips. "In that case, we need to stop these nymphs and head home as soon as possible. My mother lives in the town that holds Nighshade's plant. When will they poison the water?"

"They plan to do it in a week's time. I'd be willing to bet that's also when Nightshade will regain his human form."

Gabriel crossed his arms over his chest. "Care to share how they're planning to poison the water?"

Elizabeth glanced over at Rose, who nodded. "They plan to use the toxins from the dyes and textiles. They're just barrels of factory waste, and they'll need several barrels to cause any actual damage to the water. The danger lies more with the poison... Manchineel leaves. Just a handful can render an entire river toxic. I will retrieve the leaves since they still trust me."

Rose curled a lock of hair around her finger. "But I'm useless in a fight. How are we going to do this without getting killed?"

Elizabeth bit her lower lip. "Well... I have a comrade who is a former member of the military. I'll help you with magic lessons, and I'll try to convince him to help with combat training. We'll start tomorrow."

Rose's jaw dropped open. "Your friend was in the military? I thought nymphs hated humans."

A halting laugh escaped Elizabeth's lips. "He's not the biggest fan of humanity after what he witnessed in battle, but he used to be one of their allies... I'll do my best to convince him."

Elizabeth turned her gaze to Gabriel. "As for you, if you want to make yourself useful, you'll need to learn how to fight. Rose, you'll have your lessons after your workday is done. We can search for weak points and potential hiding places in the factory. Both of you will meet me at the largest tree in the forest. It's just past where the train tracks split."

Gabriel stared at Elizabeth blankly, and she sighed. "Gabriel, I'll retrieve you from work and show you the way there. We can't risk you wandering aimlessly around nymph territory. Rose, we'll go there together after work tomorrow night. For now, both of you will need to get some rest."

Elizabeth stood up from the chair and headed for the door, but Rose stepped in front of her. "Wait. What about a cure for Gabriel?"

Elizabeth's gaze flicked to Gabriel. "I'm not familiar with remedies for Manchineel poisoning and asking around could arouse suspicion. If apothecaries weren't bordering on extinction, that would be your best option."

"What about the library?"

Elizabeth's jaw opened and closed and her brows knitted together. "You can read?"

Rose huffed and crossed her arms over her chest. "Of course I can."

Elizabeth muttered, "I didn't mean to offend you, it's just uncommon for a woman of your....status. In that case, try researching there."

She pushed Rose aside and let herself out of the room without another word.

Rose locked the door behind her and whirled around, her voice rising to a yell. "Why didn't you tell me about the Manchineel poisoning?"

His jaw worked, and in two quick strides he'd crossed the room so that their faces were inches apart. He stared down at her and shouted. "How about you tell me why you hid that book from me in the library? Were you worried I couldn't handle knowing that Nightshade is alive?"

She shouted back at him, her teeth bared in a mockery of a grin. "You're changing the subject. Answer my question. I would have done anything to help you find that antidote."

He broke her gaze and mumbled, "That's what I'm afraid of."

"What exactly do you mean by that? Are you insinuating that I would resort to violence like my father or like Nightshade?" She leveled a frosty glare at him.

"I was worried that you might go...too far if my life is on the line. Or that you might abandon the fight against the nymphs trying to help me. I couldn't live with that." He clenched his teeth together in a forced smile that did little to ease the tension in the room.

"I can't believe you don't trust me." Tears brimmed in her eyes.

"Odd. That's precisely how I felt when you hid that book from me."

He walked past Rose towards the door, but Rose grabbed his wrist. "I've told you already that I'm sorry, and I meant it."

With her hand still on his wrist, he whirled around and used her grip to pull her in close. "Sorry will need to be shown in actions, not words. That's why I won't apologize for hiding the information about the tree. I would lie again in a heartbeat if I thought it would protect you."

Rose sighed. "As would I."

Gabriel placed a hand to Rose's cheek. "I know. That's why I would trust you with my life, but I can't trust you with my heart...yet."

Rose placed her hand on his. "Perhaps we should be more honest with one another."

He traced her jawline "Perhaps you should be honest with yourself first."

"Care to elaborate?"

"I think you already know exactly what I mean," he said before disentangling from Rose and exiting the room. The door swung shut.

What does he mean by being honest with myself? Why must he be so infuriating? She frowned down at the dirt wedged under her fingernails and the dust clinging to her arms. She flushed. *He kissed my hand like this? What does it matter? He admitted he doesn't love you.* She ran her fingers through her filthy hair and glanced over at the washroom.

Maybe a bath will help clear my thoughts and the caked on grime. She ran a hot bath, and as she sank into the steamy water, some of her worries faded away as the heat soothed her sore muscles. She scrubbed her skin raw with the bar soap, but she couldn't erase her worries. Her mind roamed to the Manchineel tree. *What are the side effects of the poison? Is it even poison? Can he be cured?*

Visiting the library on a workday was out of the question considering she left the factory far too late for it to be open before or after work. She'd have to wait for a day off at the end of the week, but that's when the nymphs would attack.

She tangled her fingers in her hair. *I need to help him, but how? I can't quit. If I leave Elizabeth alone in the factory, and she gets attacked, I couldn't live with myself...* She sank her face into the water.

But maybe Gabriel can leave his job to conduct research now that we know the coal mine isn't the nymph's hideout. Yes, that could work.

Once the water went cold, she drained the bath and changed into nightclothes. She sank into bed and was asleep before she had the chance to set any alarms for the morning.

* * *

ROSE AWOKE to the sound of slamming drawers. She rubbed at the grit in her eyes and stared out at the curtains. She didn't see the sun, but if Gabriel was already rushing around, then she must have overslept.

She threw off the covers, pulled on clothes, and bolted out of the door. Her pulse raced as she ran down the stairs, but when she saw the time on the clock, it read 4:00AM. She rubbed her eyes. *No, that can't be right. Gabriel's up early?*

Her jaw clenched as she felt all eyes on her again. Gabriel clomped down the stairs, and she noticed the dark circles under his eyes. *Did he sleep at all?*

He'd left his shirt untucked and nearly tripped on the bottom step. As he shuffled over to the front desk, she intercepted him.

"You're up early."

Gabriel groaned and ran a hand through mussed hair. "I didn't sleep well. I was up the whole night."

"You could just quit now that we know more about the nymphs. It would give you time to research an antidote."

"Perhaps I shall, but not today. We may need more money for the journey."

She bit her lip. "Oh. What about the savings?"

He sighed. "That's limited, and our trip has been rather expensive."

She thought back to his reactions when paying for the coat and the food. "Is that because of me?"

His lips quirked up in a small smile. "It's not your fault. Now get your food so you can go to work before you're late."

"Yes, sir," she said with a mock salute that made him roll his eyes.

On her way to work, anticipation vibrated through her body like electricity. She wanted the workday to end so she could get to training, and it showed through in her work.

Her hands moved with a surprising amount of grace. When Elizabeth came to fetch her, she looked over at her stack of nets, and her jaw dropped. It was three times the amount she usually crafted.

Elizabeth's eyes widened when she took in Rose's pile of nets. "Impressive. How did you manage to make so many?"

Rose shrugged. "I guess you were an excellent teacher."

Elizabeth snorted. "Or you're an excellent thief."

Rose scoffed. "I would never."

"Sure you wouldn't. Now, let's collect our money and get going." She beckoned Rose to follow her with a wave of her hand, and they exited the stuffy room.

Rose gulped the air outside of the walls of the factory. The air here still scraped at her lungs, but there were still hints of pine and the faint scent of earth that the musty workrooms lacked.

Elizabeth watched Rose in amusement, but said nothing. "How do you do this every day for years? I already want to climb the walls every time I'm in there."

Elizabeth shrugged. "You get used to it, but it takes a toll on your body. Why do you think I'm so short?"

Rose cocked her head to one side. "Aren't you younger than me?"

She shook her head, causing a few strands of pale brown hair to break free from her ponytail. "I'm about the same age as you, or rather the same age in nymph years, not human years."

Rose cupped a hand over her mouth. "How old would that be in human years?"

She stared up at the sky for a few moments. "I believe about fifty human years, give or take a few years. We live as long as our plants, so it depends on the lifespan of the plant."

They continued along in silence, waiting for the area surrounding the factory to clear to avoid anyone from following them.

Once the other women got on the streetcar and the area near the factory went quiet, Elizabeth and Rose crept through the streets, crawling closer to the forest on the edge of town. They passed the dark library and a rundown hospital.

Further down the road, freshly painted homes and bright shops were replaced with shabby-looking shacks with broken and boarded up windows. A chill ran down Rose's spine.

She gripped at the fabric of her skirt as they walked, keeping her eyes glued to Elizabeth's back.

When Elizabeth had described a *forest,* she'd expected more trees. A small cluster of a dozen trees with an evergreen tree that towered over her at almost three times Rose's own height comprised the sad excuse for a forest.

Elizabeth pressed a hand to the massive tree. "This is it. We're going to meet here every day for training. It's about as remote as you can get in this city. Few people come out here because this is where vagrants like to wander. If one of them sees us... Well, no one would believe them anyway," Elizabeth said with a wink.

"Are you sure? This feels a bit...exposed." Rose twirled a lock of hair around her finger.

Elizabeth waved it off. "It should be fine, but we're in Nightshade's territory, so we should still be cautious. If another nymph catches me training *you* of all nymphs, it will be more difficult to carry out our plan."

Rose leaned against a tree and Elizabeth flinched. "I will give you something to practice before I go to fetch Gabriel, but first get off the tree."

Rose stood up straight. "Sorry."

"Good. Now, watch carefully because I'm only going to show you this once."

Elizabeth held out an arm, and it changed before her from tanned skin to a light brown bark that matched the color of her hair. The bark became rough with ridges like the evergreen tree behind her. The effort made Elizabeth's face turn red, and sweat trickled down her forehead, making her blink.

She turned the transformed hand over before Rose. "This is the easiest magic to do. Changing parts of your body into their original shape. You want to imagine that part of your body returning to nature."

Rose closed her eyes.

She pictured her fingers turning into bark like Elizabeth's hand and felt pins and needles go through her arm, but she frowned when she opened her eyes to see that only the color of her hand had changed.

Elizabeth bit her lip. "What plant did you imagine just now?"

Rose stared down at her green arm. "Yours. Why?"

She laughed. "No wonder it didn't work. Our natural states won't be the same. You have to think about *your* plant for this to work."

"But I don't know my plant."

Elizabeth pressed a finger to her temple. "Your name is Rose for a reason. I might go by Elizabeth, but my nymph name is Evergreen."

Rose smacked her fist into her palm. "Oh. I suppose that makes sense. Let me try again." This time when she closed her eyes, she pictured the white roses from the greenhouse with their silky petals and the spiky thorns growing along their stems.

When a ripple went across her skin, she cracked an eye open and let out a squeal of delight when she saw her now green hand covered with thorns. "I did it."

Elizabeth placed her hands on her hips. "You did, but you still have a long way to go. Keep practicing changing it from plant to flesh until I get back. Here. I'll show you how to swap back to human form."

Elizabeth's hand changed back into flesh before her eyes. It looked more like a mirage than actual flesh. "How do you do that?"

She shrugged "I guess I just imagine what the human form looks like and then picture forcing the bark to hide, to return to the tree. It's always uncomfortable, like slipping into clothing that's too tight."

Rose pressed her lips together. "It feels the opposite way for me. I feel more at home in my skin rather than the thorns."

She placed a hand on her hips. "That's probably because you've spent more time living as a human. I mean, if your powers just activated, you aren't even old enough to grow wings, but at least that means changing back should be easier for you."

A small smile touched Rose's lips. "Let's hope you're right. I don't want to be stuck this way."

Rose closed her eyes and imagined her hand as it had been before the transformation—pale, slender, and fleshy. Heat raced its way across her skin.

When she opened her eyes, her hand had returned to its normal state. She flexed and stretched the palm, turning it over and prodding the skin. "It really worked." The words came out breathy, and she reached for her throat. "Did I do something wrong? It's hard to breath." She took large gulps of the night air and wiped her sweaty palm on her skirt.

Elizabeth said, "Since you haven't practiced before, transformation might take a lot out of you. However, doing this will build your strength and stamina. "

Rose huffed. "No kidding. You could have warned me."

"You would still need to practice regardless. Just be careful not to pass out while I'm gone."

"I will." Rose drew her focus back to transforming as Elizabeth slipped away to retrieve Gabriel.

* * *

I can't believe she learned to transform so quickly, even though she seems to have lived most of her life as a human. She really must be Belladonna's child. The magic she emanated when she transformed was almost on par with Nightshade. A shudder went through her body despite her wool coat and long skirt that nearly reached the thin dusting of snow on the ground.

I don't know if even her raw talent is going to be enough, and the bosses are...a force to be reckoned with themselves. They haven't caught on to us...yet. I don't think they know she's a nymph, but if they learn what she is... Unease sat like a lump in her chest, and she picked at her nails. They'd gone to extreme measures to quell the last rebellion.

One of their supposed human allies had turned them in. The sounds of their screams and the scent of char as they were executed invaded her mind. *As a warning to anyone else who wished to leave Nightshade's army.* Those were the words they'd said as her friends were reduced to stumps and ashes while they were forced to watch.

If they couldn't win here, this could be the end for them. *The training has to be enough. I can't witness something like that. Not again.*

It couldn't just be Nightshade. They'd have to broach a truce with the humans if they wanted a chance at any sort of peace. One thing she hadn't told Rose was that Elizabeth was part of the reason they'd chosen to attack.

The town wanted to cut down her little clearing of trees to construct a building in about a week's time.

I'm damned either way. Let the humans kill me or get killed by my own kind because my views don't align with Nightshade's. Killing off all the humans makes us just as bad as them. This thought still raced through her head when she reached the coal mine.

Gabriel would have to train twice as hard as Rose to have any chance at surviving this, not to mention there was his sickness to account for. She kicked a stray rock on the dirt road.

What Gabriel had said about the Manchineel tree didn't add up. Its poisonous air lasted a few days at most. Even Manchineel curses only yielded mild hallucinations.

The weight of the dark magic pressing down on him got stronger whenever he was close to Rose.It reminded her of a familiar bedtime story that she'd thought was just a myth used to scare children.

After a nymph's lover betrayed them, they'd cursed their lover's present, a mirror, so that anyone who came into contact with it would fall ill. The sickness worsened as you fell in love with someone and when your lover died, it passed on to your new lover. That's where it got its name…the Lover's Curse. *Was it possible that this curse was the true culprit of his illness?*

She picked out Gabriel's brown-blonde hair and smaller stature in the crowd of tall, bulky men. His gaze stared off at nothing as he dragged his feet.

If they didn't do something about his sickness soon, he would die. If it was the Lover's Curse, it would kill him and then make Rose its new host unless the creator of the curse dispelled the magic or one of its hosts died alone.

When Gabriel walked away from her, his eyes searching the dark night, she weaved through the throng to get closer without being spotted.

When she was in earshot, she put her fingers in her mouth and whistled once to catch his attention. She lowered her face into her open palm when he kept wandering. She whistled once more, louder this time.

He turned towards her, his gaze narrowed as she searched the darkness. He was almost within her reach when his forehead wrinkled, and he spun on his heel to leave.

She called out, "I'm over here" and ducked out from behind the building, yanking him into the shadows by the collar.

He flushed and adjusted the shirt. "Sorry. I wasn't sure if your image was real or imagined."

Elizabeth bit her lip. "It's okay, but try to be more aware. If I'm seen with you, they'll know I've betrayed them. Did you remember to cut ties with the coal mine?"

"Yes. I let them know today was my last day."

She sighed. "Good, that means we'll have more time to train you, and you can look for a cure. Come on. Let's take you to Rose before she faints from over-exertion."

She gestured for him to follow, and they snuck away toward the training grounds, staying in the shadow of the buildings.

But the clunk of his steps behind her made her teeth clench together. She whirled on him, and he pinwheeled his hands to keep from falling down.

"What's wrong?" he whispered.

"Make your steps lighter. You sound like a galloping horse," she hissed.

After her remark, his tread was less of a clomp and more of a light crinkle.

When they reached the training ground, Rose laid back in the dirt, her right hands braced as she lifted her head to the sky, taking deep breaths of the night air.

Her entire arm from shoulder to fingertips was green and covered in thorns, and a smile spread across Elizabeth's face.

Hope bloomed in her chest. *Perhaps we stand a chance after all.*

CHAPTER 14

*R*ose stood at the center of the clearing, drenched in sweat and gasping for air. Her left arm was green and coated with vines.

Elizabeth gave Rose a slight smile. "Rose, take a break while I work with Gabriel."

Rose fell back to the grass, arms outstretched.

Elizabeth turned her hand into a solid piece of bark. "Now, it's your turn to train. Get into a fighting stance. I want to see how you do with just your hands."

Gabriel hesitantly balled his hands into fists, holding them out in front of him and crouched slightly. "Okay. Go ahead."

A gust of wind rippled his shirt and Elizabeth blurred before him. A flash of brown was the only warning before wood collided into his right arm, scraping his skin. "You'll have to be faster than that."

He stepped back, raising his arms again for her next attack.

This time, he picked out her moving towards his right arm, and he dodged to the left. She sliced through the space where his arm had been, but she stayed on balance, crouched low to the ground. Meanwhile, his legs had gotten too far apart, and his ribs were in front of her.

He tried to turn to face her, but she shoved the side of his torso with her arm, and he tottered off balance, placing his hands out to break his fall to the dirt.

His palms stung as they scraped against the grass and dirt, and when he looked up, she pointed the tip of her transformed arm at his throat. "You waste too much movement when you dodge. If this were a real battle, you'd be dead. Now, you try to attack me."

Attack with what? He thought.

But before he could open his mouth to voice the question, she created a staff of thick bark before his eyes. Her face flushed red and her breaths came in heaving gasps from the effort. She struck out at the air, hefting it with ease, and then tossed it at him.

He fumbled with the staff, and it clattered to the ground, eliciting a sigh from Elizabeth.

She nodded at the staff. "I want to see if you're any better with that. Try to hit me."

Maybe if I surprise her I can hit her? Without warning, Gabriel thrust the weapon up at her throat.

She stepped back to avoid the blow and grabbed the arm holding the weapon. She locked his wrist and twisted his hand into an unnatural position.

He yelped and dropped the staff. "Nice try, but you're signaling your moves with your body. You want to keep your stance low and aim even lower. Try to keep your elbows in when you thrust the staff."

Gabriel pulled his elbows in and stood with the staff held out in front of him.

Her gaze skimmed over him, appraising him like a pig at the market. "Watch my stance and try to copy it."

She got into a low crouch like the one she'd used to dodge his attack. Her feet were squared off. One hand covered her face, and the other hovered just below her stomach.

Why do I have a feeling that I'll just look like a fool if I try that? His gaze shifted from her body to his as he crouched down as low as he could go and placed a hand in front of his face and groin like she had.

Her frown as she circled him and the feeling of his legs shaking as they tried to keep the stance told him he was doing something wrong. When she gave him a good shove, he fell right over.

"That was better, but you're too stiff. You want your center of gravity low, but the rest of your body should be light so you can dodge or strike at a moment's notice. Get up and try again."

He got back into the stance, but this time he didn't crouch as low, and he didn't lock his legs. It felt less forced.

She tapped his back to straighten it and gave a few quick swipes to see if he could get out of the way fast enough. His legs were still too slow, but he dodged the strikes she'd aimed at his arms, chest, and head. "That's better. Let's try again, but this time I'll move a little faster."

This time, he couldn't see her at all when she slashed at his leg. The force made him cry out, and she aimed a jab at his side. He lifted the staff to block it, but he was too slow to avoid the strike entirely.

The sharp bark grazed his ribs. He inched his foot back as she went for his leg, but he tripped over his feet, temporarily losing his stance.

She levelled a blow at his head, so he sidestepped. But it was a ruse. The arm stopped mid blow and moved to block while her other arm thrust forward, getting him square in the stomach.

His ribs vibrated from the force, and he rubbed at the tender flesh. She'd stopped before she'd done real damage, but that was going to bruise in the morning.

He gritted his teeth, trying to push past the pain and focus on the movement of her hands and feet.

She kicked out with her leg to sweep him off his feet and he slid back, keeping his elbows in as he thrust his staff towards the leg she wasn't using to kick, but in the process he'd favored his front leg, taking him off balance.

Her transformed arm connected with his front leg, and he fell forward. He had to drop the staff and throw his hands in front of him to avoid landing chin first, and his chest landed right on the staff, knocking the wind out of him.

She stood over his prone form, taking even breaths while he struggled to get air in his lungs. The fight hadn't even phased her.

When he didn't get up right away, she shouted, "You're going to have to do better than that. Again!"

He grimaced and pushed up from his spot up on the ground. "I don't think my body can handle any more bruises."

His legs shook beneath him. "If you want to survive this, we have to work until you collapse from exhaustion."

"My legs are already barely holding me. Perhaps I should continue this tomorrow?"

She snapped, "Our time is limited. You need every second of training you can get. Now take your stance."

He picked up the staff and took his stance again, but one of his legs buckled beneath him. Gabriel placed a hand on the leg and straightened it out.

Elizabeth shot him a pitying look. "I'd like to let you rest, but we don't have the luxury of time."

Gabriel dusted himself off. "I understand. Do you have any advice to keep me from losing my balance?"

Her gaze drifted to his wobbling legs. "Don't leave your stance. When you dodge, make sure your legs move in an L, not a straight line so you don't trip. Always aim low when you kick."

She did a couple of mock kicks to show him and then demonstrated how to move forward, backward, and to the side. She moved in a way that didn't allow any opportunities to trip over her own feet, and her kicks were low enough they'd be tough to dodge.

He adjusted his stance to mirror what she'd shown him and waited for her next attack. She went right for his legs with a swift kick. He moved his leg out of the way like she'd shown him. But he couldn't move with the same grace she had, and his feet tangled together. He fell to the dirt.

She smoothed out the lines forming on her forehead with her thumb. "Again."

He forced himself up, and took his stance, but a flash of green caught his attention and he turned to look at Rose. All he caught was a glimpse of green fingertips before he was knocked to the ground. "Don't focus on your lover, focus on yourself."

Rose's entire face flushed, and her gaze turned to Elizabeth. In unison they both shouted, "We're not lovers!"

Heat warmed Gabriel's cheeks. *Somehow I don't think us answering in unison did much to dispel her impression of us.*

Gabriel felt Rose's gaze on him now as he practiced, and he caught a second wind of energy. *I have to do this for her. I can't hold her back.*

Despite his already shaky legs and sore ribs, he managed a couple more sparring matches with Elizabeth before his legs turned to lead weights and he collapsed to the dirt ground.

Once he was spent, he observed Rose's training as she transformed her arm over and over until she also fell to the ground covered in sweat, her chest heaving as she tried to gulp air.

Elizabeth looked from Rose to Gabriel and then back again. The clock tower chimed, alerting them it was midnight. "That's all for today. We'll do this again tomorrow," Elizabeth said.

Rose recovered first, and she walked over to Gabriel to pull him up from the floor. They supported each other as they half-crawled, half-walked back to the hotel.

Even Rose's footsteps stomped along, her usual energy completely gone.

When they arrived at the hotel, they had just enough time to bathe and catch a few brief winks before she would go back to work and he'd go to the library for research.

* * *

ON THE WAY TO WORK, Elizabeth's mind raced. *That training session was a disaster. I spent the entire time working with Gabriel. All Rose did was transform over and over again, but she needs to learn to fight. I need Ivy's help. He's far better at this.*

Elizabeth wasn't sure how she'd convince Ivy to join her, but she knew there was one thing her comrade would agree on: Nightshade had gotten out of hand.

If he was using Manchineel's leaves, that meant he was injuring one of his closest allies just to spite the humans.

And his plan meant poisoning the water that the water nymphs were connected to. The water nymphs would die, and those growing closest to the lake's banks would get injured from the poisoned water.

He'd gone too far this time.

Perhaps having Rose at our side can give the others confidence to rebel against Nightshade. To tip them over the edge. As a descendant of Belladonna, she had the potential to become even more powerful than Nightshade, but not in a week.

Gabriel wasn't particularly strong or observant, but he was clever. He'd tested stances and strikes with the methodical manner of a scientist trying out new theories. But his movements were slow and clunky. *Maybe Ivy will know what to do with him if I can get him to help us. If anyone can whip them into shape, it would be him.*

She dug her nails into her palm when Rose stepped onto the streetcar. Even with the glasses she used to hide her eyes, her silky, black hair and pale skin stood out in the crowd.

Elizabeth waved her over and patted the seat down beside her.

Rose skimmed the crowd and lowered her lips to Elizabeth's ear. "Have you spoken to your ally yet?"

"Not yet, but I shall speak with him soon."

She murmured a "thank heavens," and they spent the rest of the trolley ride in silence.

The workday passed in a blur as her thoughts circled between strategies to gain supporters and what she would say when she saw Ivy. *What am I supposed to say? Hey, I found Nightshade's biggest enemy. Want to risk your life helping train this nymph halfling so she can help us overthrow Nightshade?*

Elizabeth frowned down at the sweater she'd been sewing. Several stitches were crooked. As she attempted to fix the error, her thoughts traveled back to their haphazard plan.

How are we meant to foil Nightshade's plan and gather allies without him knowing?

Magnolia had sent an urgent message to her: "He's regained Hawthorn by force." If that were true, it was only a matter of time before Nightshade ordered the attack.

She didn't relish losing her neutral stance, but perhaps the leader's impression of her as a harmless, subservient girl could help them get the information and the following they needed.

Laurel and Cedar were the fastest workers, and when they got up to leave early, she hissed. "Laurel. Cedar. I need to talk to you about something"

Cedar kept walking. "Not while the bosses are here, Evergreen."

"I understand. I'll speak with you later."

Laurel turned to face Elizabeth and sat down beside her. "What did you want to talk about?"

"Do you trust me?"

Laurel placed a hand over hers. "Of course I do. You've saved me from more than a few lessons in my more rebellious years. Why?"

Elizabeth bit her lip. "How do you feel about the plan to poison the water?"

Laurel's gaze searched the floor for onlookers, and she lowered her voice. "I'm not fond of it, but we don't have much of a choice, do we?"

"But what if we did?"

Laurel tucked hair behind her ear. "I'm listening."

"I may have a powerful ally, a descendant of a powerful nymph that's willing to help us stop the poisoning, but we'll need more to join us to succeed. Do you think you can help?"

Laurel bit her lip. "You're treading dangerous waters, but I'd prefer dangerous water over a raging fire. I'll see what I can do, but if it gets too dangerous I'm out. I don't want to become another...lesson."

"I understand. Thank you."

Her lip curved up in a smile, and she rose to leave just as the clang of metal alerted them to someone ascending the stairs.

A weight eased in her chest. At least Laurel still had some fight left in her. Perhaps the others would too, if they knew they stood a chance. The remaining workday passed in a blur, and soon the sun had set and she exited the building with Rose close behind.

Elizabeth tapped Rose on the shoulder as they exited the factory. "Meet me at the usual place. I have an errand to run beforehand."

Elizabeth watched Rose walk towards their usual meeting place and then walked in the opposite direction to swipe a Manchineel leaf.

ose arrived at the training ground alone, but Gabriel trailed not far behind her. He peered down at an open book on medicine as he walked.

"Any luck finding an antidote?" she called out, and he looked up from his book just in time to step to the side, avoiding a gnarled root.

"I found something, but you're not going to like it." Gabriel slammed the book shut. "Much like the tree, the antidote only grows to the southeast. In our hometown."

She bunched the fabric of her skirt. "Maybe they sell it at a market somewhere?"

He shook his head. "It has to be fresh."

"Then maybe we should-"

He cut her off. "Don't even think of suggesting leaving before the battle. You know as well as I do that we can't."

She crossed her arms over her chest. "Well, at least one of us has to look out for your well being."

He ran his fingers through his hair. "And what if the antidote doesn't work? We don't know for certain if it was the poison. It could be a curse from Manchineel or even from Nightshade. There are far too many unknowns. An entire town of people could lose their lives and we can't sacrifice them for me."

Rose tapped her fingers against her skirt and jutted her lip out in a pout. "You're right, and I hate it. I don't want to choose between an entire town and you..." Her voice trailed off. *Because I'm tempted to choose you, but I know I shouldn't,* she thought.

Gabriel cleared his throat, bringing her attention back to him. "Would some training take your mind off of it? You've only been practicing your magic and I'm fairly certain the only punches I've ever seen you throw were at me."

She flushed. "I don't like to fight. It's only because you say such inappropriate things."

"That's only because we're unable to put the words into actions without attracting unwanted attention." His gaze trailed from her head to her hips, warming her despite the winter's chill.

"If you're trying to get me to fight you, it's working." She changed her left arm into a thick stem covered in thorns, but it was still shaped like an arm and hand.

He held up his hands. "While I appreciate your enthusiasm, I wouldn't produce much of a fight unarmed, but I can help you practice your stance."

She moved to cross her arms over her chest, but then stopped herself when a thorn pricked her. Instead, she settled for shooting him a death glare. "I suppose... as long as you don't get carried away."

He placed a hand to his chest. "Me? Never." A smile tugged at the corners of his mouth. "Put your legs far apart and then bend your knees like this."

Her gaze shifted from him and then back to her own feet. "Is this right?"

"Not quite. I'll help you."

He moved over to her side and pointed at her right knee. "You want both feet rooted like a tree. Can I adjust you with my hands?"

Rose gulped. "I suppose, but be careful where you put those things."

His hand skimmed her knee and wandered down to her foot, pressing her feet into the ground.

"That feels more stable."

"Good, then do that with your other foot. I'll adjust your back next. If that's okay with you?"

"Yes." Her voice came out a squeak.

Then he was behind her. His hand pressed against her lower back, forcing her to stand taller. "You want your back straight. You're slouching."

He gave her a slight shove. She didn't fall over.

"Can I attack like this? What about moving?"

He rubbed his arm. "That part I don't remember as well, but I'll try. First, you'll want to make an L shape with your legs, and since you favor your left hand, your left foot will face forward. The heels of the two feet should line up."

Rose slid her right foot back and Gabriel walked over to face her. "How does that feel?"

Her legs felt grounded, but her calves were already burning. "Weird, but oddly sturdy. Can we spar?"

"Only if you promise to go easy on me and if you find me something to use as a staff."

Rose searched around until her eyes came upon a tree with a loose branch. "Maybe we can break that branch off." She reached up to tear off the broken branch, but Elizabeth's voice stopped her.

"I know you aren't about to rip a branch off one of my trees." Rose turned to see Elizabeth carrying something wrapped in a silky cloth.

Before Rose could ask, Elizabeth unwrapped the cloth to reveal a single leaf. "This is a leaf from the Manchineel tree. Remember what they look like because we'll need to destroy every last one of them, but you can't touch them unless you want to get burned."

"What about your ally? The one meant to train us," Rose asked.

"I'm going to speak with him once I know you can spar without killing each other. He'll be more likely to help if he can see your abilities up close. Understand?"

Rose and Gabriel nodded.

"Okay then. Let's get started. Gabriel, today you're going to spar with Rose, and I'll give you both instructions on combat. Rose, that means you'll need to manifest a weapon."

Before Elizabeth could explain how to create the weapon, Rose closed her eyes and pictured the vine whip she'd created before, how it felt in her hand.

Warmth spread through her palm, and a thorn pricked her palm. She opened her eyes to see a long, thin staff covered with thorns.

Elizabeth looked from Rose to Gabriel. "Interesting. Let's see what you can do with it. You're going to spar with Gabriel today, but make sure you don't cause any serious damage with those thorns, okay?"

Rose was already moving into the stance Gabriel had taught her, but Elizabeth held up a hand to stop her. "Give me a chance to arm him first."

"Sorry." Rose looked at Gabriel through hooded lashes.

A muffled laugh escaped his lips when he caught her staring. "Don't worry, you'll get to beat me up soon."

Rose watched with wide eyes as Elizabeth created a weapon for Gabriel. Sweat beaded on her face as she formed the staff and then ran a hand along the bark to smooth it.

Maybe it's more difficult because she's modifying the tree for her weapon? Rose thought.

After the staff was done, she threw it at Gabriel. Then she sat down to watch.

"Go ahead. Have at it. I'll intervene if it gets too dangerous." Elizabeth plopped to the ground to watch.

Rose took her stance and inched towards Gabriel. Once she was close enough, she tried to imitate Elizabeth's previous movements by aiming low towards his legs.

Gabriel scrambled back and blocked her weapon just before it could hit him.

Next, she faked a blow to his head. He raised his weapon to block, and she went for his chest. She tried to stop short, but it still grazed him, tearing a hole in his shirt and drawing blood.

Pride and worry warred within her, and she lowered her weapon. "Gabriel, are you o-"

Gabriel charged her, striking her square in the chest. The blow was so forceful that she fell to the ground, stunned.

He pressed the staff to her throat. "Checkmate," he said with a smile.

Rose let out a huff. "I stopped because I was worried about hurting you." Rose pointed at the cut with her chin.

He looked down at the torn shirt and the minor wound. "I can handle far worse than this, Rose," he said, but his heavy breaths and sweat-stained shirt told a different story.

"I suppose, but I rather like you alive."

He wiped at the blood. "When we face the nymphs, you know you won't be able to stop because someone is injured."

She pursed her lips. "It's because it's you. I don't want to hurt you."

"I don't mind getting roughed up a bit if it's you."

She stuck her tongue out. Her mind shifted to how Elizabeth had modified her staff. *Elizabeth modified her weapon for Gabriel. Maybe I can do the same, so I don't have to worry about slicing him with thorns.* Holding up a finger, she said, "Wait. I have an idea."

She pictured the roses people bought in stores, the ones with the thorns cut off. She imagined the same thing happening to her weapon. She closed her eyes to concentrate. When she opened them, the staff's surface was smooth.

Elizabeth's jaw dropped, but she didn't say anything.

They continued sparring. With the smooth staff, her movements became quicker and quicker until Gabriel struggled to block them.

After a few rounds of struggling to keep up, Gabriel started predicting her moves. He couldn't block all of them, but if he rightly guessed it was a fake blow, he'd use that opportunity to hit her first. He'd even gotten faster, and his sturdy stance made him hard to knock down.

When they'd finished their bout, Elizabeth said, "I'll be back in a moment. Keep practicing until I get back," before disappearing from the clearing.

* * *

THEY'RE PERFECT SPARRING PARTNERS, Elizabeth thought as she veered to the east and the outskirts of town. Rose was fast and light on her feet, but there was little strength behind her attacks. Gabriel was slow and clumsy, but his technique was excellent.

Gabriel was getting better at predicting her jabs and parrying them. Not to mention Rose's magic was growing in leaps and bounds. Rose had only seen Elizabeth modify her own weapon once and was immediately able to duplicate the effect, modifying her staff for Gabriel.

She dug her nails into her palm. *Ivy has to help. We need his knowledge to make this work, and I can't fight him. Not after everything we've been through together.* They only had two more days before they would need to confront the nymphs and stop their plans. If he didn't agree to help, there was a good chance that they would fail.

The higher ups knew her plant's location because they'd helped her protect it from the human settlement, but only she knew the location of his plant. That would give Ivy an advantage in the battle that she'd never have: he would be harder to kill.

Ivy's plant had grown around a building so old that the chimney had scorch marks and the wood had started to rot. The exterior of the building was covered in a thick layer of moss, and half of the roof had caved in. It lacked electricity, running water, and heat. Not surprising, considering the building had been abandoned several decades ago.

She knocked on the front door, but there was no answer. Elizabeth crawled through a broken window and looked up to see green eyes staring down at her.

He brushed copper hair from his forehead and yawned. "What do you want at this hour, Evergreen?"

When she stared at the ivy sprouting from his ungloved fingertips, he hid them behind his back and cleared his throat.

She looked back up at him, her hands balled at her side. "I need to show you something. But before I do, you need to promise you won't say anything to Nightshade or anyone at the factory."

He lowered his head, so they were at eye level, his eyes bright with mischief. "Now, you've piqued my interest. You know how much I hate Nightshade. What is this about?"

She bit her lip. "Remember how Nightshade mentioned to be on the lookout for a powerful nymph?"

"I vaguely recall that. She was Belladonna's descendant, I believe. Why?"

She shifted her weight from foot to foot, but didn't speak, and his lip quirked up in a lopsided grin. "Oh, Evergreen. You've found her?"

Her face heated, and she nodded.

"And what are you planning to do with the girl?"

Her heart hammered in her chest. "Remember the plan to poison the water?"

"I do. Many nymphs were whispering of revolution, but I doubt they would be successful." His half-smile turned to a full grin, and he placed a hand on her shoulder. "If you're planning a revolution, count me in. You know how much I adore foiling Nightshade's precious plans." He ruffled her hair, and she cut him a steely glance.

"Can you stop doing that? I'm not a child anymore and I'm not that much younger than you." She smacked his hand away.

"But dearest Evergreen. I've seen far more in my sixty years than you have in your fifty."

She crossed her arms over her chest. "I know, and you don't have to bear the weight of that alone." She placed a hand on his arm.

Ivy's eye color darkened, so it was almost black. "No nymph should have had to endure the abuse they've suffered under Nightshade's rule. He's controlling us with fear, and it needs to end before more die."

She squeezed his arm. "And we will stop him together, but I need your help training our new allies."

He gazed down at her with a wan smile. "I'll do what I can if it's for you." He gestured at a sword sitting in the corner of the room. "Should I bring weapons with me?"

"You might want to."

"Done." Ivy deposited a revolver, a pouch of gunpowder, and a sword into a large sack and slung it over his shoulder.

Training was going to get interesting.

* * *

They'd been practicing for what felt like hours when Elizabeth returned with a broad shouldered, muscular man that moved with the lithe grace of a cat. Judging from the ivy sprouting from his fingertips and the sword poking from his bag, this was the ally she'd spoken of.

The distraction made him drop his guard and Rose caught him square in the chest with her staff, knocking him back several feet.

The man's piercing green eyes burned a hole into Gabriel's skull.

He turned to Elizabeth and hissed, "Are you siding with *humans* now? Fighting Nightshade I can understand, but why are we helping a *human* after what they've done?"

He spat the word human like an insult and then pointed at Rose. "And your powerful ally is half human too? Care to explain?"

Elizabeth held up her hands in a placating gesture. "She is powerful despite being half human. This is Belladonna's child, Rose."

He narrowed his eyes. "Not what I was expecting, but I suppose that one makes sense. What about the human?"

"The human has a name," Gabriel shouted.

Elizabeth's shoulders bunched. "And the loud mouthed human is her companion, Gabriel. Manchineel cursed him or poisoned him. We aren't sure which."

Ivy cracked a smile. "Interesting. I'd love to know what he did to incur a nymph's wrath, and I'm surprised Belladonna would let her blood be diluted. She was a powerful nymph. Perhaps she went soft."

Elizabeth looked to Gabriel and Rose and then back to Ivy. "Will you do it?"

He let out a sigh. "I suppose I don't have a choice. They won't get anywhere with their current abilities."

"Thank you, Ivy."

"Don't mention it." Ivy lowered the sack to the ground with a light thud and unpacked the sword and gun.

Ivy turned the gun over in his hand as he spoke to Gabriel. "From what I saw in your fight, you'll need something like this. You're too slow to wield a sword or staff. Even a fast human wouldn't be faster than the slowest nymph." Then he scoffed. "And let's face it—you're not even a fast human."

He threw the gun at Gabriel.

Instead of catching it, Gabriel moved directly out of the way and let it drop to the ground. "Are you insane? What if the gun went off?" he said.

Ivy just laughed and opened his hand to reveal several bullets. "And I rest my case. I removed the bullets before I threw you the gun. I'm not an imbecile. I saw you wield the staff."

Elizabeth tapped him on the shoulder and whispered something in his ear. "Depending on how your... condition progresses, we might just have you wield this for intimidation purposes. If I give you any bullets you'll be under close supervision by someone the bullets won't kill. Understand?"

"I understand, but do I really have to use this thing?" Gabriel picked the gun up off the ground with his thumb and index finger like it was a rabid animal likely to bite him at any moment.

"Yes, and you need to hold it properly." When Gabriel awkwardly wrapped his index finger over the trigger, Ivy held his hand out.

"Here, give it to me." Gabriel dropped the gun into Ivy's palm. Ivy wrapped his index, middle, and ring finger around the handle and his right thumb faced forward towards the trigger.

"You want to make sure you've got a firm grip on this, but keep your thumb just below this here," he said, running a finger along the metal chamber that held the bullets. "That is, if you'd like to keep your hands."

He placed his other hand over the top one, the second thumb resting just below the first.

He held the gun towards the ground. "You want to make sure you're holding this out and down when you aren't using it so you don't accidentally shoot yourself or someone else and keep a firm grip with both hands."

Gabriel squinted at his grip, memorizing how he held it. "I think I understand so far, but what if they get close to me?"

Ivy slid a hand along the top of the gun. "This is a long-range weapon. If they get too close, you unload the weapon and throw it as far away as you can. We'll work on your ability to dodge so you can hopefully avoid that. You can practice by trying to catch me. If you think you can."

Gabriel sighed. "I'll try."

Gabriel ran towards him, but before he could get too close, Ivy ran backwards without taking his eyes off Gabriel. Gabriel got too close, and Ivy chucked the gun into the darkness and far out of Gabriel's sight. When he turned back to Ivy, he was gone.

Forest green eyes popped out from behind a tree. "Too slow," he said into Gabriel's ear.

Gabriel whirled around, punching at Ivy's shoulder, but Ivy grabbed Gabriel's hand and used his momentum to throw Gabriel to the ground. Gabriel fell face first into the dirt.

Gabriel pressed up off the ground with a groan. "Did you have to throw me that hard?"

"Yes. You should've known better than to throw a punch while you're off balance."

Gabriel brushed hair and dirt from his face. "I suppose you'll want me to practice with the revolver now, but I don't know where it is."

"I'll retrieve it."

Ivy walked off into the darker patches of the clearing and came back with the gun in hand. He pressed it to Gabriel's palm. Once Gabriel was holding it the way Ivy wanted, he nodded in approval. "I'll give you five seconds to put distance between us. Don't get caught." Then he was a blur of motion.

Gabriel bobbed and weaved backwards, but he couldn't anticipate where the trees were like Ivy had. His heel bumped right into a thick trunk, and when he pivoted, his arm scraped against rough bark.

He turned his back to Ivy and ran. When a flash of green moved to his right, Gabriel pointed the gun at it.

Instead of finding purchase, he cried out as Ivy grabbed his wrist and twisted it at an unnatural angle. He yelped and the gun clanged to the floor.

Ivy scooped it up and pointed it right at Gabriel's head. He wagged a finger at him in disapproval. "Bad move. Don't turn your back to the enemy and don't shoot point blank. That's how you'll get shot with your own bullets."

Gabriel ran a hand through his hair. "I suppose I panicked."

Ivy placed a hand on his shoulder. "If you feel yourself panicking, focus on just one thing you can do to buy time, whether that's throwing the gun or causing a distraction of some sort. Do not lash out in panic."

Gabriel surveyed the area. "So in this case, perhaps throwing a branch or stray rock could serve as a distraction."

"Precisely, but right now I want you to focus on something else before I hand you off to Evergreen over there. Your dodging was pretty horrible, so I'll teach you a trick."

Ivy took the same stance Elizabeth had taught him. "Use your back leg and your peripheral vision to look for obstacles. If your heel touches it, you should run straight instead of back or to the side if possible. Where there's one obstacle, there are likely to be others."

Gabriel took his stance, but he could barely see anything in the darkness shrouding the clearing. "Are you sure this will work? I can barely see anything."

"You'll get it with time."

He cupped his hand and shouted, "Elizabeth, it's time to swap."

Elizabeth swept Rose's legs out from under her, knocking her on her back and ending their spar. "I'll be right there."

As Elizabeth jogged over, he waved at Gabriel. "Elizabeth will help you. Just keep practicing with the gun. I'm going to work with Rose now."

* * *

Ivy's smug smile mocked Rose every time he caught her off balance, dropping her to the ground for another face full of dirt.

Rose slammed the staff down towards his foot, but he dodged to the side and grabbed her weapon, pulling it forward until it was out of her grip. "Don't just rush in like a horse with blinders. You have to plan your attacks."

He held out his staff to give it to her, and the moment she had it back, she stabbed at his windpipe. He backed up a couple steps, avoiding the blow. "Temper, temper. Look for an opening before you attack. And stay in your stance. If you're off balance, you'll fall."

"But I tried that, and it didn't work with Elizabeth. She still beats me every time," she whined.

He held up his hands in surrender. "That's because we have had years of training. This is only your first time training with me."

Her lip jutted out in a pout.

"Fine. Try it your way. I'll indulge you, but I won't go easy on you."

Rose aimed for any vulnerable part she could find from his neck, to his eyes and knees. All the while, he kept an amused grin on his face, blocking her like he was swatting away a troublesome fly.

When she aimed for his groin, he skidded back. "That was dirty. I think I rather like you."

"Unfortunately, the feeling isn't mutual." She huffed, and slumped over, feigning a loss of energy.

He edged closer to her, and she tracked him in her peripheral vision as checked on her. "Are you ready to listen to—" his words were cut off when she launched herself at his neck. He caught her attack just in time to soften her blow and their fall.

"That was clever, but, let's see if you can find an opening *and* keep your balance next time."

"I suppose." She crossed her arms over her chest, and he laughed.

"I know you're even younger than little Evergreen over there, but let's try to be adults."

"I'm not little," Elizabeth shouted from across the clearing.

"You are from where I'm standing," he jibed.

"Sorry. Let's try again. We'll focus on some basics. I'll show you how to turn someone's strike against you. Attack me."

Rose's grip on her staff tightened. "Gladly."

She lunged forward with the staff, and he knocked the blow aside and grabbed her wrist, then twisted it until she let go with a yelp. "When you attack, let your opponent's momentum bring them close enough for you to disarm them if you can. Now I want you to try the same. Hand me the staff."

Rose tossed the staff, and he grabbed it out of the air. "Get in your stance."

She crouched, and he aimed a strike at her arm, but she was ready this time. Rose slid to the right and knocked the staff to the left. Once he was close enough, she grabbed onto his wrist and twisted until it fell to the floor with a thunk.

He whistled. "Nice one, rookie." His gaze flickered to the clock tower and then back to her.

"We have enough time to focus on one more tactic and this one is really important, so pay close attention."

Her brows knitted together. "I have a feeling you're trying to run me ragged."

"You'll thank me for this later. Now what do you do if someone grabs you from behind?"

She stared blankly at him. "No idea, but I'm sure you'll enlighten me."

"Just come here. Now face your back to me." She turned, and the hairs on her arm raised.

He wrapped his arm around her neck with a firm grip that made her breaths come in gasps. She pulled at his arm, but it wouldn't budge.

She felt around for his foot and stomped on it. His grip loosened slightly, but she still couldn't wriggle free.

"Think about what else is vulnerable." He whispered into her ear. She lifted her heel up to his groin, but he dropped her and backed away before she could make contact.

"Not bad, but there's one more thing you can do if your arms are free. Here, go ahead and grab me."

Rose had to stand on her tiptoes to wrap her arm around Ivy's neck. "First you want to grab onto the hands on your neck so they don't move. Then drop down to the ground until your center of gravity is lower than theirs."

He crouched down until his lower back nearly aligned with hers. "Then step inside their stance."

His feet went in between hers, and he tugged her arms tight against him. Then he lifted her up on his back. "Once they're on your back, you can just turn like you're looking up at the sky. They'll drop to the floor."

Instead of dropping her, he crouched back down so she could slide off him. Rose released him and then they swapped places, but as she was easing Ivy onto her back, Elizabeth yelled out, "Someone's here. Hide."

Ivy and Elizabeth ducked behind the trees in the clearing, and Ivy tugged Rose behind a bush, but Gabriel just stood there. Rose cupped her mouth. "Gabriel hide. Now."

A strange man covered with ragged clothes approached passing a hand through grimy hair. Gabriel didn't budge—his blank gaze fixed squarely on the unknown vagrant. "Damnit Gabriel," she cursed under her breath.

A silver object gleamed with the streetlamp flame. The disheveled man shouted. "What do you think you're doing in my territory, boy?"

"Damnit, Gabriel…" Rose cursed as she sneaked through the underbrush and towards the shifty vagabond. When she was close enough, Rose dove at his knees.

He landed to the floor with a yelp, the silver object skittered through the air. A metal rod he'd used for a cane slid across the floor. "Please—please don't hurt me. It's your territory now! I'll leave, I promise!"

Rose raised herself to her feet. Glaring down, she barked, "Say nothing of us to anyone, and you will find no problems. Understood?"

When he met her red gaze, he gasped. "You're... you're that nymph! The one he's looking for!" He shuffled backward on all fours."

She reached up to her face, but didn't feel her glasses on her temples. "Wait." Rose held out a hand, but he ran away too quickly for Rose to stop him.

When Ivy came out of hiding, his lips were puckered. "How could you be so dull? If he had seen us together, our plan would be dead in the water."

Rose hugged her arms to her chest. "What would you suggest? Let that filthy vagrant intimidate Gabriel? We have no idea his intention. For all we know his plans included theft if not murder. He had a weapon for the gods sake!"

Ivy shouted, "He had a rod for a cane, Rose!"

Her voice matched his, "And a rod can still kill, Ivy! I did what was needed."

He reared his hand back, and Rose shrank away from him, expecting to feel the sting of a smack, but instead Elizabeth wrapped her hand around Ivy's. "Don't. It was impulsive, but she thought he was in danger."

Her gaze turned to Gabriel. "I'm more concerned that Gabriel didn't run. What happened?"

Sweat beaded down his forehead, and his hands shook. Rose placed her hand over his. "Gabriel. Please, talk to me. Tell me what happened."

He squeezed her hand back, but it was such a slight touch that for a moment she thought she'd imagined it. "Sorry. I-I'm not sure what happened. My vision went black for a moment and when my senses returned, Rose had tackled that man."

Elizabeth pursed her lips together. "We still have a chance. They didn't see or hear Ivy and I, but this means I can no longer associate with you in public, Rose. You'll need to leave the factory. You'll train with Ivy tomorrow instead."

Ivy spoke through gritted teeth. "I'll train you, but if you do anything else like that again, I will abandon this mission. I'm not keen on dying for a lost cause."

Rose bit her lip. "I'm sorry."

"I don't want words. Show your apology with actions," Ivy spat and stalked off.

Elizabeth placed a hand on Rose's shoulder. "He may be harsh, but he's right. We've already lost too much. If we lose, it would destroy the already dying embers of rebellion. Many of our kind would be punished by Nightshade's hand. Remember that before you act."

The town's clock tower chimed to signal the midnight hour.

Elizabeth placed a hand on Rose's shoulder. "That's enough for tonight. Rose, you will meet with Ivy at sunrise tomorrow. Gabriel, you will meet us here after the library closes. See if you can find any information on nymph curses. Now, go get some rest. You'll need it."

Gabriel and Rose headed back to the hotel covered in scrapes and bruises and eager to get some rest.

CHAPTER 16

Gabriel had only caught a few precious moments of sleep before the clanging metal of his alarm clock woke him. He groaned and hit the metal button to shut the obnoxious contraption off before rolling out of bed.

He ran a hand over his face as his mind flickered to last night. *I still don't understand how I blacked out like that. It was like being asleep standing up.*

Sleep had been no reprieve either. The alcohol by his bedside table and the intense training had pulled him into a deep sleep, but his dreams had been plagued with frightening images. The most memorable was a nymph with green wings. She had curled a gnarled finger and said, *Your death will come soon, but it won't be swift.*

He shivered despite the crackling warmth from the fireplace. When he crept towards the fire, he glimpsed himself in the mirror. He was too pale, and a sheen of sweat covered his face.

He splashed water on his face and wiped his forehead with a towel. Then, he pinched his cheeks until they had a slight rosy tinge before leaving his room.

When he opened the door, he was met with Rose's red eyes.

She scanned over Gabriel with her lips pressed together. "You look pale and there's sweat on your face."

Gabriel wiped away the sweat. *Damn, I thought I'd gotten all the sweat. What's wrong with me?*

"I guess it must have been from the fireplace and the lack of sleep." He offered an uneasy laugh.

Rose fiddled with the fabric of her skirt. "Promise me you'll take it easy today?"

"I promise." He yearned to take her hand and reassure her, but he was certain she'd feel heat radiating from him, so instead he settled for walking with her to the door. *If she knows you have a fever, she'll never leave.*

Every muscle in his body still ached from training, and Gabriel longed to crawl into bed and fall asleep until dark, but research was more important. As Elizabeth had said, it could have also been a curse from Manchineel even if it was unlikely, and Nightshade had threatened to curse him if he'd gone back on their deal. He'd refused to kill Belladonna and uphold his end of their bargain, so it could have been a curse from him.

When he stepped outside his hopes of researching nymph curses were dashed by the sound of an ear-piercing scream and a woman's voice shouting, "Help! The mines have collapsed!"

CHAPTER 17

As the sun set over the horizon with no sign of Gabriel, her heart pounded in her chest. *The library has to be closed by now. Where is he?*

She was too distracted to focus on her training. Ivy's blows rained down on her body, leaving her arms and legs sore. "You could be gentler with me, you know."

"Not a chance. I want you to learn how to use those thorns to hook weapons. Let's go again."

Ivy lunged at her with the sword again. She lunged at the blade with her thorny staff, hooking the blade, but the sound of padding footsteps approached, making her turn her head.

Ivy said, "Hi, Evergreen," and yanked Rose forward, making her fall to her stomach with a tug of his sword.

Ivy's smile fell, and his sword thudded to the dirt. "Is something wrong?"

Rose looked up to see Elizabeth's hair plastered to her face. She panted, and her words came out in puffs. "Nightshade knows you're here, Rose, and his allies collapsed the mine when they found out Gabriel was working there. I saw the smoke from the factory. We'll have to attack tonight."

Rose glanced at the clock, and she dug her hands into her hair. "The library closed over an hour ago. If Nightshade is back and Gabriel is running late, we need to search for him. Elizabeth, you check the library. Ivy, come with me. We need to check the mines."

Elizabeth grabbed Rose's shoulder. "Be careful. We're treading dangerous territory."

"I will, I promise. Now, hurry. We need to find Gabriel before one of Nightshade's allies does."

When she tried to run in the direction of the mine, a muscular hand smacked into her chest. "How about you let the former soldier take the lead on this one?"

"Fine, but hurry," Rose commanded and wrenched his hand away.

He muttered, "You're going to be the death of me at this rate. Let's go."

He moved quietly from building to building, blending in with the shadows as he walked.

A massive cloud of acrid black smoke rose from the collapsed cave, and Rose pinched the bridge of her nose to stifle a sneeze. Massive boulders blocked the entrance, apart from a tiny hole. Several men grabbed shaken up miners and pulled them through the small exit hole.

Among those helping the miners was a soot-covered Gabriel.

Rose sighed with relief. *If you were just a little more selfish, I wouldn't have to worry about you so often.* Her gaze darted to Gabriel and then back to Ivy.

Ivy scanned over the area. "I don't see any nymphs. You can go get him, but be quick."

"Aye, Aye, Captain," Rose said with a salute that earned her an exasperated sigh from Ivy.

"I don't know how either of you have survived this long," he muttered.

She ignored him and ran right up to Gabriel, wrapping her arms around him from behind. He tensed, but then turned to meet her with a gaze that stared through her.

A weak smile touched his lips. "You sure you want to hug me right now?"

The scent of char and salt clung to him, and she looked up to meet his eyes. "I don't mind the smell, but I do mind you rushing into danger. Again." She cuffed him on the wrist.

Unbothered by her chastising, he smiled and brushed back a strand of her hair. "I won't apologize for helping these people, but I'm sorry that I made you worry. I'll be more careful as long as you promise to do the same."

"I will. I promise." Rose squeezed Gabriel tighter and then glanced over in Ivy's direction to see a pointed green glare.

"We should get back to Ivy now before he rings my neck. I'm afraid to ask… Did you go to the library at all today?"

"Well.." He rubbed the nape of his neck and it came away with coal dust and sweat.

Rose placed her hands on her hip. "This is your own life. Do try to take finding a cure more seriously."

She turned and strode over to Ivy. Gabriel trailed behind her.

Rose's hands shook as they made their way to the clearing, and Gabriel grabbed her hand in his. His hands were warm as a furnace as she twined her fingers with his. They'd survive this together.

AFTER THE SUN HAD SET, Elizabeth led them all to Ivy's residence to discuss the plan. Ivy's grim frown, illuminated by moonlight, set the somber mood. "Due to some... unforeseen circumstances..." His gaze flickered to Rose, and she gulped over the lump in her throat. "We will carry out our plan earlier than expected, so it would be best if you and Gabriel avoid fighting if possible. Since the Manchineel isn't native to this area, it will take longer for them to get more of those. Our top priority is to destroy every single leaf." Ivy bared his teeth in a tight-lipped grin. His eyes focused on Rose. "Let's also keep in mind that some of his allies are more like hostages. I'd like to avoid unnecessary casualties."

The annoyance coming off Ivy in waves made her stomach do flips. "I understand. What do I need to do?"

"Once we get to the factory, you and Gabriel will stay back. I'll knock the guards out with this." He held up a glass bottle with a clear liquid inside.

Rose squinted at the concoction. "What is that?"

Gabriel took a step back, knocking into Rose. "Where did you get chloroform?"

Ivy gave a furtive smile. "I may have snagged some from the house of an ex comrade-in-arms. Don't worry about it."

Gabriel took a shaky breath. "What else do we need to know?"

"Once we're inside, you'll need to search for where they're storing the Manchineel leaves and destroy them and spill any barrels of textile waste. Understood?"

"Yes," Rose and Gabriel said.

"Good. Then let's go. We don't have much time."

Ivy and Elizabeth led the way to the back entrance of the textile factory with Gabriel and Rose bringing up the rear. Ivy placed a hand on Rose's chest. "Stay by this building while we knock out the guards."

Rose and Gabriel hung back, their backs against the wall of a nearby building, watching while Elizabeth and Ivy crouched down, creeping towards two nymphs approaching the door.

"You sure this is the right stuff?" one of the men said. "It doesn't look very poisonous to me."

The other man's gaze darted around, searching for potential eavesdroppers. "That's the point. It looks harmless, but it'll wipe out the humans. It'll be a slow, painful death for the town's residents, which is exactly what *he* wants."

The first man eyed the small glass jar filled with a few shiny green leaves, but he didn't question his comrade any further. They walked towards the door, but as the first man reached for the handle, Ivy and Elizabeth rushed the guards from behind and covered their mouths with the chloroform-soaked cloths. The guards struggled momentarily, their arms and legs flailing, but alarm quickly dissolved as the effects of the chemical hit them, and they slumped to the ground.

Ivy snatched the vial from the unconscious nymph's hand. Then he waved a hand, beckoning for Rose and Gabriel to follow. They stayed out of the view of the door, and Ivy placed a hand on the handle. "Rose. Gabriel. Try to stay out of sight once you're in. If you appear at the same time we do, it will raise suspicion."

Elizabeth glanced around the clearing before she spoke. Her voice came out a whisper. "Rose, they should be keeping the poisons with the dyes, so start there. Gabriel, you will be the lookout for her. Don't join us until we give the okay."

Gabriel's expression remained vacant, and he stared in the direction of a row of stumps near the factory. Rose elbowed him. "Focus." She whispered, and he shook his head.

"Sorry. I heard her, but my sight was just...preoccupied."

Ivy glared down at the two unconscious guards. "We can't risk them waking up while we're in there. Elizabeth, look away." Elizabeth turned her head to the side, and Rose watched open mouthed as he slit the guard's throats, leaving only stray twigs and berries from their respective plants behind. He wrinkled his nose in distaste and wiped blood from the knife. "It should take some time for them to regenerate. Now go."

Rose headed for the dyeing rooms with Gabriel following behind her at a crawl. She kept to the shadows of the room, but she lost sight of him as she rushed down the corridors.

Rose heard approaching footsteps and ducked behind a nearby column. She covered her mouth to quiet her breath as the nymph walked past her hiding place. *Did Gabriel hide because he saw the nymph before I did, or was he caught?*

Her heart hammered in her chest, and a small whimper escaped her lips. The nymph let out a "hmmm" and got close enough that she could see pine needles lining his arms like hairs.

She held her breath and shrank against the cool iron. A slight shock went through her when she touched the metal, and she emitted a yelp before she could stop herself.

"There you are." He reached out to grab her and Rose kicked at his leg. When the man fell she dashed towards the dyeing room at top speed trying to create distance between them, so she could form a weapon. The nymph's steps thumped behind her, but he hadn't screamed for help yet.

There was a dead end up ahead, and she tucked into the small hallway, pressing her back to the cold brick. Her thorny staff finished taking shape just as the nymph came back into view.

He didn't see her hidden in the shadowy corner. Good.

Rose took her stance and stayed just out of his peripheral vision. She swung the staff at his neck, and she gritted her teeth as her staff dug into his flesh. He opened his mouth to scream, but it came out a wheeze.

She wrenched the staff from him, but he didn't drop.

The only warning was a slight twitch in his right hand before he wrapped his hands around her throat and pressed down on her windpipe. Rose clawed at his arm with her nails, trying to break free. Spots danced across her vision. She kicked out with her feet, aiming to catch his toes, but her aim was poor, and he lifted her off the ground. She glanced down at the now useless staff. It dissipated as she lost concentration, but she remembered Ivy's words from training: *Aim for something vulnerable.*

She reached her hands out to his face and pressed her fingers into his eyes. His grip loosened on her neck, and she dropped to the floor coughing and gagging.

He thrashed about, his throat working painfully as he tried to utter a scream, but only wheezing and hissing noises came out. When she'd regained her breath, she sprouted thorns from her fingertips and approached the man on the floor.

She grabbed him by his arms and dragged him into the corner. Her fingers pressed against his neck, and she closed her eyes as she ran the sharp thorns into his flesh. *It's only destroying his body, not him,* she reminded herself as wheezing turned to gurgling.

When she opened her eyes, he only gave off faint tremors and then laid still. Pine needles were left in his place. *You didn't have a choice. He would've killed you if he'd had the chance.*

She muttered a "Sorry" to the pine needles before moving down the corridor and towards the dyeing room with Gabriel nowhere in sight.

As a room filled with vats of purple and blue dye came into view, footsteps alerted Rose to another nymph's approach.

Rose ducked behind a large tapestry that had been hung up to dry. From her hiding spot, she caught glimpses of guards coming around the corner. Their presence sent a shiver down her spine, like an unseen presence pressing down on her.

Does that mean they can sense me too? I hope not.

Hairs rose on her arm when one of the men looked in her direction and laughed. "I think we have an intruder in our midst. Come out, little mouse."

She dropped to the floor, inching her way to the exit. She crept from tapestry to tapestry and crawled under work tables, trying to avoid being spotted. Her heart hammered in her chest as the group came closer, too close.

"Come out," the larger man said again.

Rose focused on her hand with an effort that made her limbs burn and her head feel light, but she got the desired effect. A short, thin staff with thorns only at the edges appeared in her hand. It was just the right size for throwing.

When he was close enough that she was sure she wouldn't miss, she threw the staff at him, and heard a growl as it connected with his skin.

Rose kept a close eye on him as she retreated into the darkness, ducking behind a vat of dye.

"You're a feisty one. I'm going to get you for that." He pulled the spiny staff from his forehead. His teeth gritting together in a grimace.

I hoped that would cause more of a distraction. I should've just kept running.

Her breath grew ragged, and she sucked wind as he drew closer. When she could hear the vibrations of his laughter he said, "I've found you." She bolted away on shaking legs, but at that moment she made a grave mistake, turning her back on the enemy.

He caught her by the collar and lifted her off the ground from behind. This man was far larger than the first, and he had comrades. Her limbs grew stiff as a porcelain doll's.

The men laughed, and the large one holding her dangled her like a hunting trophy. "I don't know why Nightshade was so bent on getting rid of you. You don't seem that dangerous to me, child of Belladonna."

He knows who I am. This isn't good. How do I get out of this? She turned her head to see her staff on the floor. It hadn't disappeared. At least not yet.

If I can just get him to drop me, I can use the staff to keep them at bay long enough to run.

Rose flailed her legs backwards. She couldn't see him, but maybe she could hit her target. The first several swings did nothing.

"What are you-?" His words turned into a shout when her foot connected with his groin. He dropped his grip, and she fell to the floor. Rose crawled along the ground, towards the staff. She tossed it at the larger man's neck and ran towards the spinning room before his comrades could come to assist him.

"Gabriel! Gabriel! I could use your help right about now."

From the corner of her eye, she saw a hand coming towards her. It wrapped around her mouth, and she was pulled back by the waist.

She elbowed behind her, but stopped short when a familiar voice whispered, "I thought the goal was to save me, not kill me."

He released his grip on her mouth, and she leaned back into the warmth of his arms. "I'm glad you're-" He pushed a finger to her lips, stopping her next words just before the other men passed by.

They crouched behind a massive pillar, away from the eyes of the threat.

The large man waddled instead of walked. His hand smacked against a nearby wheel. "I'll get you for that, you wench." Rose pressed her face into Gabriel's chest when she saw the dark look in the nymph's eyes, and the lacerations on his arm. She'd missed.

Gabriel absentmindedly ran fingers through her hair, calming her.

The man yelled, "She couldn't have gone far. Go. Search for her, now!"

Rose gripped Gabriel's shirt in a vice. She was thankful for the cover he'd found between two massive machines. They pressed into the pillar. Two of the nymphs got painfully close, but they turned away without seeing them.

"I think they've escaped, Spruce. I don't see them anywhere."

The larger man narrowed his eyes as he searched the room. "She's got to be nearby, so go check the adjacent rooms." The group of nymphs filtered out one by one, and the larger nymph went back to his post in the dyeing room.

Once the nymphs were out of earshot, Gabriel leaned into her ear. "You have a knack for getting into dangerous situations. How did you go from destroying the poison quietly to being chased?"

She wrinkled her nose. "Coming from the one who nearly got elbowed in the throat because he surprised me."

How are we supposed to get to the leaves with him standing guard, she thought.

"We still have to get to the poison, but he can sense me. He'll know if I'm in the room. You'll have to do it."

He pulled her into his chest. "Why do I have a feeling you're about to suggest something ludicrous?"

She bunched the fabric of his shirt in her hands. "We should split up. They don't know you're here, and if they're chasing after me, maybe you can find the poison unhindered."

He narrowed his eyes at her. "And what do you plan to do if they catch you?"

She planted a kiss on his cheek. A small white rose bud sprouted from her palm, and she plucked it, depositing it into his hand. It was all she could manage if she wanted to have any magic left for the nymphs. "If this disappears, come find me."

Gabriel grabbed her shoulder. "It's too dangerous."

"What other choice do we have? We have to find that poison. You can't outrun them, but maybe I can."

With a last squeeze of his hand, she crawled out of the safety of the pillars.

Once she was far enough away to avoid getting Gabriel caught, she cupped her mouth and yelled. "You looking for me, ugly?"

The large nymph snarled and locked eyes with Rose before barreling after her along with the henchman.

Once the nymphs were out of sight, Gabriel ran into the empty dyeing room. He moved slowly, just in case there were other guards, waiting in the wings.

However, after scouring every inch of the room, he came up empty handed. The leaves weren't there.

* * *

Ivy gripped Elizabeth's sweaty hand to keep her calm. Before they entered the room, he bent down to whisper in her ear, "Just let me do the talking."

A shudder worked its way up her hands and arms, and he gripped her in a vice and hissed, "Get a hold of yourself," as the first guard came into view.

When Ivy and Elizabeth approached, the guard narrowed his eyes at them. "I'm surprised the boss sent *her* with you. What's the weakling doing here?"

His shoulders lifted in a shrug. "You'd never believe it, but she's excellent with a staff."

The man looked at Elizabeth with disbelief, and she shrank under his stare.

"It's her first important assignment, so she's just nervous, right?" Ivy said with an easy smile and placed a hand on the small of her back.

"Oh. She's your entertainment." He wrinkled his nose. "Not my type, but to each their own."

Inwardly Ivy cringed at the thought of anyone using her like that, but a grin spread across his face. "Yup. But anyway, I brought the leaves. When are we moving forward with the plan?" Ivy asked.

The muscles in man's jaw worked. "You're late. Most of them are already on their way to dump it straight into the river water just upstream from here, so you'd better hurry if you want to join the others. Follow me, they're waiting outside." He started leading them to the door.

181

Once the man's back was turned, Ivy grabbed a cloth damp with chloroform and placed it over the man's nose and mouth. Evergreen held his arms as the man struggled and flailed until he finally slumped to the ground.

Elizabeth's nails dug into her palm. "If what he said is true, that means Rose and Gabriel won't be able to find the rest of the poison. I'll go signal them. You take care of him."

Elizabeth placed a finger into her mouth and gave three sharp whistles that echoed through the walls of the factory. When there was no response, she ran towards the dyeing room. *Please let them be okay*, she thought as she raced off, her legs moving faster than her brain.

That was a mistake. She ran right into her boss, the one who'd picked on Rose for her lack of productivity at work.

He glared down at her. "What are you doing here? You weren't supposed to be here for this part of the plan."

She bit her lip. "I forgot something at work, but when I came around back to get into the factory, Fern's and Woody's bodies had been destroyed. I came here to warn everyone," she said with a surprising amount of confidence despite the half-truth and the sweat beading down her back.

He considered her for a moment, hesitating, until a man raced past him with several scratch marks on his arms, yelling, "Intruders!"

"I'll evacuate my men. We'll discuss this further at a later date," he said and stormed off in the opposite direction of the dyeing room.

That's strange, she thought.

Elizabeth ran to the dyeing room as her lungs burned in her chest, glancing around as she ran, but she didn't spot any other nymphs. *Where are the guards?*

As she slid into the dyeing room, she heard muttering. Gabriel stood in the center of the room sliding dyes off of tables, making them clatter to the floor. His fingers dug into his scalp. "It has to be here somewhere." His gaze darted off to the left. "Shut up, Lara. No one asked you."

Elizabeth clomped towards him, hoping to get his attention before coming into striking range. His head swiveled to her, his pupils massive. "It's not here, and the flower is gone. Rose needs help."

A chill shivered down her spine, and she bridged the gap between them in two strides, gripping his shoulders in a firm grip. "I know. I just found out. What do you mean Rose needs help? What did she do this time?"

He rocked back and forth on his feet. "Rose is distracting the guards. She did it so I could find the poison and told me if the rose disappeared to find her."

Elizabeth pinched the bridge of her nose. "They're already heading to the river. Do you at least know where she went?"

He pointed a shaking hand to a long corridor. "She ran towards the other end of the factory, but that's all I know."

She huffed out a breath. "Well, we need to find her, and quickly. I told them there was an intruder, so they're searching the building."

Elizabeth signaled Rose again with three long whistles and heard a weak, quick whistle in response. They followed the noise to a hallway that led to a side exit and saw two angry nymphs standing near a large pillar.

Rose clung to the pillar with thorn tipped fingertips about fifteen feet off the ground. Her gaze met Elizabeth's, and she smiled. "If you want to capture me, why don't you come up here and get me."

The larger nymph spat. "When I get you, I'll make you regret crossing me."

"*If* you can get me," she teased.

The man below gripped the pillar, trying to claw his way up, but he only made it a few inches before he slid down, landing to the floor with a thud.

Elizabeth held a hand against Gabriel's chest. "Stay here," she whispered and crept towards the two henchmen. She snuck up behind the smaller man and wrapped one arm around his neck and placed another on his mouth.

He struggled against her, and the larger nymph turned around. "You tr-"

The nymph's words cut off as Rose let go of the pillar, flying downward and landing feet first on the other nymph's neck. He tumbled to the ground and Gabriel rushed in to help Rose with the large, stunned nymph.

Rose pressed her fingertips to the nymph's throat as he laid there, dazed and blinking. "Any chance you'd rather work for us?"

Elizabeth pressed her lips together. "Don't bother. Hemlock is the least likely person to abandon Nightshade. Destroy his physical body. A slice in between the shoulder blades should sever the spine which is quick and painless. The other option is taking the head off."

He wheezed out a weak, "I can help."

"You mean like how you helped me when I worked here?" Elizabeth wrinkled her nose. "Not a chance. Do it."

Rose gulped. "I'm sorry. Gabriel, can you hold him?"

Gabriel held the nymph's arms still as Rose went around to his back. She used her thorn tipped fingers to feel around for the part that Elizabeth had been talking about and buried her fingertips into the base of his skull. Red stained her fingers and she fought back nausea as he whimpered and flailed until her nails went deep enough for the body to slump in Gabriel's grip.

Gabriel released the imposing man and he disappeared, leaving behind hemlock leaves and a few stray branches.

Elizabeth created a sharp stake of pine wood, and Rose turned away when she brought it down towards the man's neck, but the sickening wet thud told her all she needed to know.

She didn't meet Elizabeth's gaze when she spoke. "Let's get going. Ivy's going to the river with some of the stragglers, but he can't stop the nymphs alone."

Gabriel and Rose tailed Elizabeth through the factory, hiding behind crates or in dead end hallways when other nymphs got too close. Rose and Gabriel hid in a storage room near the exit. There was a small hole in the door, and Rose pressed at it with a nail.

"Wait here until everyone has left. We'll try to convince the other nymphs along the way," Elizabeth whispered.

A few moments after they'd shut the door, the remaining nymphs approached and Rose pressed her face to the hole.

"Did they find the intruder?" Elizabeth asked.

A young nymph about Elizabeth's age shook her head. "No, but you should have seen the damage they caused." She shivered. "They destroyed Hemlock's body."

Elizabeth squeezed the girl's hand. "That is scary, but I think our boss is still scarier."

She smiled. "You have a point. I'll be glad once this is all over. I really don't like the idea of attacking humans like this, but I know we have to if we want to survive."

Elizabeth's gaze darted around as the other nymphs filtered out of the factory, and she leaned in to whisper in the other nymph's ear.

Rose couldn't hear what Elizabeth said, but she could make out the girl's response. "If there was another way I would welcome it, but I don't think any nymph is that powerful."

Elizabeth forced a laugh and brushed her palms on her skirt. "You're right. Maybe it was just rumors after all." Elizabeth left hand in hand with the girl nymph.

Rose and Gabriel waited behind the pillar until the rest of the nymphs left the factory. Then, they came out from their hiding spot and trailed behind the straggling nymphs, trailing them to the water supply.

CHAPTER 18

*R*ose and Gabriel followed the nymphs past the train station, past the clearing in the trees and the abandoned buildings. In the distance, there was a river with a copse surrounding it.

They continued toward the horizon with the half-destroyed forest and tiny stream of water. The river ended just outside the city and connected to a large tower that resembled a water tower she'd seen in one of her books.

Rose spotted Ivy in the distance pushing a barrel with the larger of the two groups of nymphs, and Elizabeth chatted with several young girls and a boy with a wicked grin who looked even younger than Elizabeth. Her heart squeezed at the sight.

Nightshade was exploiting children for his own gain... just like the factory had.

Maybe the humans and nymphs aren't that different after all. She dug her nails into her palm. She couldn't think about that now. This was about survival, not who was right or wrong.

Her lungs protested her fast pace, but they needed to pass the other nymphs, to intercept them before they reached the river. Rose turned back to see Gabriel a good ten feet behind her. She waved a hand, beckoning him to move faster.

The massive barrels slowed the group's pace, and Rose shrouded herself under cover of buildings and the occasional tree as she ran to the river. Her lungs gasped for air and sweat poured down her arms and legs. She kept looking over her shoulder to ensure she hadn't lost Gabriel. The rushing of water whooshed through her ears as she reached grass just before the source of the river.

When Rose chanced a look back, the group of nymphs was behind them, but they were gaining quickly.

What do we do if Ivy and Elizabeth can't convince the others? she thought.

They didn't have time for a Plan B. "Come on, let's go. We should meet them before they reach the water just in case." She grabbed his hand, pulling them out into the open.

Once they were standing in front of the river, exposed to the approaching nymphs, she whispered, "Gabriel. What if they're all afraid to join us? What if it's just us stopping Nightshade?"

He spun her around to face him, their chests inches apart. "Have more confidence. You're a powerful nymph, and you have a human ally on your side already. We will make it through this."

"Together?" Rose whispered.

He gave her hand a brief kiss and his burning emerald gaze met hers. "Together. Now show them what a truly powerful nymph looks like."

Rose squeezed his hand and then turned to face the approaching mass of nymphs. She allowed magic to course through her fingertips, forming the thorny staff in her hand as she walked. She set her lips in a thin smile and stood to her full height.

When there were only a few feet between them, Rose stood with arms outstretched, blocking their way. She boomed, "I can't allow you to continue any further. Poisoning that water will kill countless humans and all the water nymphs connected to that river!"

One of the larger men laughed and elbowed Ivy. "You and what army, wench?"

Beside him, Ivy looped an arm around the man's neck, and pressed a knife against his throat. "This army."

Elizabeth shouted, "This is the nymph I told you of. She's Belladonna's child. If you want to be free of Nightshade, now's your chance. Join us."

Eight of the youngest nymphs, children, turned on the older nymphs. Their hands fashioned into weapons crafted from their plants.

But two of the nymph's beside Ivy turned on him. Ivy held the nymph he'd captured as a threat.

"You'd dare betray Nightshade?" the one with a knife to his throat asked.

Ivy's lip quirked up in a half-smile. "He turned on his comrade Manchineel to get the poison for the water, and he's killed several of us for not obeying him like lap dogs. Do you really think he won't turn on you the second you're no longer useful? The second you speak a bit too loud?"

Murmurs went through the crowd. Several nymphs abandoned their barrels and joined Rose and Gabriel.

The captured man spoke again. "He's kept us safe for years. I won't turn my back on him now."

Ivy pressed the knife down until it broke flesh, and blood trickled down his skin. "You sure about that?"

A shiver went down the man's spine, but he raised his head. "I refuse to turn traitor."

"If you stay with Nightshade, you are the true traitor," Ivy said and slid the knife across the man's neck. The nymph gaped, and his body twitched as Ivy dropped him to the floor.

The younger nymphs hesitated and Rose stepped towards the group. "We don't wish to harm anyone, but we have to protect the water and the forest- no matter the cost. We'll fight for the peace and safety of all nymphs, not just a select few."

The women and children whispered to each other. A young girl pointed at Gabriel, her eyes wide. "If what you say is true, why is there a human with a gun here?"

Rose glanced at Ivy and Elizabeth. Elizabeth was the one who spoke up. "We won't just bring down Nightshade. We'll also make peace with the humans, so we'll need a human ambassador, won't we?"

Another young nymph girl ran up and wrapped her arms around Rose's leg. "I'm tired of the fighting and the *lessons*."

"Me too." A young boy with the same snow white hair as the girl joined Rose's side. "I can't leave my little sister behind."

Another wave of nymphs left barrels behind and joined their coup.

An older woman tossed a glare at one of the larger nymph men as she left Nightshade's army behind, clutching a vial of leaves to her chest.

The male nymphs stood there, shocked, as their forces abandoned them. "You too, Maple?" one of the men asked.

She puffed out her chest. "Yes. He allowed someone to pull leaves from Manchineel's branches without permission. Do you understand how painful that is? It's inexcusable behavior."

He sighed and followed after Maple, running a hand through his hair. "I suppose you're right...this time."

All but ten nymphs joined their side. Ivy and Elizabeth had helped turn the tides, but they still needed to deal with the remaining forces. "Gabriel, stay here and protect the children."

Gabriel scooted back a few steps and placed a few bullets into the gun. Rose wrinkled her nose at the iron smell of gunpowder.

Rose stepped forward, towards the remaining nymphs. "I'm giving you one last chance to relinquish the poison. If you take another step near the river with that," she pointed at the leaves, "we will show you no mercy."

One of the remaining enemy's gazes scanned the crowd, his dark eyes shadowed. "If you think I'll let a few women and children hinder me from fulfilling Nightshade's mission, you're mistaken."

He ran towards the river with the vial in his hand, but Ivy followed in a blur of motion, diving for his waist. The man fell to the ground, and the vial was flung from his grip. The glass container rolled across the ground.

Ivy's knees pressed against the man's ribs. The man tried to push

Ivy's legs, and he pinned his hands to the ground. "That's some stunt you pulled. Too bad it was futile."

The man's lip curled up in a sickening smile. "Are you sure? Look around you."

Rose pulled her gaze from Ivy to see nine nymphs racing towards the river, poison in hand.

"Ivy, Elizabeth, try to take down as many as you can."

Rose whirled to face the nymphs before her. "We'll need your help. You five are too young. You'll stay here while Gabriel guards you. I need the rest of you to fan out in groups of three. Do whatever you need to do to stop them from reaching the water."

Several small groupings of nymphs including the boy with the snow white hair raced away at different angles, zipping towards the water.

The first group ran towards a nymph getting dangerously close to the water, and the other went further out to the nymph that had run downstream.

After the first group tackled a nymph to the ground, Rose knelt down next to two nymph girls that looked about Elizabeth's age. They hadn't moved an inch.

"You two. Come with me."

The two nymph girls she'd requested followed her to one of the slower nymphs pushing a barrel of waste.

Rose pointed a hand at the man. "Grab him."

The man turned towards the sound just as she tried to hook his leg with the spikes on her staff, but it caught on the fabric of his pants instead, and he tore it free.

He lashed out at her head with a fist covered in spiny leaves. She moved her head to the side, but he extended the length of his weapon, and a bladed leaf nicked her neck. She placed a hand to the wound as blood seeped from the cut, and the girls came around to his side, pinning his arms behind his back.

He struggled, flailing against them. "That was the wrong choice."

Rose brandished the thorns on her fingertips. "Close your eyes. You won't want to see what happens next." Once their eyelids squeezed shut, she dug her hands deep into his neck. He screamed and flailed, but eventually his body went limp.

When all that was left was spiny leaves, she said, "You can open your eyes. Let's go see if the others need help."

The young nymph girl with auburn hair wrinkled her nose at the leaves on the ground. "Was what you did truly necessary?"

Rose placed a hand on the girl's shoulder. "Unfortunately, yes. If we hadn't done that, he would've just tried to poison the water again."

Rose turned to the side and spotted Elizabeth with her arms wrapped around a nymph's throat while the white haired boy held his arms and a girl with light brown hair held his legs.

The smaller of the two girls beside her pointed her shaking finger at the only nymph still approaching the water. "That's one of the bosses from the factory. How are we supposed to defeat him?"

Rose balled her hand at her side and forced a smile. "We'll do this together. I'll distract him, cut off his path to the river. When I do that, come from behind and try to immobilize him."

She took off in a sprint after the man, her heart pounding in her chest and the hand that held her weapon dripping sweat, but his form grew closer. Her legs burned, but she pushed herself to keep going until she was able to pass him and cut him off with just a few feet of grass between them and the river.

The man narrowed his eyes at her when she stood before him and held out her arms. "You think a pitiful half nymph like you can stop me?"

Gripping her staff and digging her heels into the ground, she held the weapon out. "Maybe not, but I have to try."

His lip curled up in a snarl. "I don't have time to play with you, so I'll take my leave. If you try to stop me again, I'll kill you."

He darted to the left, and she slid to the side, blocking his path with a smile. "Then I guess you'll have to kill me."

His eyes darkened. "Gladly."

His arm turned to a thick bark and he lashed out at her face. She brought the staff up to block, but the force of the blow made her slide back until her heel was only a couple feet from the water.

"Nowhere to run now. Last chance to surrender."

Rose caught a glimpse of the girls out of the corner of her eye, but forced herself to stay focused on the nymph in front of her. She straightened her back and bared her teeth in a grin. "I've never been one to back down from a fight."

"Have it your way th- what the hell?" Thin branches wrapped around the arm holding his weapon and roots snapped up from the earth to grab onto his legs. He balled his fist and swung at Rose with his remaining free hand, but she ducked under the blow and slammed the staff into his side, and a crack sounded at it connected with his ribs.

"You tricked me, you damned wench. Nightshade will hear about this."

Rose approached him with her weapon brandished. "Who said you'll live to tell the tale?"

His face went white "You wouldn't!"

She pressed one of the staff's thorns into his neck. "Why wouldn't I? You would've done the same to me and my comrades if you'd won."

Rose sliced into the side of his neck and a shrill scream tore from the younger girl's throat as blood poured from the wound. He writhed against their grip, squirming and bucking until his skin went white and his body laid still.

The girls let go of his unmoving form as it transformed into a massive hunk of bark, but their work still wasn't done. She bent her knees to meet the eyes of the two girls. "I'm sorry you had to witness that."

Without missing a beat, the older of the girls stepped forward. "While I don't like hurting other nymphs, I understand why we had to. He would've poisoned the water otherwise. Right, Anise?"

Anise ran a hand along her braid. "You're right, Bergamot. He was a danger to the humans and nymphs at the factory too."

Rose pursed her lips. "I'm sorry you had to endure that sort of treatment. Once we've disposed of the poisons we'll discuss that in our proposal with the humans."

Anise's voice shook. "Are you sure that they'll listen to reason?"

Rose placed a hand on her shoulder. "They'll have to if they don't want something like this to happen again."

The forest was silent now that the immediate threat had dissolved, but they weren't in the clear yet. If the loyalists lived, they could come back and do the same thing again. "Do either of you know where that nymph's plant is?"

Anise and Bergamot looked at each other. After a long pause, Anise said, "I know where some of the other's plants are, but not his."

Rose unclenched her jaw. "I'm concerned about them trying this again. Is there any chance that they'll regain their human forms before tomorrow afternoon?"

Anise placed a hand on her hip "It's unlikely, and if you're planning on killing them I want nothing to do with it. Killing them would make us no better than Nightshade."

Bergamot's lips turned down in a frown. "That's not true, Anise. He often killed humans trying to help us and killed our friends for standing up for themselves. You know that. We're just keeping the dream of peace alive."

"By killing?" Anise crossed her arms over her chest.

A sigh escaped Rose's lips. "We can attempt to reason with them one last time, but if they still refuse to denounce Nightshade, we'll be left with no other choice. If they attack during negotiations, we'll have more than Nightshade to worry about."

* * *

Anise, Bergamot, and Rose gathered up the discarded poisons. They pushed a barrel away from the water, heading over to the growing crowd of nymphs with Ivy and Elizabeth at their center.

A dozen barrels and a handful of vials sat in the middle of the crowd of nymphs.

The crowd looked on at Rose expectantly and her gaze darted to Elizabeth. "They want to know what your plan is now that we stopped them from poisoning the water," Elizabeth whispered.

"Of course, right." Rose cleared her throat. "Thank you, everyone.

You all did well in stopping the immediate threat, but if we want permanent peace, we will need to form an alliance with the humans. Hiding in the shadows isn't serving us any longer. The more they know about us, the better our chances of survival."

A nymph with green eyes like Ivy's shouted out. "And what's to stop them from just slaughtering us?"

Rose held up her hands. "They are more like us than you think. We can reason with them and protect the nymphs living here."

Gabriel stepped forward to stand beside Rose, and she linked her hands with his. "Gabriel saved me from entrapment in a glass prison. Even going so far as to risk his life. A human woman named April died saving me from a fire. There are good humans out there, and I truly believe most of them will see this as an opportunity to gain an ally and friend, not an enemy."

One of the younger girl's raised her hand. "How are we going to convince them?"

Gabriel cleared his throat. "We value our medicines, animals, and livelihoods. If you can aid the town with those things, you have a good chance at convincing them."

Elizabeth's arm shot up. "We can help grow plants and communicate with the animals."

Rose gave a slight smile at Elizabeth's enthusiasm. "Good. We can bring that up tomorrow. But before then we need to dispose of the poison safely. Any ideas?"

Elizabeth pressed her lips together. "The leaves aren't toxic if they're dried or burned, but the smoke can be dangerous. You don't want to be near it once the flame is lit. The waste usually goes to a mountain of garbage on the outskirts of town. The tins contain dangerous poisons from the dyes, so there aren't many safe ways to dispose of it."

Rose walked over to a barrel and grabbed the handle of the dolly that held it. "In that case, I'll need a few of you to help me cart these barrels to the dump. Gabriel, you'll come with me. Elizabeth and Ivy, can you take care of the leaves?"

Elizabeth grabbed a vial from the floor. "We'll take care of it, friend."

Rose's eyes crinkled at the corners. "Thank you."

Rose turned back to face the crowd. "Let's dispose of this and then we'll deal with the remaining threats to our negotiation."

CHAPTER 19

$\mathcal{A}$ cold sweat broke out on Gabriel's forehead and his vision swam as they walked to the garbage heap. His fingers felt stiff from the cold, but he felt like he was burning up despite the dusting of snow on the ground.

The stench of rotten food and chemicals swarmed his senses and he placed a hand over his nose as the dump came into view.

Images of Lara danced across the corners of his vision, and he blinked in an effort to banish them. The effects reminded him more of the mirror than any poison, and what the fake Lara had said about the mirror killing her played through his mind.

But Rose shattered the mirror, so it couldn't be affecting me, could it? He thought as he continued along the path. He didn't dare drag a barrel. His leaden arms and legs weighed him down more with each step, and when Rose looked back at him, her smile wavered.

He mouthed. "Later."

Her gaze lingered for a couple more seconds before she turned around.

They quickly wheeled the barrels in and poured the liquid onto the trash heap.

An hour later, they were back near the river.

Rose gathered everyone in a circle. Girls stood on their toes, eagerly awaiting her next words, and Gabriel's heart raced in his chest.

But the next words out of Rose's mouth caused his jaw to drop. "Tonight, we will find the nymph's whose bodies we destroyed and we'll kill their plants before the negotiations tomorrow. It's the only way to ensure they won't contact reinforcements."

A young nymph girl pointed a finger at Rose. "That's just like the bad man."

The girl's brother patted her head. "That doesn't sit right with me. They were our comrades once. Isn't there another way that doesn't require bloodshed?"

Rose crossed her arms over her chest. "If you have a better idea, I'm open to suggestions."

A girl spoke with a small, wavering voice. "Some of us can try talking to them... alone. Maybe they'll listen to one of us when they aren't being forced to choose between two powerful and frankly terrifying leaders." The girl's gaze drifted to the floor. "One of the boys... he was a friend of mine. Please let me talk to him first."

A sigh escaped Rose's lips. "If you can convince him to reject Nightshade, I will allow him to go free."

The girl's eyes shone. "Thank you. You won't regret it." She raced off in the direction of the factory.

Gabriel's gaze drifted back to Rose. "As for the rest of Nightshade's loyalists, we need to find their plants. Does anyone know where the other nine plants reside?"

Ivy leaned against the tree. "I know where two of them are. I'll try talking to Birch and Maple but I doubt they'll leave Nightshade's side." He walked off, blending into the darkness of the night.

Elizabeth scraped her shoe against the dirt. "I know where our boss's plant is. I'll take care of him myself."

Rose grabbed Elizabeth's hand and whispered something Gabriel couldn't hear. A small smile turned up the corners of her mouth. "Thank you. I needed to hear that," Elizabeth said and ran off.

Rose turned to the rest of the group. "Find any of the nymphs you know. Tell them we plan to negotiate. If they still refuse to leave Nightshade's side...you know what to do. When you're done, meet back here and be careful."

* * *

IT WAS a few hours later when they'd all made it back to the clearing. The girl that had asked about her friend returned with red rimmed eyes and fingertips that smelled of ash.

Rose's throat ached. "I'm sorry."

The girl's friend held up a hand, stopping her from saying anything else. "Don't."

Rose turned from the girl's words like she was avoiding a blow. A weight settled in her stomach as she faced the crowd of hollowed out eyes and slouched figures. "I know what many of you just had to do wasn't easy, but sometimes that's the price of peace."

Anise spat. "You speak like you understand, but have you ever had to kill a friend with your own hands?"

Rose narrowed her eyes at Anise. "No, but I've lost a friend because of this war."

Elizabeth stomped over to Anise, and Anise shrank back despite them being roughly the same height. "I put my life on the line for this, and so did Ivy. We're her friends, and we could have died in this battle. This is a war, and it won't be pretty. Rose gave your friends every chance to make the correct choice. You can either accept that and choose the right side or see yourself to the door." Elizabeth's face flushed, and her shoulders clenched up near her ears.

Rose stepped forward to stand beside Elizabeth, placing a hand on her shoulder. Elizabeth's posture relaxed. "Elizabeth is right. We've done all we can. We cannot not allow hatred to thrive or else it will destroy lasting peace, choking it like a strangler fig does to a tree. Tonight, rest. You've all earned it. We will meet in the town square at dawn tomorrow for the negotiations," Rose said and turned to leave.

Elizabeth placed a hand on Rose's shoulder, stopping her. "Be careful when you get back to the hotel. There's a good chance Nightshade knows where you're staying now."

Rose's gaze swiveled to Gabriel's. "In that case, perhaps we can trouble you for a place to sleep?"

Elizabeth's lip quirked up in a half-smile. "Sure, but I'll warn you it's a bit cramped and it's not as nice as the fancy hotel."

Rose laughed. "I used to live in a garden shed. Trust me we'll be fine. Right, Gabriel?"

Gabriel laced his hands behind his head. "I'd much rather have my creature comforts, but I suppose one night won't be the death of me. If I scream in my sleep, I apologize," he said with a dry laugh, but his eyes held no glint of humor.

When they reached the hotel, Gabriel ran in to gather some of their belongings and a change of clothes before they made their way to Elizabeth's home.

But the building was more hovel than home. The shack was composed mostly of slanted wooden boards and rusty nails. One cot lay on the floor with no frame and the floor was coated in a thick layer of dust.

As Rose went to sit down, something with a long, thin tail skittered across the room and she let out a yelp. "Was that a rat?"

Elizabeth shrugged. "Probably. You get used to it."

"I had no idea you were living like this."

She smiled. "It doesn't really bother me. Although, I miss living in the forest. I tried to warn you."

Her gaze searched for the rat, and she spotted a hole in the wall. "Do you think it'll come back?'

"Probably. Why? Are you afraid of it?"

Rose pursed her lips. "Perhaps."

She scrambled backwards on all fours and grabbed onto Gabriel's leg with one arm. Her arm pointed at a hole in the wall. "You're sleeping near that in case it comes back."

Elizabeth sighed. "You can sleep on the cot with me, Rose. Sorry, Gabriel."

Gabriel shook his head and smiled at Rose. "It's fine. It'll only be for one night." He lowered himself onto the floor and laid on his back, gazing up at the ceiling.

Rose kept glancing over to the wall as she settled into the cot next to Elizabeth. Despite the plop of a water leak and her scare with the rat, she quickly drifted off to sleep.

* * *

THE SOUND of screaming jolted her awake, and her head snapped in Gabriel's direction, searching the dimly lit room. He writhed on the floor, and a steel flask that smelled of ether rolled across the wood, knocking into her knee. *Oh, Gabriel. It was worse than you let on, wasn't it?*

She climbed on top of his flailing body as he thrashed out and pinned down his arms. She lowered her head to his. "Gabriel. It's just a dream. Come back to me."

At first he didn't respond. He bucked underneath her, and she jerked her head back when he almost slammed his face into hers.

When she placed a hand on his forehead, it was burning up. "Gabriel. It's Rose. Please wake up." Her voice cracked on the word "please" and his eyes flew open.

But he stared past her to the discarded flask and wrinkled his nose. "You should have killed me instead of making me into what she hates, Nightshade." The chill in his voice made the hairs on her arms stand up.

Rose pinched his arm. "It's Rose. I don't hate you and Nightshade isn't here. Snap out of it."

Tears filled her eyes, and the hard look in his gaze softened. "Rose?"

"Yes, Gabriel. It's me. Why would I hate you?"

His voice choked. "Because I'm becoming like your father."

Rose's voice cracked. "No. You aren't!"

He rubbed her shoulder and nodded to the flask. "You wouldn't say that if you knew what was in that flask."

Rose's gaze flickered to where it had fallen. "I figured it out the second I caught a whiff. How long has this been going on?"

"It's been happening since we got on the train, and I'm sorry I kept it from you. It helped me sleep and numbed me to the hallucinations."

"Why didn't you tell me?" Her hand traced his jaw, and he tensed under her touch.

"I didn't want to worry you, and I didn't know how you'd react considering your father's... predicament."

She placed her hands around his. "You're nothing like him. You're selfless, silly, and kind to a fault. You even risked your own life trying to save April's life and mine. But I am taking this away from you," she said, plucking the half-empty flask from the floor.

He ran a hand through her hair. "What was your father like?"

She bit her lip.

"You don't have to tell me about it if you're uncomfortable."

Rose shook her head. "I want to talk about it, but only to you."

He smiled, and she leaned her head against his chest. "His inner nature was twisted long before a drop of alcohol hit his lips. It just lowered his ability to hide his wicked side. You aren't like that, but I always worry I might be. Especially considering my short temper."

She felt his chest move as he laughed. "You may be impulsive and ill-tempered, but you're also incredibly caring and empathetic. Completely unlike him."

Pink light streamed through the gaps in the wooden wall, and Elizabeth arched her back and stretched her arms up on the cot beside them. *How did she sleep through all that?*

Her hooded eyelids turned to Gabriel and Rose. "Someone's having an extra good morning, but could it wait until I'm not in the room?"

Rose flushed as she looked down and saw she was still straddling Gabriel. "It's not what it looks like."

Gabriel put an arm around her shoulder. "Please do explain what it looks like."

She narrowed her eyes. "If the curse doesn't kill you, I will."

He clucked his tongue. "Temper. Temper."

Elizabeth gagged. "Before I have to endure another minute of this, it's almost sunrise. Are you two ready to go to the square?"

Rose stood up. "Yes, of course."

Elizabeth scanned over her filthy clothes. "Not in that you aren't. Get changed."

Her face flushed as she looked down at her bloodstained attire. Elizabeth threw a change of clothes at her, and she looked over at Gabriel. "I'm not changing with him looking at me."

Elizabeth threw her hands up and then walked over to Gabriel, forcing him to face the opposite wall. "Oh, for goodness' sake, turn around."

"You seem to have a knack for ruining all my fun." But he turned around with just a mock pout and she quickly slipped into fresh clothes. Once she had changed and cleaned up the best she could, they left for the square.

* * *

THERE WAS ALREADY a small crowd of people gathering at the square, their eyes wide as they stared at Anise who stood atop a box shouting, "Come one, come all, to see real nymphs in the flesh."

While her method of drawing the crowd wasn't exactly subtle, she had to admit it had been effective.

When Anise saw Rose, she stepped down from her pedestal. As she passed by Rose's ear she whispered, "I'm giving you a chance. Make sure you keep your end of the bargain."

Rose's palms were sweaty, and she wiped them on her skirt before climbing atop the shaky wooden crate. As she looked over the crowd, her mouth went dry. "Hello everyone. You may be wondering why we've gathered you here today."

A woman shouted, "We're hoping to see these imaginary nymphs your friend has been screaming about."

Rose rubbed her fingers into her temples and glimpsed Anise's mischievous smile in the crowd. "I assure you we aren't imaginary and many of us aren't happy about the comrades we've lost so you could build this city."

A man shouted, "If nymphs are real, then prove it."

Rose's gaze flickered to Elizabeth. "Very well." Rose focused on her hand and thorns protruded from her fingertips. Pale skin turned to a rich green before their eyes.

Several people in the crowd gasped. Women covered their mouths and a small girl whispered, "They're real."

"Now that we've got your attention. We'd like to broach peace with you. Many of our people were murdered to create this city, and more still are dying every day. The trees razed to make way for factories are our graveyards and your factories and homes are cemeteries to us."

A young girl tugged on her mother's skirt and muttered, "But we didn't know."

Rose smiled at the young girl. "We're aware that many of you may not have known our existence. That's why we wish to make you aware. We don't wish to fight, but we refuse to lose anymore lives. We need to come to an agreement that will benefit both nymphs and humans."

Rose held out a hand, gesturing to Elizabeth and the other factory workers. "We've been working amongst you for years. You may recognize some of my fellow nymphs in the crowd, including the one that will be negotiating our terms."

Rose beckoned Elizabeth forward and stepped down from the pedestal. As they passed one another, she placed a hand on Elizabeth's shoulder. "You know the nymphs here better than anyone. I trust you to know their best interests."

Elizabeth cleared her throat as she stood in front of the pedestal. "In exchange for our safety, we can offer knowledge of natural dyes in every color, even green, that won't harm the environment."

Murmurs went through the crowd, and a woman said, "What about medicine?"

"We can show you natural medicines that even your doctors and herbalists aren't aware of."

Gabriel addressed the crowd. "They can also assist doctors with the healing of animals. Many of them can communicate with them, so they'll be able to pinpoint what treatments they need. They can even keep the wolves away from villages and livestock."

"Truly?" A man asked.

Elizabeth mouthed "Thank you," and then said, "Yes. It's one of our specialties, and we can help you create factories that don't cough out air that stings your lungs, and we just ask you don't harvest our plants."

"But we still need plants for survival."

Elizabeth held her hands up. "It wouldn't be a ban on the harvesting of all plants. Only some contain souls of nymphs, and we can even help you grow plants to harvest, but we'll need your cooperation. Can we count on you?"

The first to step forward was a woman with clothing that appeared permanently dusty. "I'll join you. I'm tired of the smoke from the factories."

A man came forward next. "And my horse has been sick for ages. None of the doctors know what's wrong."

One by one, humans in the clearing stepped forward to join Elizabeth. Rose joined the group and whispered, "Nicely done."

Elizabeth held her head high. "Thank you everyone for your cooperation. We will write up a formal agreement and meet back here in a few day's time."

The crowd dispersed and Elizabeth grabbed Rose by the hand, breaking free from the crowd to approach Ivy. "Stay with the others until the crowd is gone, just in case one of Nightshade's allies or one of the humans try to attack," she whispered.

His lip quirked up in a half smile. "Yes, madam leader. I'll be right behind you."

Rose frowned. "Why are we leaving so soon?"

Elizabeth scoffed and her gaze lingering on Gabriel's form a few feet behind her. "Because despite his earlier words, his face is whiter than the snow on the ground and his eyes are haunted. I'll accompany you to the hotel so you both can change and pack, then you should get back to Florida to get the arrowroot for his cure, and Nightshade still needs to be dealt with."

Rose's mouth opened in an "O."

Gabriel caught sight of them staring at him and hurried over. "Are we leaving?"

The short run had left him winded, and his face was moon beam pale. She reached out to grab his hand and it was hot as a fireplace. "Yes, Gabriel. We need to go to Florida to get the antidote for you."

His eyes fixed on a point in the distance and his grip on her hand tightened. "That's probably best."

He gripped her hand with white knuckles as she towed him along to the hotel.

The person at the front wrinkled his nose at Rose and Gabriel's filthy clothes. Then, his gaze darted to the mailboxes behind him, and he pointed to Rose. "If my memory isn't faulty, you're that factory worker. Rose, right?"

Trepidation edged into her tone. "Yes, why?"

He reached into the stack of letters behind him, organized by room and pulled out one addressed to her. He held out a letter to her, and her blood froze in her veins when she saw a seal with green wax vines adorning the envelope. "This was delivered for you."

Beside her, Elizabeth froze. She whispered, "That's Nightshade's seal."

Panic climbed into Rose's throat as she tugged at the seal and ripped open the letter. Gabriel glanced over her shoulder as she read it.

Dear Rose,

I'm holding your mother hostage. Consider it payment for stealing my allies and ruining my plans in Pennsylvania. If you'd like to see her alive again, return yourself and Gabriel to me. I'll take your lives instead. If you don't respond to this letter and don't arrive here, I will kill her. You have two weeks. Your time starts now. I'm eagerly awaiting your arrival.

Sincerely,
Nightshade

ROSE'S HANDS SHOOK, and she dropped the letter. *He'll be the one losing his life if I have anything to say about it.*

She gripped Gabriel's arm, her nails digging into his skin. "We need to leave. Now."

Gabriel turned to the man at the desk. "We'll be checking out today."

The man gestured to the stairs. " Once you've cleared out your rooms, just come here to turn in your keys."

Rose raced up the stairs, not bothering to see if Elizabeth and Gabriel followed. When she got to her room, she threw her clothes and belongings in her bag haphazardly.

After taking one last look around the room, she ran off to retrieve Gabriel. He sat on his bed with his belongings stuffed into his pack that had several pants' legs sticking out. A glass of amber liquid was halfway to his lips.

She placed her hand on her hips. "And I thought I was thick headed. What are you doing?"

He whispered, "I needed the images to stop. They're getting worse."

She snatched the glass from his hand without meeting his gaze. "Let's go. We need to hurry if we're going to catch the next train, and we can't have you incapacitating yourself. You're the only one who knows how to handle the horse."

"I suppose you're right. This time," Gabriel grabbed his bag and slung it over his shoulder. Rose led Gabriel down the stairs. Elizabeth waited at the bottom of the stairs, pacing back and forth like she was trying to make a hole in the floor.

Rose stood in Elizabeth's path, stopping her frantic loping. "Thank you for your help so far, but I couldn't possibly ask you to continue on with us any further. It's too dangerous."

"I'm going to help you, and there's no chance of you stopping me." Elizabeth puffed out her chest, a comical look for someone who barely reached her shoulders.

Rose stifled a snicker then pressed her lips together in a frown.

"What about the negotiations? What if Nightshade's remaining allies retaliate or if you aren't there to hand over the written treaty?"

She glanced down at her feet. "Ivy or Anise would be better able to handle either of those situations. He's a better fighter, and she's a better negotiator. Besides, you need someone to keep your impulsive tendencies in check."

Rose glanced back at Gabriel, who swayed slightly on his feet, "We don't have time to talk about this. We need to go. Now. If you're joining us, grab your belongings quickly and meet us at the train station. If you aren't there by the time the next train arrives, we're leaving without you."

Gabriel reached out to squeeze her shoulder. His grip was so weak that it made her shoulders clench.

Gabriel got the bit in the horse's mouth and the reins attached in record time. The horse trotted as they made their way to the train station, jostling her about like a leaf in a rainstorm. Her stomach squirmed so much that she almost didn't hear Gabriel say, "Rose, what about the letter?"

She kicked at the wall of the cart and cursed when her head smacked into the wall. "How long will it take for the letter to arrive if we send it at the train's first stop?"

"Maybe two to three days, why?"

Rose's forehead creased as she weighed her options. "We'll send the letter then. The longer my mother is with Nightshade, the more danger she's in. Our time is better spent catching the next train."

Her voice cracked, and he reached back to place a hand on her leg. "We'll find her before he can hurt her."

"You don't know that," Rose's lip trembled.

"I don't."

She bit her lip so hard it drew blood, and the metallic tang coated her tongue. "I'll kill him when I find him." The words left an acrid taste in her mouth, and the rest of the ride to the station passed in silence.

When they got to the station, a long line sprouted from the ticket counter, and she tapped her foot in impatience.

"We can't make the line move faster Rose, relax."

"How am I supposed to relax? My mother might be dead and you're getting sicker by the minute despite how you tried to hide it. What if we don't make it out of this because of a stupid line?" Her voice rose to a shout, and several people turned to glare at Rose.

Gabriel ran a hand through his hair. "We'll make it through this. I promise."

"I can't lose her. I can't lose you."

He gathered her into his arms. "I know. I don't want to lose you either."

She muttered against his chest, "I shouldn't have let her stay. I should have forced her to leave that place."

"You did your best, Rose."

"But what if it wasn't enough?" Her voice was so weak that he'd barely heard her.

He whispered into her hair. "You've done more than enough. You are enough. No matter what happens next. Okay?"

"Okay." She pulled away from his embrace and wiped away the start of tears as the line moved up.

Gabriel kept Rose behind him as he approached the desk. "What time does the next train arrive?"

"You just missed getting the last ticket for this train, so the next one won't leave for about an hour and a half."

Rose opened her mouth to say something, but Gabriel placed a hand on her shoulder. "We can wait for the next train. It won't kill us," he said.

"If it kills us, we'll know who to blame," she said, shooting a glare at the ticket clerk.

The man placed a hand over his mouth to hide a smile. "We'll take two tickets for the next train, please. Thank you."

The man laughed. "Sounds like your woman is as wild as a stallion."

"And as violent as one," he added.

Rose elbowed Gabriel and the man's mouth dropped open.

As they walked away, Rose's stomach grumbled, and she looked up at Gabriel. "Do you happen to have any food?"

He let out a sigh. "When we get on the train, I'll get you whatever food you want, but until then try not to snap at anyone else."

"Yes, sir." She gave him a little salute that made him smile, and they sat down on a nearby bench while they waited for the next train.

Gabriel sat on the bench with his head in his hands, trying to calm the woozy feeling spreading through his body. He raised his head when Rose said, "Why is Ivy here?"

He'd raised his head too quickly and Elizabeth's face swirled as she sighed. "Because he refused to let me go alone, and he insisted on seeing Nightshade's downfall in person."

Gabriel peered down at the grime still wedged underneath his fingernails. *We should've stayed and bathed,* he thought with a grimace.

Rose sat down beside Elizabeth, begging for the nuts and seeds in her hand like a stray dog. Ivy's gaze darted around wildly, scanning for threats as he loomed protectively over Rose and Elizabeth.

Elizabeth extended out a handful of nuts to Rose with a smile. "Do you want some?"

Rose snatched up the offered food greedily. "Thank you," she whispered before shoving the food into her mouth, making her cheeks puff out like a squirrel's. It made him smile despite the nausea settling in his stomach.

His vision edged in black, and he wiped away sweat from his forehead. The world swayed behind him, and he blinked, trying to correct his distorted vision.

A shiver shook his body through his wool coat, and this time he didn't stop Rose as she reached out to place a hand on his forehead. She jerked her hand away like his skin had burned her. "Gabriel. Are you okay?"

His breaths came in huffs, and he latched onto her wrist. He could feel her wrist, but only barely, and he couldn't see her. He managed a weak, "I'm sorry, Rose," before his vision went dark, and he felt and saw nothing.

* * *

ROSE'S HEART dropped into her stomach as Gabriel collapsed into her lap.

"Gabriel. Gabriel," she said, but he didn't respond. His eyes moved back and forth beneath closed lids. His chest rose and fell with erratic movements.

She glanced at Elizabeth whose face had gone pale.

Panic crawled up her throat. They needed to do something. His skin burned beneath her fingertips.

Elizabeth broke the silence by asking, "Is—is he breathing?"

"Yes, but it sounds like he's struggling to draw breath and he's burning up. We should have left sooner." She gripped the bench so tightly her knuckles went white.

Elizabeth placed a hand on Rose's shoulder. "What's done is done. Right now our goal should be to keep him alive until we get back to Florida. When we get on the train, let's look for the icebox. Something cold might help with the fever at least."

She buried her face into Gabriel's shirt. "I'm sorry. You were always smiling, even like this. I shouldn't have listened to you. I should've helped you and damned the consequences. It's my fault you're like this."

"It's not your fault. He wanted to help the others just as much as you did. It was his choice too," Elizabeth said.

The train screeched to a halt in front of them, and Ivy and Rose supported his shoulders, hauling him upright. They placed Rose's tinted glasses on his face as they carried him aboard.

The train personnel's glance kept shifting from Ivy to Gabriel, and his lips parted in a question but Ivy, ever the smooth talker, said, "He had a little too much to drink."

Ivy flashed a toothy grin, and the conductor frowned, "Alright. Just make sure he stays out of trouble," he said before collecting their tickets and waving them aboard.

Ivy and Elizabeth helped Rose get Gabriel to their seat. They laid him flat on their assigned bench, his back rested against the plush surface.

Ivy brushed sweat soaked hair back from Gabriel's forehead. "Rose, go ask for a washcloth and have them soak it through with cold water."

He turned his gaze to Elizabeth. "See if you can get some ice from the kitchen's icebox, but be inconspicuous about it."

He beckoned them closer with a hand and lowered his voice to a whisper. "Don't let on that he's ill. They might panic and kick us off the train. I'll stay and watch over him until you return."

Rose took one last look back and then headed towards the kitchen with Elizabeth.

Her empty stomach rumbled as they neared its entrance, but the thought of food turned her stomach. *How long will he last if he can't eat or drink?*

Rose tapped a cook on the shoulder to get his attention and then batted her eyelashes at him. "Excuse me, sir, but do you know where I could get a cloth for washing? I really would like to clean off a bit."

The man looked her up and down and rubbed at the scruff on his chin. "Young lady, I'm not sure why you're asking here for a wash-cloth, but you'd need to go to a different car to get something like that. We don't have those here in the kitchen."

She stuck out her lip in a slight pout and forced a slight quiver. "Can you show me the way? I'm worried I'll get lost again."

The man's gaze softened. At that moment she knew she had him hook, line, and sinker. "I'll take you there, but we have to be quick. Okay?"

Rose wiped her eyes. "Okay." She allowed her voice to crack for good measure. It wasn't hard when she thought of Gabriel's current state.

He led her off to a different car, and as they walked away, she turned around and gave Elizabeth a wink. Now, it was up to her to get the ice.

* * *

ELIZABETH SQUIRMED in her seat amongst the women dressed in jewel toned skirts and dresses as she listened in on Rose's conversation.

The crack in her voice would've had me convinced, she thought as Rose led the man away and gave Elizabeth a quick wink.

Elizabeth moved quickly with measured steps, sneaking past the busy chefs while crouching close to the ground. She hid behind cabinets and under tables as she made her way through the kitchen unnoticed.

As she hunched under the table, she saw a chef pull meat out of a wooden cabinet. Inside it, there was a massive hunk of ice. *But how do I get some without getting caught?* She searched the room for anything that would distract them for a moment, and the flames cooking the food gave her an idea.

She cupped her hands around her mouth and took a deep breath through her nose, hoping she could throw her voice convincingly. She raised her tongue to the roof of her mouth and then shouted, "There's a fire in the engine room. We need to evacuate, now!"

The chefs turned to look at each other for a moment in disbelief. Then they rushed out in a panic. Now was her chance.

As soon as the room cleared out, she grabbed an oily cloth a chef had been using to wipe pots and pans and opened the icebox. Thankfully, the ice hadn't melted much yet.

She grabbed an icepick from the top of the cabinet and chipped off a few large chunks and wrapped them in the cloth, carrying it so the ice didn't touch her hands. She slid the door of the icebox closed and then loped out of the kitchen.

Rose stood beside Gabriel, a wet washcloth pressed to his forehead. Rose's body shook with silent sobs as she approached. His closed eyelids moved back and forth and an occasional mumble escaped his throat, but he didn't wake.

Elizabeth's heart squeezed as she approached with the already melting chunks of ice. *I hope he lives for her sake.*

With a sheepish smile, she held out the bundle for Ivy. "It's not much, but hopefully it helps some."

Ivy cocked his head to the side. "I take it the false fire in the kitchen was your distraction?"

Elizabeth bit her lip. "Perhaps. It worked rather well. Humans also appear to fear fire."

He shook his head. "You're something."

Rose and Ivy sat Gabriel up and placed a chip of ice in his mouth, being careful to make sure he wouldn't choke on it. As it melted on his tongue, his eyes fluttered, but he didn't wake. They fed him a few more ice cubes and inserted a couple of cubes under his armpits and on his forehead to try to bring his body temperature down.

Anything they did would only be a temporary relief until they figured out what was ailing Gabriel. If it truly was Manchineel's poison, then this wouldn't end until they found an antidote, and if it was a curse, they'd need to find a way to reverse it.

When they lifted Gabriel up, a small ring fell out of his pocket and clinked to the floor. Elizabeth picked it up, examining it between her fingers.

She held up the ring for Rose to see. "Are you married to him?"

Rose shook her head. "No, I'm not. He was married, but his wife got sick and died."

Elizabeth blinked. "I didn't know he was married."

A frown tugged at her lips. "She died of a strange sickness. One time when Gabriel was hallucinating, I heard him talking about a mirror. He asked the hallucination of Lara how the mirror could have killed her. He'd given me a mirror too..."

Rose's voice trailed off.

Elizabeth tensed. *If there was a mirror involved, maybe it is a curse after all.*

She pursed her lips together, mulling over the words before she dared utter them aloud. "Was there anything unusual about this mirror?"

Rose's hands bunched her skirt. "When I kept it in the greenhouse with me, it drove me mad, made me hallucinate, but we broke the mirror. Belladonna told us it would weaken Nightshade, so we could kill him. After that, the hallucinations stopped."

Images of a mirror and tales of a curse ran through her mind. One that got stronger the more you fell for someone. She placed a hand on

Rose's shoulder. "A mirror wouldn't weaken a nymph, but it could hold their magic."

Rose's pale complexion went grey. "Wouldn't breaking the mirror destroy any magic it held?"

Elizabeth bit her lip. "We can't be sure."

Rose ran a hand along Gabriel's arm. "Do you think Nightshade cursed the mirror? Is it doing this to him?"

Elizabeth put a hand over Rose's. "I don't know, but there's no use fretting over it now. If it is a curse, then we'd need the magic of the nymph that cast it in order to break it"

The spark in her eyes faded. "Oh."

She squeezed Rose's hand. "You'll need to eat to keep up your strength. Why don't you go get some food? We'll look after him for awhile."

"Thank you," she whispered, and stood up to head towards the dining car.

Elizabeth waited until she was out of earshot and then turned to Ivy. "I didn't want to worry Rose, but I think we might be dealing with *that* curse."

"What makes you say that?"

"She mentioned a mirror he'd given to his previous wife. That wife died of a rare illness and he's gotten sicker as they've gotten closer to one another. Sound familiar?"

Ivy gasped. "That sounds exactly like the Lover's Curse."

CHAPTER 20

*R*ose had only picked at her food as thoughts of curses and death swirled in her mind. *How many more have to die in this war? We've lost so many, and I can't lose him. Can't lose my mother.*

She glared down at the coins, a reminder that without him, she'd never have made it this far and yet she'd let him get so sick. She picked at the bread and sipped at soup, but the scent of fish normally mouth-watering now turned her stomach.

After eating only a few mouthfuls of bread and several sips of soup, she pushed the plate forward and paid before returning to Gabriel, her stomach still rumbling.

Ivy and Elizabeth stood at Gabriel's side. He shivered on the seat, but didn't stir. Her heart lurched as her gaze raked over his pale skin, and she dragged her feet over to the bench.

When Ivy and Elizabeth went back to her seats, Rose laid her head on his chest. "Please don't leave," she whispered, blinking back tears.

The moment the words left her mouth, his breathing became even more jagged, and she clutched his wool coat, burying her face into the fabric. Despite the pulse racing in her chest, her eyelids grew heavy and fluttered closed.

* * *

ELIZABETH'S NECK craned to observe Rose from her seat. Gabriel's fever had burned through damp towels, leaving them warm and damp with sweat. His skin was paper white and his breathing labored. He didn't open his eyes. *Should I have kept them apart? We still aren't sure if it is the Lover's Curse, and if it isn't, I'll have denied her what might be his last moments and worried her.*

Elizabeth gripped the backrest of her and Ivy's bench as the sound of metal on metal assaulted her ears. She ground her teeth together as the train came to halt.

When the train hissed to a stop, she stood up and approached Rose's sleeping form. Dried tears ran down her face, but she looked peaceful. Elizabeth gave Rose's shoulder a shake. "Rose. Rose. Wake up."

Her eyes blinked open, and her arms stretched. Her mouth parted in a slight yawn. "Are we home?" Rose's gaze flickered to Gabriel beside her, and she pursed her lips together.

"Has he woken at all?"

Elizabeth hid her face behind her auburn hair. "No, he hasn't. I just wanted to make sure you can send a letter to Nightshade before we leave. This is a longer stop, so you should have enough time."

Rose clutched Gabriel's shirt. "I have to leave him behind?"

Elizabeth bit her lip. "Yes, but only for a short while. The post office is just down the road."

Rose loosened her grip on Gabriel. "Keep him safe."

Elizabeth steadied Rose as she struggled to get upright on shaky legs. "I will. Now go and don't forget your ticket stub to get back on."

"Right." Rose felt for the ticket in her jacket pocket and her finger caught on a few loose coins from her job at the factory.

"I've got it. I'll be back soon."

Each step she took towards the post office sent another thought that wedged a knife into her heart. *He wanted to stay behind. If I'd let him, he might be okay.*

Another step. *He might've found a cure faster if he hadn't gone with me.*

Another step. *We promised we'd stay together, but I've left his side twice now.* By the time she reached the post office, she wished to run back to the train, back to him, but she had to do this. Her mother needed help too.

Because you let her stay behind. Two people will die because of you. She blinked her eyes against tears, but there were no tears left.

She stomped the rest of the way to the post office. Heavy footsteps turned to a gentle gait when pointed towers, waving flags, and the massive arched glass windows came into view. The imposing building sat just a few blocks from the train station and mail carriers shuffled in and out of the building, leaving there by foot, horse, and car.

The scent of paper and ink filled the air as she stepped through the front door, and she took deep breaths to savor the smell that reminded her so much of the library.

Behind the wooden counter at the back of the room stood a man with stick thin arms and thick glasses. His eyes examined her as she approached, and she cleared her throat to get his attention. "Hi. I'm here to send a letter."

He blinked. "Do you know where you'd like to send it to?"

"It's just south of King's Road. The address is 249 Route 1 in Oak Lawn, Florida."

"Very well. I'll get you a letter and pen. Do you know what you'd like written on the letter?"

Rose's face flushed pink. "Am I not permitted to write it myself?"

The man's stuttered. "I'm sorry I didn't realize a woman of your status…" his voice trailed off.

She clenched her teeth together and turned her lips up in a forced grin. "Status doesn't equal intellect."

"My apologies." He darted to the back of the mail room and soon returned with a pen, paper, and envelope. Her frustrations poured onto the page, and her hand cramped as she wrote. Her lettering left much to be desired, but it was legible.

Dear Nightshade,
I'll be there in a few day's time. If you believed I would tuck my tail and run,

you were sorely mistaken. If you've harmed her in any way, know that I will not allow you to live to tell the tale. You will truly witness the thorns of this

Rose.

Sincerely,

Rose

A weight lifted from her chest as she folded up the letter and sealed the envelope before returning it to the post office worker. "Thank you," Rose said and let the few meager coins she had on her person clink to the counter.

Once he'd retrieved the letter from her and let her know it would be shipped out, she gave the man a slight smile and thank you before returning to the train.

* * *

HIS MIND WADED through a thick fog that dragged his limbs down as surely as lead weights. His eyelids remained glued shut, but he heard everything.

ROSE STAYED AT HIS SIDE, begging for him to stay alive, and each word pressed down on him, stealing air from his lungs. He cried out in his mind, *I'm still here, beside you,* but the words refused to form on his lips, to leave his mouth.

SOBS WRENCHED FROM HER THROAT, sending a knife through his heart, and he longed to comfort her. That thought thickened the mist into a soup.

HE DIDN'T KNOW how long it had been when Ivy and Elizabeth's voices penetrated his mind. The first was the gentle cadence of Elizabeth's

218

speech. "I didn't want to worry Rose, but I think we might be dealing with *that* curse."

Ivy's rough voice reached his ears. "What makes you say that?"

"She mentioned a mirror he'd given to his previous wife. That wife died of a rare illness and he's gotten sicker as they've gotten closer to one another. Sound familiar?"

"That sounds exactly like the Lover's Curse."

That's why the mist is getting worse. I have to tell her, but how? The forces dragging him under only grew stronger until the screech of brakes sounded and Rose left for the post office.

A few minutes later the fog eased, and he kicked and clawed at it, screaming out. He tried to think of leaving her behind, forgetting her, and the fog eased. He opened his eyes and saw cloudy images of Ivy and Elizabeth. He turned his head and saw red eyes approaching him.

* * *

ROSE ARRIVED on the train to see Ivy and Elizabeth hovering over Gabriel. Her heart fluttered in her chest when she heard a weak, "Rose."

She ran over to their bench, brushing past Ivy and Elizabeth. "When did he wake up?"

Elizabeth bit her lip. "A few moments after you left the train."

She knelt down beside him, gripping his too warm hand in hers. "Gabriel. You're awake."

"Yes, but it feels like wading through fog."

"We're on the train. We're going to get you the antidote."

Gabriel tried to sigh, but it came out a wheeze that turned into a cough. "I need you to listen. No antidote will cure me. As much as you wish to care for me, I need you to keep your distance. Can you do that for me?"

Her lip quivered. "But why?"

"I can't explain. Just promise me, so we can survive this together."

Her hand gripped his. "I promise."

He touched a hand to her cheek. "In case I don't survive this, I want you to know-"

Elizabeth placed a finger to his lips. "Don't."

Her stony gaze told Rose that she was hiding something.

She traced circles on his hand. "When I've cured you, you'll tell me."

A shadow of his usual smile touched his lips. "Yes, but now I'm feeling tired again. I need to rest."

Her throat burned, but all that came out was a whispered, "No. Please stay."

But his eyelids already fluttered closed.

HER STOMACH GRUMBLED in protest as she picked at another meal of bread and soup. She wrapped her parched lips around the glass of water, but only sipped it. She brought the mostly full glass to Gabriel and handed it off to Elizabeth.

She went to Elizabeth's seat, but her gaze kept slipping back to his sleeping form as Elizabeth forced water past his lips.

Looking at his prone form made her thoughts drift to the journey ahead. *How will we get home from the train station in Lullin? I don't know how to handle his horse. Does Ivy or Elizabeth know?*

"Please. Please be okay," she pleaded as she curled up in a ball on her seat. The seconds felt like hours as she leaned against the bench. Ivy wrapped a comforting arm around her, but it felt stiff and awkward.

"We'll get him better," he said so flatly that it only worsened her longing for him. She wanted to touch him, care for him like he had when she'd been poisoned. *I can't help him. I'm the poison.* She pressed her fingers into her eyes.

Sleep clawed at her body, but her mind refused to rest.

Dark circles had formed under her eyes by the time the train reached its last stop, Lullin. The closest stop to her home. *I have to face yet another death that I caused.* The thought made her shoulders stiffen.

Once they'd gotten off the train, Ivy rounded up the horse and hauled Gabriel into the mail cart with Elizabeth's help.

Ivy conversed with the horse like he was a person. When he asked, "How do I harness you?" The horse neighed and pointed his head at the harness.

Ivy stroked the horse's mane and whispered "thank you," as he hooked him to the cart.

She paced back and forth, throwing an occasional worried glance at Gabriel who laid flat on the back of the mail cart

Over an hour later, they were ready to go. Rose climbed into the mail cart, and Elizabeth pulled herself up, her skirt catching on the wood. She tugged it free and bumped into Rose. "Sorry," she said and then crawled to the back. She sat with her feet hanging off the edge of the tiny vehicle as Ivy steered.

The cart bumped along and Ivy had to jerk the reins, hissing a "Stop that. We're in a rush." when the animal lowered his head to graze on some wildflowers for the fifth time.

As they passed through the town, Rose's mouth went dry.

The pile of ash that used to be April's hotel made her chest squeeze, and April's smile flickered through her mind.

Elizabeth rubbed Rose's back, and she looked down to see wet tears dropping to the fabric of her skirt. "I know. He's taken so much from us all," Elizabeth whispered.

Rose spoke between hiccuping sobs. "It was my fault. My friend died trying to save me when that inn burned down."

Thinking of the choking smoke and burning flames made her clutch a fistful of fabric near her chest. She wished she hadn't run. She should have hugged April's mother and cried together with her then, but she'd been too afraid. She'd thought April's mother would blame her for April's death. She still blamed herself for April's death.

Rose wanted to apologize for running, but they didn't have the luxury of time now.

I'll come back and apologize to you properly, but first I have to face the nymph that caused all this carnage...before he steals my family from me.

When they arrived at the next inn, only a few street lamps lit the town.

Rose and Elizabeth hefted Gabriel's limp body from the carriage and dragged him to the back door of the hotel to avoid unwanted questions or unexpected hospital trips.

They leaned Gabriel against the wall, and she pulled two hairpins from her messy bun. She pried the first pin apart, bending it into an L, and removed the piece of rubber on the end. The other remained closed as she bent it and she stuck it in the lock, using it as a lever. As she angled the other pin into the lock, she kept her ear close, listening for soft clicks.

When the door creaked open, they peeked their head in. Ivy beckoned them to the stairs and hauled him up to their room.

After Ivy had settled Gabriel into bed, Rose and Elizabeth snuck over to the women's bathing area.

Scraping away the grime and stress with lukewarm water helped make the stress fade away. She turned to Elizabeth, who still washed off her arms. "Elizabeth? Do you think we stand a chance against Nightshade?"

Elizabeth tugged at her lower lip. "I'm not sure if Ivy or I would be of any use on our own, but perhaps together we stand a chance. But we'll have to stick to the plan. Don't let him manipulate your emotions. If you distract him long enough, I might be able to sneak past his guard to destroy his plant as long as you don't try to destroy him yourself."

Rose crossed her arms over her chest. "I don't know if I'll be able to keep a level head if he's harmed my mother."

She placed a hand on her shoulder. "Ivy and I will be there to remind you of what needs to be done."

Rose gazed down at the murky bath water. "Thank you. I don't think I could've done this alone."

They finished bathing in silence.

After they'd dried off and dressed, Rose grabbed a washcloth from the bathing room and soaked it in some cool water. She knew it was important to keep Gabriel's temperature down, even though nothing they'd done had any lasting effects.

When she got to Ivy's room, she gave three quick raps on the door. A yawning and shirtless Ivy cracked open the door to greet her with a, "Yes, Rose?"

She turned away, her face beet red. "Um... I brought a washcloth for Gabriel."

Ivy smiled. "He's lucky to have someone who cares so much about him." He took the cloth and ducked back into the room. "Did you want to see him?"

Her heart squeezed at the thought of Gabriel's last words to her. "I shouldn't."

"Fair enough." He entered the room and pulled the door shut behind him.

Rose paced in the hallway until her muscles ached and her eyes burned, begging for sleep. She pulled open the door to see Elizabeth already in bed, the covers pulled up to her neck.

Rose crawled into bed in her nightdress, but a million thoughts raced through her mind, and it wasn't until the skyline began to turn grey that she drifted off to sleep.

The feeling of knees pressed to her chest and the sound of Elizabeth crouched over her sleeping form saying, "Rose, wake up," was what jolted her awake the next morning.

Rose shot up so quickly that she nearly hit Elizabeth's face. "What time is it?" She looked out the window and saw that the sun had barely risen, sending bits of soft yellow light into the room.

"It's nearly seven. Get dressed and ready," Elizabeth said as she hopped off Rose's chest.

Rose groaned. "Now I know how Gabriel feels when I wake him too early." She shoved the covers off and rubbed grit from her eyes as she slunk out of bed.

By the time she'd gotten dressed and packed, Elizabeth had already made her bed and rushed out of the room. Rose stuffed her nightdress into her bag and made her way to the back door. Ivy passed Gabriel off to her and Elizabeth, and they snuck out to the stables.

Shortly after they hauled Gabriel into the mail cart, Ivy arrived with an armful of food. Her stomach grumbled as he approached with the offerings of bread and fruit.

Elizabeth tore off a piece of bread and shoved it in her mouth. When Rose didn't touch the food, she nudged her shoulder. "I know you're worried about Gabriel, but we need to be at our best if we want a chance at defeating Nightshade."

Rose sighed. "I'll try." She tore off a piece of bread and nibbled away at it. Elizabeth pressed an apple into her hand and took two small bites.

That was all she could eat before her stomach did flips that made her feel ill. She handed the rest of the apple to Elizabeth. "Let's go."

Ivy and Elizabeth shared a look. Ivy stretched his arms up. "I suppose we can leave now."

He hooked the horse to the cart and they were off.

Rose heart squeezed anytime her gaze caught on Gabriel's prone form. She stared out at the forests that crowded the area as they neared Gabriel's home, but images of her mother's death, of Gabriel's death, cycled through her mind as they drew closer no matter how she tried to distract herself.

The town that held Gabriel's home looked too normal. People continued along with their daily routines. Couriers delivered mail. People went to work or clothing shops on foot or in a buggy. A crowd of people waited in line at the hospital. But...something felt off.

The hairs on her arm stood on end as they approached Gabriel's home.

Broken shards of glass shone in the grass near the front door. Rose cursed under her breath. "How did he find this place?"

Her back stiffened, and she held a hand out to stop Elizabeth from approaching the door. "I think my father is here. He can be violent, so be careful."

Elizabeth cocked her head to one side. "Can one human really be that dangerous?"

Rose dug her nails into her palm. "This one can be, so be on high alert."

"Okay," Elizabeth said with a touch of disbelief hitching her voice.

Rose reached out her hand for the doorknob. For a moment, she froze, afraid to turn the door. She dug her nails into the doorknob. *I'm stronger than him now. I can and will face him.*

She took a deep breath in and then turned the handle to reveal... her father.

He carried a bottle in his hand filled with alcohol, and a ruddy crimson blush stained his cheeks. The air reeked of wheat that had taken a turn. When he caught her gaze, he flashed a slick smile that made bile rise in her throat.

"How did you find this place and where is Mother?" Rose shouted, being careful not to get too close.

Her father's lip curled up in a snarl. "Let's just say when I told the doctor my wife was missing, he pointed me in the right direction."

Thorns sprouted from Rose's fingertips, and her vision blurred in red. "What did you do with Lailah?"

John let out a gravelly laugh that sent shivers down her spine and made her heart race in her chest. "When I finally found my missing wife and tried to bring her home, the ungrateful wench bit me. Another man saw me dragging her home and offered to take the bitch off my hands."

Rage boiled over in her chest, and she closed the gap between them in an instant. The sound of Elizabeth screaming, "Rose, stop," made her hand freeze with her fingertips on her father's neck.

Instead of digging the thorns into his flesh, she grabbed him by the collar. Her tone was ice cold when she said, "If Lailah is dead because of you, I'll make sure you regret it. Death will be too light a sentence." Then she threw him to the floor like she was discarding a piece of trash.

His face went white, and he scrambled backward. The haughty look he'd had before vanished. "You're a monster."

"No. I believe that title is reserved for people like you, and I refuse to stoop to your level."

Rose took in Gabriel's old living room. Her father had tainted it with littered beer bottles and empty cigarette cartons. She wrinkled her nose at the sight. He'd moved in here. *He has some nerve.*

"However, we can't risk you escaping. Ivy, Elizabeth, let's tie him up and then we'll go. Ivy, do you still have chloroform from before?"

Ivy rifled through his bag and snatched up a small vial of it. "Why don't you let me handle this part?"

Rose stepped to the side and he tackled her father to the ground in a flash of movement, pinning him with one arm while the other forced the chloroform to his mouth.

After a short time, her father slumped over, and Rose's gaze darted to him. "I'll bring Gabriel inside as well. He'll have to stay here since he's in no condition to travel."

Elizabeth jogged over to Rose's side. "I'll help. Gabriel can be a bit difficult to carry alone."

When they went back out to the carriage, Rose grabbed some old rope that had been left near a post. *Perfect.* Rose grabbed the rope in one hand and hefted Gabriel in the other.

Elizabeth bore the brunt of his weight as they dragged him back to the house and led him over to the bedroom.

Her muscles strained as they lowered him to his bed, and her fingers brushed against the bare skin of his arms. The heat made her body tense, and she pulled away from him. She turned to Elizabeth. "Can I have a moment alone with him?"

Elizabeth blinked. "Are you sure that's wise?"

"Perhaps it's unwise, but it's needed."

She bit her lip. "I'll be just outside if you need me."

Once Elizabeth had left the room, Rose leaned down to place a kiss on his clammy forehead. "I'll be back for you. I promise."

She gave Gabriel's hand a quick squeeze before exiting his room. *You shouldn't make promises you can't keep,* her mind warned. The thought squeezed her heart, and she walked right past Elizabeth.

"He'll be okay, you know."

Rose gave her a wry smile. "Don't feed me false hopes."

Elizabeth's lips parted, but didn't say anything else.

In the living room, Ivy hauled her father's limp body into a chair. Rose held out the rope she'd seen near the horse. "Here. Use this to tie him up."

Rose's breath hitched in her throat as he secured the last of the rope. *We have to face Nightshade next.* She memorized Elizabeth's and Ivy's faces. *I'm unsure what unseen entities the nymphs speak to, but if you're listening, please protect them.*

Rose straightened her back and lifted her chin. "Let's go," she said before walking to the mail cart.

They steered the mail cart in the direction of the medicine man's, no Nightshade's, home. The scent of brine and freshly turned earth filled her nose, making her heart race and her palms grow damp with sweat.

Ivy slowed the cart to a stop and Rose's hands shook at her side. She paced in front of the stable as he led the horse in.

Her heart hammered in her chest in time with each step that brought them closer to Nightshade's home.

In the distance, Rose saw a flash of white, and squinted her eyes, picking up her pace so she could see the details.

As they rounded a corner, long dark hair came into view. *No. No. No. It can't be. Please no*, she thought.

A pale figure laid unmoving on the floor, hair splayed about framing a pale face. Rose broke into a run. Distantly she heard the words "stop" and "trap" in Elizabeth's voice, but her brain only saw that her mother's skin was pale, too pale.

A hand grabbed her wrist, and she yanked her arm, trying to get free, but all she felt was a sharp pain ripple up her shoulder.

Rose whirled around and locked eyes with Elizabeth. "Don't stop me!" she yelled, but Elizabeth only tightened the grip on her wrist.

Elizabeth spoke through gritted teeth. "This is probably a trap. He's hoping you'll run to kill him yourself. Use that to your advantage. Make him believe you came to kill him, alone."

Tears stung Rose's eyes. Elizabeth was right. Rose sniffled and wiped away tears. If she wanted this to end, they had to stick to the plan. There would be time to mourn later.

Thorns poked out from underneath her fingernails. Once Elizabeth was out of sight, she cupped her mouth and shouted. "I'm going to kill you for this Nightshade! Come out, you coward."

"The only coward I see here is you. You threatened me in your letter, but let's see if you can keep your little promise."

A flash of black eyes and pale skin came from the herbalist's home. "If you want to kill me, you'll have to come and get me, little nymph."

Rose approached the home tentatively, but a woman's voice echoed in her mind, stopping her. *"Be cautious. Nightshade is a snake and his den contains poison."*

Rose's brow knit together and she glanced around, searching for the source of the noise.

"Who are you and why are you helping us?"

"Because he plucked my leaves to poison the water. It was like having my fingernails torn off several times. All for his misguided plan. Make his death slow for me." Her slithering voice sent shock waves down her spine.

"Gladly. Where is his plant?"

"It's on the side of the building with white flowers and berries the color of night."

"Can you relay that to Eliza...Evergreen, the nymph girl in the forest?"

"I shall."

"What are you stalling for? You said you were going to kill me. I'd like to see you try." Nightshade's voice broke her connection with Manchineel.

Rose bent her knees, falling back into her stance. She held her hand out, brandishing it as she entered Nightshade's home. "Show yourself!"

The vines that weaved along the wall of the home rippled, joining together until he appeared before her. "Gladly," he said with a smirk, and she slid her foot back.

"Running away so soon? I thought you intended to kill me if I harmed your mother." Anger and frustration burned her throat, and her arm twitched.

Stick to the plan. You need to distract him, but how? She searched the room, but there were only plants, a pestle, and some vials. She'd have to move closer to throw them at him.

She didn't see the poison Manchineel had spoken of, and her teeth ground together. *How am I supposed to avoid what I can't see?*

Rose narrowed her gaze at Nightshade. "Why did you kill my mother? You were supposed to keep her alive until I got here."

His dark pupiless eyes gleamed with humor and he flashed a grin that revealed razor sharp teeth. "I didn't like the tone you took with me in that letter, so I killed her as punishment. Consider it payback for...delaying my plans for Pennsylvania. She thrashed and shouted your name even as I forced the poison into her body. A pity you couldn't get here soon enough to see it."

Rose dug her fingernails into her palm. *Don't react. Just buy time.* "You said I only delayed your plans. What makes you think you can regain control?"

He clicked his tongue. "I thought you came here to fight, not talk?"

Rose gulped. "I did."

"That sounded rather unconvincing. You're trying to stall and that just won't do. I guess I'll have to kill you quickly."

So much for playing it safe.

Rose's palm heated as she formed her thorn covered staff.

His lip curved up into a slick smile. "Belladonna gave you her magic. That will make this more interesting." The slight move of his left arm was her only warning before he darted forward.

She held the staff out, prepared to block him, but he ran past her. His hand gripped a small string dangling from the entrance of the hut. "Goodbye little nymph girl."

The string snapped down. The wood creaked, and she looked up to see shiny green leaves raining down on her. *The poison.*

Rose's eyes widened, and she ran to the exit. "Elizabeth. Run!" Rose shouted.

She darted after Nightshade, ducking and weaving, trying to avoid the poison fluttering dangerously close to her skin.

Halfway to the door, a leaf seared her skin, and a scream tore itself from her through. She peeled it off with her fingernails, and threw it to the ground like a hot coal, but not before it left a welt behind.

Rose pushed forward, but the leaves swayed closer, getting more difficult to avoid with each step. Another leaf settled on her leg and then another on the back of her neck. Each one slowed her pace as agony washed through her.

The only thing pushing her forward was the need to get out. She was a few steps from the door when one got her ankle, burning through the thin stocking. "Elizabeth, Ivy, help!"

Her vision tunneled on the exit as she hobbled to the entrance. Her left leg went numb as she glanced back to see the last few leaves drift to the floor.

A woman with pale green fingertips approached her. Her attire was the same shiny green as the poisonous leaves. Her fingers wrapped around Rose's hand and dragged her forward as her legs burned in protest. "Come with me. Now."

*E*lizabeth crouched next to the nightshade plant, her hands cupped around the small flame engulfing the match. She held it up to a dryer leaf under a purple bell-shaped flower. The fire licked it harmlessly; the flame refused to spread. She narrowed her eyes at the small fire. "Just light already," she muttered.

The words "Elizabeth run!" pulled her from her task.

Her head swiveled in the direction of the sound, and she glimpsed pale skin and dark hair approaching. *You had one job!* she thought as she nursed the pitiful flame, trying to will the leaf to dry out faster, to go up in flames.

Her heart pounded in her chest, a quickening countdown to her demise. *Come on. Please hurry.*

A spine chilling laugh echoed through the trees. "You're out of time, traitor,"

She shuddered but didn't turn to face him. The leaf caught fire and started licking at his plant, consuming it one leaf at a time. Elizabeth stood before the plant, arms spread wide. "Actually, you're the one who's out of time, murderer."

Nightshade looked down at his hand as burn marks appeared.

"You conniving little wench." He lunged for his plant, but she shoved him back, her heels digging into the ground.

He stumbled back several steps, and flames spread quickly to his torso. He didn't have much longer. She just had to keep him away from the plant. *Where is Ivy when I need him?*

Elizabeth looked over at Nightshade's plant and smirked. "This is a fitting end for you after all the nymphs and humans you killed with flames."

Nightshade let out an ear-splitting scream, and his flaming body hurtled towards her. Ivy appeared from the brush and slid to a stop in front of Nightshade, ivy extending outward from his fingertips.

"If you want to get to her, you'll have to go through me."

"Gladly." Nightshade lunged at Ivy with sharp, violet fingernails.

Tendrils of ivy shot out from his hand, wrapping around Nightshade's arm and squeezing.

"Too slow," Nightshade said as a small untouched branch of the Nightshade plant sailed through the air towards Elizabeth.

"Evergreen, move," he shouted.

He crashed into her, pushing her out of the way, and the branch hit him in the chest, digging through flesh and sinew.

Ivy's body dropped to the floor before Elizabeth. "You monster. How could you?"

"That was intended for you, but don't worry, you'll be joining him soon." His body fell apart in clumps of ash. "I'm not the only one who harbors resentment towards humans. We'll see how long your fragile treaty lasts." His dark eyes bore into hers as the last of him disintegrated, leaving only blackened branches behind.

She fell to her knees, her hand hovering over where Ivy had fallen. "We'll come back for you, Ivy. Please stay safe until then."

Shiny leaves appeared in her peripheral vision, and her lip curled back. Elizabeth turned to see Manchineel approaching with Rose wrapped around her arm. Rose's limbs were dotted with leaf marks and welts.

Her hand balled into a fist at her side, a jolt of magic thrumming through her fingertips. "Why does she have evidence of poison from your tree?"

She scoffed. "Why would I help you kill Nightshade only to injure your friend?"

Elizabeth huffed. "I suppose you make a fair point. How do we treat her?"

"You'll need a poultice of arrowroot. There should be some in the greenhouse. Help me carry her there."

Rose gripped Elizabeth's shirt. "What about Gabriel?"

"Gabriel should return to normal now that Nightshade is dead." Rose's hand dropped from her shirt.

I hope, she thought. Elizabeth supported Rose's other shoulder as they carried her to the greenhouse. "You'll be okay. We're going to make an antidote for you," Elizabeth said.

Rose whimpered but said nothing. Her eyes were shut, and one of her legs dragged in the dirt. Elizabeth looked down to see angry red marks along her ankle.

Nightshade's former home was littered with fallen leaves splayed around like miniature corpses, and she cringed with each crunch underfoot.

Across the room, she spotted a table, but it had scatterings of Manchineel leaves covering it. Manchineel held out a hand. "Take a few steps back."

Elizabeth obliged and then Manchineel ran a hand along the table, knocking vials to the floor with a crash. Several leaves fluttered to the floor. "Bring her here."

They helped Rose get up onto the table and laid her on her back. Manchineel held up a finger. "Take care of her clothes while I gather the arrowroot and a pestle and mortar. We're going to need one."

Elizabeth tore the stocking from Rose's skin with only weak, muttered protests. Then, she searched the shelves for a pestle, being careful to avoid any remaining leaves. Hidden behind a vial of dark red liquid, she found a small metal pestle and a mortar and placed it on the table beside Rose.

Manchineel returned with a brown root whose shape resembled

an arrow. Elizabeth moved to grab the root from Manchineel, but she smacked Elizabeth's hand away. "We need some water first. There should be some containers with collected rainwater here."

She placed the root on the table, and her finger skimmed the room. "Ah, there it is." She strode over to a metal barrel not too far from the entrance and dunked a glass vial in.

"Now we use the pestle on the arrowroot and mix in some water. If we apply it to the wound, that should help with the pain and burning."

Elizabeth watched as Manchineel prepared the poultice with expert precision, but a question still nagged at her mind. "If you didn't side with Nightshade, why allow him to use you for poison?"

Manchineel's grip on the pestle tightened. "I didn't allow him. He burned a part of my tree, so I'd be too weak to take human form. Too weak to fight him. He was never the same after Belladonna betrayed him."

Elizabeth's jaw dropped. "I thought he betrayed Belladonna."

"Nightshade attempted to kill the leader of Belladonna's forest as revenge for leading humans into our forest to destroy it, but his actions almost killed Belladonna in the process. She gave him back his mirror with a nasty little curse on it as payback...There it's finished," Manchineel said and held out the poultice for Elizabeth.

"Wait. Belladonna cursed the mirror?" Elizabeth asked as Manchineel applied the poultice to the wounds on Rose's arms, and she slathered the mixture onto her legs and ankle.

"Yes, but that's a story for another day. I'm sure that mirror is long gone by now."

Elizabeth bit her lip. "What if it isn't?"

Manchineel's hand stilled. "Then, the owner of the mirror would suffer a fate worse than death."

Elizabeth's nails dug into the table. "Would the magic be tethered to the mirror or its owners?"

Manchineel ran her tongue along a pointed tooth. "I do not know. I didn't craft the curse. Why do you ask?"

Elizabeth gulped. "There's someone I need you to meet. How much longer can you keep your human form?"

Manchineel looked down at the pink burn mark on her wrist. "Perhaps an hour at most. My plant is still severely damaged."

"That should be enough time." She grabbed onto Rose's arm. "Rose, we need to go so we can help Gabriel."

Rose's eyelids fluttered open. "What about my mother?" she said weakly.

Elizabeth thought back to the too still woman from before. The tips of her fingers had already been blue and she hadn't uttered a single breath. "I'm sorry, but she was beyond help."

Rose's lip quivered. "Can we bring her body with us? I want to give her a proper burial."

Elizabeth's gaze flickered to Manchineel. "Would you mind helping with the body?"

Manchineel's lip curled up in a snarl. "I don't particularly care for humans, but I suppose I can do that much for the nymph girl who killed my oppressor. Can you load her into the carriage on your own?"

Elizabeth glanced over at Rose, trying to push herself up from the table. "I should be able to. The mail cart is waiting at the stable near the edge of the forest. I'll meet you there." Elizabeth slung Rose's blistered arm over one shoulder and tucked the pestle and remaining arrowroot under her other arm.

Rose's weight made her back arc, and she gritted her teeth. "I need you to support some weight on your good leg, so I can load you into the mail cart. We still need to help Gabriel, Rose."

Rose nodded weakly and scrambled to support herself with her good leg. Elizabeth helped Rose hobble to the horse cart, and Manchineel arrived just behind them with Rose's mother in her arms.

"I'm sorry, Mother," Rose cried before inching into the cart with help from Elizabeth.

Elizabeth secured the horse to the cart the way she'd seen Ivy do and urged the horse into a canter that made the cart rock the entire way there.

When they lurched to a stop, Rose pushed her mother's hair back from her head and hugged her cold body. "Goodbye, Mother. I'm sorry that I couldn't help you in time."

Rose lingered in her mother's embrace for a moment longer before Elizabeth put a hand on her shoulder. "We'll come back to bury her soon, but for now let's go help Gabriel."

Rose nodded and stood on wobbly legs, leaning too heavily on her good leg.

When they swung open the door to the living room, Rose's father was where they'd left him in the chair, unmoving. He snored away.

When they opened the door to Gabriel's room, he breathed heavily.

Elizabeth held out the remaining arrowroot for Rose. "If he has Manchineel poisoning, eating this should help him."

Rose gripped Elizabeth's arm. "If?"

"I won't know if my assumption is correct until we try this first." Elizabeth handed the pestle and mortar over to Rose.

Rose fed him the poultice just as Manchineel entered the room. "Is this the one you wanted me to see?" Manchineel said, nodding to Gabriel.

"Yes. Is it possible he's suffering from a curse and not poison? His wife died after receiving a mirror as a gift. Rose received the same mirror, but they shattered it in a battle with Nightshade."

Manchineel approached Gabriel's bedside and placed a hand over his forehead. "The fever is unusual. That's not a symptom of Manchineel poisoning. What were the other symptoms?"

Elizabeth glanced up at the ceiling, counting the symptoms off on her fingers. "Worsening hallucinations, fever, and chills."

Manchineel pursed her lips. "The poison causes only temporary hallucinations and some swelling. Unless he ate an apple, it wouldn't cause that."

Elizabeth advanced on Rose until their noses nearly touched. "Then that means only you can break the curse." Elizabeth's gaze flickered to Manchineel. "Right?"

"Yes, but she would need to know what triggers the spell. You'd need to reverse the trigger to break it."

Elizabeth bit her lip. "If you want to help Gabriel, you need to search your mind for the trigger of the Lover's Curse."

Rose's forehead creased. "I sometimes see her memories in brief flashes, but never on purpose. I'll try to call up the memory." Rose squeezed her eyes shut. She sifted through memories until she came across one that burned her skin. She'd been upset because he hadn't trusted her. Just like she hadn't trusted Gabriel. Not with the information about Nightshade and not with her heart.

Her face flushed, and her eyes opened. "I know what to do, but I'll need both of you to leave the room."

Elizabeth shook her head. "Too shy to break the curse in front of us?"

"Yes!" she snapped.

Elizabeth held her hands up in surrender. "Alright, we're going. Right, Manchineel?"

They exited the room and once they were out of earshot, she climbed on top of Gabriel, straddling him and placed her hand on his heart. "I'm sorry. I should have trusted you when I found that information about Nightshade, and I should have trusted your judgement when you wanted to stay behind." She struggled to form the last words. "I- l love you."

Violet light seeped from his chest and entered her hands. She jerked her hand back and Gabriel's breaths evened out.

His eyes fluttered open. "So you love me, huh?"

Her eyes widened, and her face turned beet red. "You could hear me?"

"I could hear everything, Rose." He lifted his hand to her cheek, wiping away tears with his thumb. "I love you too."

She lifted him from the bed, pressed him to her chest in a bone-crushing hug. "I don't know what I would've done If I'd lost you too."

Gabriel pressed his hands against her chest. "It's good to see you, but you're making it a little hard to breathe."

Rose's face flushed. "Sorry." She loosened her grip and held him at arm's length.

"I made Elizabeth and Manchineel wait outside, so we should probably get them before they make any strange assumptions."

He leaned in to whisper into her ear. "I can gladly make those assumptions a reality."

Her mouth went dry. "N-n-ot now!"

"That implies a later."

Rose huffed and strode over to the door. "You truly are shameless."

"But you still love me anyway."

She pursed her lips. "That's true."

"May I at least request a kiss?" He pushed himself up from the bed, but his legs refused to support his weight fully.

His knees buckled, and she ran over to catch him. "Be careful. You could've hurt yourself."

"Well worth it if I could retrieve my kiss a moment sooner." She bit her lip and lowered him to the bed.

She hovered over him and pressed her lips to his. He devoured the kiss hungrily, his hand lifting to tangle through her hair and his tongue darting into her mouth. Her skin heated at his touch, and he removed his mouth from hers to trail kisses along her neck in a way that sent a delightful shiver down her spine.

When he pulled away from her, she gasped for air.

Elizabeth called out to her, bringing her back to reality. "I can hear you in there. Your father has awoken. What do you wish to do to him?"

She looked down at her hands, one gripped his shirt and the other grasped his neck, her nails dug into his skin. With a muttered "Sorry," she removed herself from Gabriel and got up from the bed, striding over to the door.

She cracked it open to meet Elizabeth's red gaze. "You can take care of my father's punishment. I trust your judgement."

Elizabeth nodded, and a grim smile appeared on her lips. "I'll make sure he doesn't hurt anyone else ever again." She left the bedroom and beckoned for Manchineel to follow.

Manchineel shook her head. "I'll be going now. I must return to my plant." She disappeared, leaving a few barren branches behind.

* * *

WHEN ELIZABETH ENTERED the living room, Rose's father was awake and trying to scream through the gag.

Elizabeth closed her eyes and produced a lone seed for an evergreen tree in her hand. She allowed magic to flow through her body and into the seed as she neared him.

"This seed that I'm placing in your body will keep you from hurting any more people. If you try to remove it, you'll die a horrible death. If you hurt anyone, the plant will grow larger until it destroys you from the inside. If you drink alcohol, the plant will poison you."

He flailed and shrieked through the gag as she sharpened her hand into a stake. She slashed through his skin, creating a hole near his stomach and shoved the seed into the wound. She placed her hand over the gash, pouring the magic into him and leaving behind just a thin pink scar.

Elizabeth untied him and curled her lip back in a snarl, "Now, get out of our sight before I change my mind about sparing your life. Don't bother trying to tell anyone what happened. They'd never believe you, anyway."

He got up and scrambled away like a frightened animal. "Just as Rose promised, you'll suffer a fate more painful than death- rebirth. The same rebirth we'll need to create peace between humans and nymphs."

AUTHOR'S NOTES

If you liked this story and would like to know what else I'm working on, you can sign up for my newsletter by clicking here. I send weekly updates, new releases, sneak peaks of new stories, book giveaways, and author events.

Thank you so much for reading this story. If you'd like more stories like this don't forget to leave a review. You can review *Gabriel is Cursed* on Goodreads, Amazon, and Bookbub.

You can also connect with me on the following social media sites to find out about fun competitions, giveaways, and writing and self-publishing tips:

Twitter, Instagram, YouTube, Facebook, Tiktok, My website

Happy reading!

JULIA GOLDHIRSH
WAR OF THE TWIN SWORDS
GEMSTONE MASSACRE SERIES
PREQUEL

ACKNOWLEDGMENTS

Wow this book ended up being the longest and the most editing intensive project I've done so far with a whopping seven rounds of self-edits, two rounds of beta readers, and three different editors. I want to start by thanking the amazing people who helped with those beta edits especially Val and Sam. They were both amazing at catching my weird POV slips and historical inaccuracies, and my mother sniffed out any of the remaining mistakes like a bloodhound. Additionally, I want to thank Kent for encouraging me to try method acting to really get to the heart of who my characters are. It was incredibly helpful. Anyone who reads this book is amazing, and I hope you enjoyed my first full-length novel. Finally, I want to say thank you to the amazing team of people that got this book ready for production and my ever patient cover artist. You can check out their services below.

Cover Artist- Sukesha Ray (She sings too!)
    Content editor- Charlotte Blowe Stanley/ N-D Scribable
    Content/Line editor- Erin/ Survivor Bunny
    Proofreader/Line editor- Willow Oak Author Services